When Theseus, ruler of Athens, returns home with his bride-to-be, Hippolyta, Nick Bottom and his thespian pals hope to contribute to the forthcoming revels by acting out their play.

Plans, however, go wildly awry when Nick's forthright simplicity is taken for the more dangerous art of subtle sophistry; an enchanting and beautifully crafted comedy ensues, while, on a serious note, through the antics of a hugely enjoyable and often outrageous cast of characters, a darker, more sinister element of human nature emerges. Theseus's bride is the captured Queen of the Amazons, who arrives in a cage shrieking, half-naked — and creates an even greater stir amongst the goggling crowds by treating Peter Quince to a peculiarly uninhibited expression of her royal disdain. But her pious sister, the chaste Emily, is the *real* shocker; thanks to her alarmingly quick wits, Nick finds himself thrown into prison where he encounters two Theban knights — and if you think along the lines of two moths falling in love with a lighted touch-paper, then you'll have an inkling of what happens when these two gallants become smitten with dear Emily . . .

Thank goodness, then, for fairy magic; for Puck the careless muddler and for Dewdrop the talking donkey, whose poignant calamities will make you laugh and make you weep — and then make you laugh again for the sheer felicitous exuberance of it all.

Publisher's note: Many years ago, Oberon, King of the Fairies, appeared to both Geoffrey Chaucer and William Shakespeare and told them his story. Here we are privileged to announce that Oberon has appeared once again, this time to Robert Watson, to whom he has retold his tale. Again, it has altered in the retelling, but for proof of this auspicious encounter we offer no more evidence than that which lies hidden between these covers.

'The humour, the warmth, indeed the tenderness of the book are sustained to the end. *Whilom* is an affecting, funny and very readable novel' – Robert Nisbet, *Planet*

BY THE SAME AUTHOR

EVENTS BEYOND THE HEARTLANDS
RUMOURS OF FULFILMENT

WHILOM

For those who have made the move north so good, and, always, for Roz, Tom, Annie, Kate and Emily.

WHILOM

ROBERT WATSON

BLOOMSBURY

First published in Great Britain 1990
Copyright © 1990 by Robert Watson
This paper edition published 1991

Bloomsbury Publishing Ltd, 2 Soho Square, London W1V 5DE

The moral right of the author has been asserted

A CIP catalogue record for this book is
available from the British Library

ISBN 0 7475 0810 0

10   9   8   7   6   5   4   3   2   1

All rights reserved: no part of this publication may be
reproduced, stored in a retrieval system, or transmitted in
any form or by any means, electronic, mechanical, photocopying
or otherwise, without the prior written permission of the
publisher.

Printed and bound by Clays Ltd, St Ives plc

I

'HILOM,' OBERON LAMENTS, 'before cigarettes, posters of pop stars, the three-pin plug, before exhaust fumes and atom bombs and cannon, even before typewriters, whilom there were men I admired, men worthy of respect. And because I remember them they are alive amongst your collar studs and laser beams, your memories of war, your dread of emptiness. They stand above your anxious, petty concerns like giants.

'It is not to record the passing of my own tribe,' Oberon weeps, 'that I am here; though I am our last breath and this, I fear, is where I reach my appointed end. I am here because I have never travelled on beyond this moment. So this is where I tell it for the last time, the story I have told so often before, that has been lost, and lost again.

'Do not expect,' Oberon says, 'my people to be the saviours of yours. If we are in the story it is simply because we were there amongst the last of our friends. And we were victims too. You will not understand us, though I believe we were necessary enough. But you have never understood and you have always lost us – which is your tragedy and ours.

'Return,' Oberon advises me, warming to his purpose, 'to the heroes who founded your world, to Theseus, the lord between legend and ledger, and to Nick Bottom, textor of Athens. All you have to do, Rob, is weave together my memories, fabricate

— 1 —

something for the gaps, and bring to the whole your mortal sense of order. I have told this to Geoffrey and William, who were closer to me than you are, so begin where they began.'

They began with the return home, I remember, so I will too.

One warm afternoon a great lord, fresh from victory, reined in his horse, thus bringing to a noisy halt his tough returning army, and gazing thoughtfully into the gentle valley just beyond the forest – gazing at the only part of the bowled landscape not flickering with the sun's heat – he said:

'I see there is one who cannot be happy.'

Those near enough to catch this remark repeated it carefully, and as it was passed along the lines the wonder increased, for no one in the entire train could make out a living soul in that green shaded valley below the road. A few stony clusters of sheep were grazing on the far slope under a walled olive grove, and they were as stiff as gravestones, but all that could be seen of unhappy humanity was the pathetic handiwork of the remoter working-folk, a few rough shacks thrown up with wood and straw and held together with dung. Such dwellings were beneath the notice of the many brave knights in the great lord's company, and yet it seemed that he did indeed gaze towards these rudimentary blots.

'My lord,' the young knight Demetrius felt invited to ask, 'where can you discern unhappiness? We see no sign.'

The governor sighed, not without a certain restrained satisfaction. 'Look again, Demetrius, and tell me what your eye says.'

Polite and petted Demetrius scanned the unpromising area intently, anxious to impress his master, as were the others who copied him. Everyone within earshot wished to participate. The object lessons in good government so freely given by their renowned lord were never taken lightly, however loopy they seemed to be. The knights knew that their own children, and their children's children, would learn the saws by heart and bless the memory of the ancestor sensible enough to pass them on. In

— 2 —

this way all his fawning retinue praised their lord for shedding his assured immortality upon them, sometimes twice or thrice a day.

Now Demetrius was ready with his report. 'I see the welcoming familiar light that Phoebus has cast for our safe return, and, lapped in its gaze, enriched by my fond gazing, I see the simple meadows I played in as a child, I see the well-stocked wood where the glad hart has multiplied unchecked in our absence to promise better sport and even greater feasts than hitherto.'

'Bravo, Demetrius!'

'Well spoke, Demetrius!'

'But seriously, boy, don't you see those cottages too?'

'I was ashamed to acknowledge them in this context, my lord.'

'You're too fastidious. Acknowledge them now, if you please, as directly as you can.'

'Then, sir,' Demetrius said stumblingly, 'it's true, the rural seat of humble swains falls within our purview, and we accept that together with the cattle and sheep and forest their purpose is to serve the general good, which is to say the good of those of us whose business it is to rule . . . er . . . for which wide bounty I give thanks to . . . to . . .' He blushed deeply. 'I cannot recall a deity to thank for the existence of such poor creatures as dwell down there – forgive me, lord.'

The governor smiled comfortably at his lieutenant's discomfiture. 'It strikes me that ever since we could smell land again your senses have gone doolally – maybe that explains the nancy diction. You were smitten with old Nedar's daughter once, if I'm not mistaken?'

Demetrius could hardly sit astride his horse now, the embarrassment was so excruciating. His lord was right, and wrong. It was marvellous that he should recall so trivial a thing as the girl Demetrius loved, so how could Demetrius point out that he'd progressed to another maiden? 'I *did* favour Helena in my extreme youth. Happily I lived to see a true beauty before we embarked against the Amazons, and throughout our long months it has been true beauty I have dreamt on, true beauty that has whipped

— 3 —

my soul almost to frenzies of adoration, true . . .' He stopped
himself abruptly. 'Not when I was preparing for battle, of course.
I mean to say . . .'

The lord's horse sidestepped and gave an impatient snort,
reminding the impulsive youth that a lesson had been about to
be delivered. He bit his tongue and lowered his head. After a
suitably impressive silence the great lord said distinctly:

'I see stone.'

Several ambitious young knights had quietly brought up their
horses to take the pressure off their friend and grab a share in
any glory that might be in the offing. All hastily scanned the
peaceful valley for stone. One noticed it in the wall around the
olives and pointed there; another saw a few rocks on the plain
and thought it conceivable that a galloping horse might stumble
and unseat its illustrious rider.

Demetrius redeemed himself by seeing what he was supposed
to see. 'I have it! That cottage!'

The others saw it now. They gasped, a little confusedly, for
all they saw was that one rude hovel had walls of rough stone
blocks instead of sticks and stuff, and that before its mean
entrance two wonky branches made a petty kind of porch,
thatched with straw.

'Tell me, Demetrius, now your eye has cleared – say why an
unhappy fellow lives there.'

'I cannot, my lord.'

'Nor I,' admitted two or three honest knights, knowing their
lord valued candour and occasionally rewarded it.

'Gentlemen, you see in this innocent valley of ours the work
of one who has ceased to offer thanks, one dissatisfied with his
lot, one who has seen visions perhaps and been transported from
his proper sphere of modest content. He has attempted to create
for himself a palace, gentlemen, and has meant no doubt to install
himself a king of currant bushes, emperor of olives and alders,
lord of the larch, the laurel and the lazy stream!'

One elderly knight actually fell off his horse at this, he laughed
so heartily. Mirth spread rapidly until all but the sullen captives

of the barred wagons were shrieking and roaring at the ludicrous prospect, so obvious now it had been pointed out.

'It is funny to us,' the lord admonished them gently when he sensed the initial flood diminishing, 'but the matter is as grave as if it affected our very Court. These hapless outdwellers are simple folk but we have a duty towards them; they are stubborn for refusing to come live within the city walls, but we shall not abandon them for that. I say there is a man, albeit a peasant, who has misplaced even that tiny degree of command which was his birthright – he no longer knows himself but believes he is some other, greater man. Yet that cannot be. No man can be more than his birth provides for. The unhappiness his pride has caused him, or must soon cause him, touches me to the quick. Demetrius, and you, you, and you – go now into the valley and pull down that pompous stonework! And take care!' He threw the last phrase up and paused until all attention returned to him instead of the dancing horses and the merry diversion. 'Take care – I do not want the little fellow harmed, nor his wife if he has a wife, nor his children if he has children. I want only the illusion removed, neatly as the bee-sting, and, to the same end, for we are coming home and shall protect *all* our people, even from those miseries so secret they do not suspect them.'

This great lord, who was not more than moderately vain and who really longed to go down in history as a just statesman rather than a raunchy club-man, was the legendary Theseus, son of the man whose name became a sea.

The stone place, which soon collapsed in upon itself with a dusty puff of silent smoke, far below, causing a patter of applause to break from the watchers on the high road, this stone place had been built by a weaver. And this weaver's father had once helped the legendary Theseus. And neither Theseus nor the weaver's father knew it. Theseus, for example, never thought to ask who had woven the marvellous thread that helped him through his greatest youthful exploit, to the heart of the labyrinth, the death of the Minotaur, and back again. And the old weaver, for example, never thought to ask just what the adamantine thread was for. All he did was pass on to his son a vision, a vision of a rare foreign beauty coming out of the forest one night with the gold from which the twine was to be fashioned. The vision was Ariadne. The weaver's son grew up believing that a similar vision would in due course come his way too.

This young, hearty, optimistic weaver, who lived in the forest a secluded but never a lonely life, was Nick Bottom.

II

NICK BOTTOM WAS a sociable enough fellow but in truth preferred the company of the forest to any other sort; the indiscriminate loud good humour that his Athenian friends expected of him was, he found, a little wearing. Once a month he was glad to put in an appearance, sell his wares, gather gossip and drink till a tidal lake surged through his innards – once a month was fun – but he valued his own thoughts too highly to turn up twice.

He began to set up his stall as usual in a shaded position between the long high wall and the tall house, where the sun was guaranteed to catch just one corner of the stall. Here Nick arranged several bright cloths of red and green and blue, so that the sun enriched their hues and drew the eye of even the most distant stroller. The sun was good for business, bad for dyes, and these specimen cloths were simply bait, the best-quality work remaining sheltered for closer examination. Nick had barely had time to unpack his patient donkey, however, before he heard rumours on the mild breeze that caused him to pause. What was that? What were they saying? Theseus returned? Theseus victorious? Almost every sentence carried along the walls quivered with Theseus.

'Listen here, Dewdrop,' the weaver said to his donkey. 'Don't move from this spot. If anyone tries to steal my samples, kick him in the ribs. If it's a woman tread on her toes. OK?'

— 7 —

The donkey blinked and twitched his lovely ears as if he hadn't understood a word.

'Well, then,' the weaver added more reasonably, 'watch this stuff for me and I promise to let you loiter where you like all the way home. Deal?'

'Fair enough,' the donkey nodded. 'Though if you're thinking what I think you're thinking there'll be precious little loitering today!'

Satisfied, Nick placed a couple of turnips on Dewdrop's feast of hay and hurried away excitedly to find his friends. That wasn't difficult. They were crowding the dimmest, coolest corner of the Bull, a corner they crowded even when, as now, the place was otherwise deserted. Robin and Francis, timid men both, started as Nick burst through the door and sent a chicken squawking, but as soon as they recognised him their faces took on an expectant, happy sort of look, as much as to say, Now we'll have fun. At the same time their hands went protectively over their pint pots, as much as to say, No you can't.

'Heard the news?' Bottom bellowed. 'The army's returned, chums!'

'We knew that yesterday,' said Peter Quince drily. 'Old news buys no drinks.'

That might have thrown the young weaver into a righteous grump on another occasion, but he had already begun to form a plan and would not be daunted by the carpenter's habitually unyielding manner. Nor was he overmuch put out to observe that Francis Flute still covered his drink with one cautious hand or that the little tailor, though he'd raised his to his lips, was endeavouring to drain it while continuing to mask it clumsily. Ale dripped up his arm and off his chin. Nick Bottom saw and refused to take umbrage, deciding instead to demonstrate generosity. Tom Snout was not on his usual stool; Nick supposed he was working.

'A drink for Tom Snout. Tom? Where is my friend the tinker – I mean to go his round.'

'Tinker's tinkling, like,' Robin Starveling muttered wetly,

— 8 —

and extremely quietly, fearing his sodden joke wouldn't be understood and he'd be laughed at for a fool instead of a wit.

'No, Robin,' complained Francis Flute, who really hadn't understood because his mother had taught him never to play with naughty words. 'Our Tom have gone outside into the back lane hereby, Nick, for to relieve himself.'

'What's more,' added Snug the joiner, seeing Starveling shyly shrinking, 'Sweet Margery what pulls our pints and pockets our pennies went out by the selfsame door as Tom not five minutes since. Make what you will of *that*, Nick Bottom!'

'By the great club of Theseus! Then I *will* stand good Tom a drink!' the weaver roared, stamping his fist emphatically. 'That Margery will have made a merry man of our tinker, if I know her!'

The truth was he didn't know her and hadn't known any woman, but none dreamt of his innocence so none could assail it. When Nick was around no one dreamt at all. At an early age he had discovered that as he was big so loudness was expected, and so long as he played it up his sense of wonder was left to grow in peace. Besides, the rest of them were almost as innocent, even if Peter Quince and Tom and Snug had wives and children.

'They say Theseus returns today,' Nick continued as he sat amongst his friends, slamming the two pints he'd drawn so hard on the table that despite two protecting hands Francis Flute's drink slapped up at his nose and made him sneeze. 'Well, my brave hearts – we must go out and meet him!'

The announcement met a silent if dribbling wall. Tom Snout returned and saw rigid faces beyond Bully Bottom's broad shoulders. He checked his buttons apprehensively.

'We are to greet our lord and governor, Tom,' Peter Quince explained with ponderous sarcasm. '*Us!* Meet *him*! I've no doubt,' he carried on, turning back to the beaming weaver, 'the great Lord Theseus has been anxious all these months apart from us. Our appearance on the road will reassure him!'

From Peter Quince this was pretty amusing, but his friends were too scared to laugh.

'We shall greet him, as it were, by accident,' the weaver said patiently, pushing the second pint towards Tom Snout and inadvertently spilling some in the man's lap the moment he'd nodded his thanks and sat down. Nick Bottom had worked out his plan between donkey and pub and was to be deflected neither by sarcasm nor spilt beer. 'We must not be *on* the road where we should obstruct his path and offend him, but if we happen to be at the road's *side* as he happens to pass, and if we happen to be busily practising a little play, and if our Lord Theseus happens – as I hear may be the truth – to be bringing home a bride . . .'

'He be, he be!' cried Snug the joiner, astonished. 'I heard it not two hours since from a man that sells rope by the harbour – Lord Theseus be marrying yet again, and this time the most fierce-somest woman as ever a man did blunder into it with!'

'Yet this is not so rare a scrap of news as to raise a shrewd man's eyebrows,' was Peter Quince's response as he struggled to hold his eyebrows down.

'Aye, you have to grant there's no surprise in that,' said Francis Flute. 'Weddings and Theseus have been frequent friends.'

'They say she've cooked and eaten the part of a man he can least bear to live without,' Snug added with a shiver. 'She relishes battle and leads a land of women who can govern themselves. They need no man but for one thing which, when they have took their pleasure, they will as lief cut off and munch on as send him home with gifts and come-agains – so I have heard.'

'Be that as it may,' retorted Bully Bottom craftily, 'the habit of his victories is still the prompt to our occasion. If we're mugging our parts by the roadside where he passes, in such manner as I've suggested, and his thoughts are filled with the joyful solemnities awaiting him, then won't he be likely to note us down and send back his man and invite us to perform our piece for profit?'

'There's something in this,' Peter Quince admitted, his manner changing all at once. 'Nick, I'm sorry I underestimated your scope. This is a foolproof plan. I see it now. We shall be made

—— 10 ——

men. It wasn't for want of skill we were overlooked before – by gum, we can act the socks off any guild in Athens, given a fair chance, but, lads, we've been ever too modest and when lesser men pressed ahead we held back, believing excellence would advertise itself. But Nick Bottom is right: we must put our show on the road. It's not enough to be good, we must be *seen* to be good. And we must get to it now, no time to waste – go, pack up your stalls and we'll meet by the gate anon, not a minute later!'

Boisterous, but not a whit less well mannered for that, the simple men carried their empties over to the counter, and Margery returned from doing her business in the lane in time to see them knot close and blush as one. Perplexed, she wished them good day, but Tom Snout was the only one with self-possession enough to return the pleasantry. The others were falling over one another in their haste to escape, as if they thought the barmaid were bewitched. Which she wasn't. But she was of course a woman.

From the city's outer gate it was a short ride to the brow of the hill. From the brow of the hill it was about three short rides to the widow's peak of the next hill. From that to the far end of the avenue of poplars was one more short ride, give or take a brief canter, and at that umbrageous spot the dusty men were obliged to dismount. They were short of their intended destination by approximately the flight of a longbow's arrow. Prudence had arrested them, for there were ladies waiting precisely where they had meant to wait.

'Who are they, Nick?'

'Did you pass them this morning? Are they jugglers, whores, or what?'

'I didn't come along the road. Dewdrop's partial to the thistles by the stream below the city walls, so I ambled in the valley.'

The ladies, being unexpected and unaccountable, had taken the wind from his sails. They presented a problem and Nick

— 11 —

hadn't planned for a problem. All were dressed in black. These then were mourning ladies, definitely to be avoided like disease. A shack of some sort had been erected near them. They had a purpose. Mourning ladies had little fun in them, added to which they were generally of note and were therefore frightening to ordinary working men. No Athenians had died recently, at least not in significant numbers. These women suggested an epidemic. As it was market day you'd hardly gather a band of dames so far from the stalls as this unless something big was afoot. It was a mystery.

'We could bypass down along the valley and return to the road some way ahead of them,' Peter Quince thought aloud.

'I find two objections to that, Peter Quince,' Bottom answered with more than his customary good sense. 'The first is that cloud rising from the farther hill – that will be Theseus, so we've no time to gain a better position and begin rehearsing before he passes by. Second – those dark ladies must be awaiting our lord too. They mean to stop and depress him with their troubles. Boys, there's advantage to being here – we may return to his tired soul all the cheer and jubilation that those lah-di-dah-di-ladies will have just wrung from it.'

Greatly heartened, the group broke out some wines and cheeses to prepare themselves. And they waited in the shade of the giant poplars, and as they waited they ate, drank, threw crumbs to the goldfinches and jays, swapped jokes, and ran through their parts. They were not nervous at this time because it was to be at most a glanced performance, caught in passing from the corner of an eye, and subject to no command. Therefore no punishment could befall them if they were wrong, no line could insult any member of Court who wanted a moment's fame, no gesture could terrify a lady who needed to bring out the protective part of her beau. They were relaxed and competent.

Meanwhile the distant cloud grew a dark monster at its centre: an army returning. The players played on.

Meanwhile the mild breeze made a muffled whistling in the dense leaves. The ladies waited.

Meanwhile Dewdrop kept an ear to the trunk of the nearest tree, and another close to the grass, all the time nodding at the stories he heard.

At last the foremost horses and riders could be seen, armour glinting in the sunlight through the reddish dust. They had halted. Now the players did begin to get the jitters, their big chance seeming imminent. But the army lingered where the mourning ladies were as if the two darknesses had fused into one mass of power and grief. And lingered again.

'We should have gone beyond them after all,' Peter Quince was heard to grumble quietly, for he was not yet so dejected as to be certain.

And still they waited. Dewdrop was trying out the bark of a tree when his master approached for an informed opinion.

'Thebes,' Dewdrop said, spitting out bark shreds, disinclined to elaborate.

'Lads,' Bottom announced, 'they won't get to their homes in Athens this afternoon, and I apologise to you one and all. We have lost trade in my foolishness.'

Because he was sincere they couldn't berate him. Instead they commiserated. After all, the afternoon had been diverting until the last tense and tedious hour. All shook hands and clapped backs manfully and then the company, minus the weaver, wended back towards Athens and evening. They might have guessed, their slumped shoulders seemed to say reproachfully, that a command performance before Theseus was not for men of their station.

'How was our sweet Margery, Tom?' Robin remembered, belatedly, to ask.

'Aye,' joined Francis hopefully, 'there's a merry tale, I bet!'

'Oh,' Tom laughed over returning embarrassment, 'she was very fair, very proper, and said she hadn't seen me slip out first. And she put her hand over her eyes till I'd done.'

'Hand over her eyes! What! This is saucy!'

'Nay, she was very sorry to interrupt my flow, so to speak, and although she laughed she was not unkind about it, and she

— 13 —

turned away and waited behind the barrels till I'd done, with her hand over her eyes.'

'Well, your wife would be proud of you,' remarked Peter Quince sourly, for even he was disappointed, there being nothing to disapprove of.

Nick Bottom and his donkey left the road to follow the valley out towards his cottage in the forest.

Theseus, the weaver thought seriously, you are a great lord but too easily distracted, and you've let down a simple man today.

'Even the wind shouldn't catch thoughts like that,' Dewdrop warned him, and the honest weaver shot wild looks about the friendly valley in terror.

III

BUT IT WAS not in order to torment the Peter Quince Amateur Dramatics and Male Voice Guild of Athens that Theseus had come to a standstill. The external circumstances that could stop a man of his awesome powers were few: weather couldn't stop him, war and wild beasts couldn't stop him. What could was what did. He could hardly instruct his horse to stomp through a large number of determined ladies in mourning, despite the flagrant ugliness of the first pair that caught his critical eye. These were both enormously fat, wart-faced, bristle-chinned dames, both duchesses who called themselves queens. He'd gone to a lot of trouble to establish a three-tiered society in which everyone had a place and value. These dissatisfied battleaxes had wanted him to install himself King of Kings because they felt uncomfortable kneeling to any-one else – and Theseus wouldn't even allow he was a king at all! So he wasn't innately sympathetic, but he had to stop.

'What troubles you, good women? Why do you darken my homecoming?'

He spoke sternly. Until then it had been a successful, diverting ride in from the harbour. Spirits were buoyant. Indeed, for several days past the men's thoughts had been wafting home ahead of them, and since reaching harbour these home-thoughts had mounted minute by minute, and hearts pounded like the sun at noon at the prospect of remembered, sustaining loved

— 15 —

ones becoming living flesh once more, to be held, to behold, to be touched by, whispered to, You're home, hero, come take your ease with us at last.

Following Theseus's impatient question a great wailing was heard, carefully orchestrated, as he was bound to appreciate. And despite their gravity the spectacle of these women as a group was not altogether unpleasant. They were sisters, wives and sweethearts, the stuff one fought for, deserving of compassion. They had stationed themselves in twos on either side of the road, and wailed with impressive co-ordination so that the drifting-forward dust, shot through with afternoon rays, took on spiritual substance even as it settled on their black gowns. With grief shaped to such a formal art, the moral strength of these mourners had to be given credit. They were a credit to the civilisation that had made them, that Theseus had made. He disliked messiness and displays of raw, ragged emotion. He believed it possible and desirable to govern everything, from people to passions. Art sprang from government, meaning from art, value from meaning, purpose from value, pattern from purpose, harmony from pattern, order from harmony, government from order, art from government . . .

'Speak,' he commanded. 'Do not fear my wrath. I am Theseus.' He sounded enormously impressive when he spoke these simple words.

'None of us is less than a duchess, lord,' the first wart-face said, trembling even so, if not from awe then from the inner wrestle not to call herself a queen and sound superior. 'If we were nothing we'd dare not appear before you. And yet it's not for ourselves, despite rank and right, that we've camped here since the first news of your return. Our grief cries louder than your victories. Alleviate our distress. Lord, we've waited till our waters are dry, eating little, praying much. We've erected a humble temple to Clementia. Help us.'

The old woman paused, choking on her tears quite as if they provided the only moisture she'd tasted in days. She struggled to recall just where her speech had been intended to end up. The

— 16 —

other women filled in with renewed decorous wailing. Theseus saw the temple, a miserable wooden hut that a passing army would soon shake to bits. These biddies ain't builders, he thought, and the thought softened his manly heart. Wealthy women *should* be impractical, and it was touching that their piety had forced them to have a go and put their uselessness on display.

'There are too few temples on this road,' he said kindly. 'I'll have one built on this very spot, framed in good rough stone, of which there's a supply near the forest back there; your Clementia shall be shaped from the finest clouded alabaster, and consecrated as soon as our celebrations are over. Are you satisfied?'

'Lord,' the other crone dared tremulously, 'there is more. Our husbands must be avenged. It is a matter of Honour.'

And so it was, though she was actually pleading for her son, Cappaneus, whom Theseus knew well. He had guessed that his pal was dead. Now he listened to the sorry tale of it.

When Theseus besieged Thebes he joined six other notables and their forces, and when the siege was prolonged left Cappaneus in charge while he led a larger force against the arrogant Amazons. In his absence things went wrong. It was not so much the deaths that demanded a reaction but the treatment afforded to the corpses. Creon, old tyrant of Thebes, had provocatively refused to return the bodies. Not only that, but the old bugger had had them chucked into a heap like so much city refuse – in Athens not even scoundrels were treated that way any longer. Creon was beyond the pale. He wouldn't even allow the rotting noble flesh to be buried, or burnt, or carted off, insisting that the heap remain outside Thebes's main gates for all to see, where half-wild dogs and any vermin could gorge themselves.

At this pitiful detail the women's cries broke out more terribly, in the disorder of individual revulsion and grief. Several broke their neat ranks and tore at the dry soil with their fine fingers.

'Enough!' Theseus exploded, and all was silence save his beating heart and the thin dust settling. 'Good women, your pain is now our pain. What you have suffered we now suffer. I thought to feast tonight, but no festivity is possible while such vileness goes unchallenged. I swear, as I am a true knight, that I will bring vengeance home to the miscreant Creon. I will bring down Thebes before I take another step towards my beloved Athens. Demetrius – the war banner!'

An audible groan, flatly unheroic, issued from the middle ranks, but it was a momentary slump. As soon as the breeze unfurled the banner and the red and awful figure of the war god Mars shone on the path, all groans were stifled, as if the god himself were glowering over them. Theseus was right again – a homecoming couldn't be all it should if there remained a pile of noble carcases stinking unceremoniously outside Thebes. And sometimes wives and children weren't as impressed as they ought to be by tales of heroic deeds in distant lands – sometimes they implied that while the men were off having fun *they'd* been short of housekeeping. A righteous fight so close to home would buck them up a bit.

Down in the valley the weaver looked up, saw the line of wagons and men on horseback, men with spears in silhouette, saw the fierce red figure on the white banner, bright as new blood as the sun struck through its fine cloth, heard a chilling cry go up and, for a heart-stopping moment, thought all the horses turned in his direction to charge him down. Then they began shrinking and bobbing as they left the path along the horizon and headed away across country towards Thebes.

'How did you know that?' Nick Bottom, trembling, asked his donkey.

'Thebes?' Dewdrop just shrugged modestly, but enjoyed the fond hand that tickled his ear.

'Why are some of the wagons continuing along the road to Athens?' Nick asked again, ever a nosy weaver.

'They'll be the captives under escort, the bronzed Amazon women you men fear so badly.'

'You're a very smart ass, my friend, but I fear no women of any sort.'

— 18 —

'That's because you've lived apart, Nick, and been blessed in solitude with trust. I fear your luck will soon change.'

Nick Bottom couldn't suppress an impromptu snort of a laugh at something he had just seen ahead. 'I fear yours just has, Dewdrop,' he said. 'Where will you sleep tonight, old chum?'

What he had seen was the stable he had recently refurbished completely reduced to rubble. He had built it of stone because Dewdrop always ate stables made of anything else, and Dewdrop had been proud of his new home and had thought himself a cut above most other donkeys and all men.

'I am crestfallen,' the donkey retorted slowly. 'My braying gods have chastened me. I shall not speak again.'

The weaver stopped laughing.

IV

BY LATE AFTERNOON the streets of Athens were jam-packed. They were nearly always crowded anyway, since Theseus had drawn in all the remnants of petty potentates and squabbling tribes of Attica, and united the lot as Citizens of Athens. It was a large and growing city, requiring extra-strong walls to hold everyone safe and snug within. Theseus had made A People where before had only been disparate families with hopelessly divided allegiances and hoary old scores to settle. To the great he had offered a share in his greatness. Not all were immediately impressed, but it became obvious to those kings who jealously clung to their autonomy that their greatness shrank rapidly as Athens grew, until at last they came grudgingly over, and agreed to pretend that they were above such titles as they owned. To the poor Theseus offered protection and a dignified position in the hierarchy. The People were to rule.

Theseus remained their Commander of War and their Guardian of the Law, but aside from that government was devolved. 'Come hither, all ye people,' he said, and they came, and came, and were slotted into the new state as Noblemen, Husbandmen, or Mechanicals – not a citizen was undervalued or ignorant of his worth. It was a brave notion. Before Theseus came along the poor and downtrodden were thought to exist to be trodden down and kept poor. He changed all that. They wouldn't become rich, but they had a share in the common humanity. Athens throve.

—— 20 ——

Theseus extended the boundaries and set up a pillar to mark their extent, inscribed on two sides so that all who could read might know. On the east side of the pillar the inscription read like this:

THIS IS NOT PELOPONNESUS, BUT IONIA

On the west side it read like this:

THIS IS PELOPONNESUS, NOT IONIA

Which is a fair sample of how Theseus's mind worked when his raw emotions didn't interfere. He admired clarity, simplicity and forcefulness. He did not admire dithering and other signs of a debilitated will. If he thought he was right then he *knew* he was right, and then he obviously had the right to act. He was also tremendously strong and had a terrifying reputation that raced ahead of him to weaken any opponents before he even reached them. Only Hercules had a greater reputation as a tough, and Hercules had gone everywhere before Theseus, which was rather irritating. Politically, though, it didn't matter: Hercules had never attempted to settle and organise Athens! In fact Hercules was little better than a yob of epic proportions. Theseus had some chance of being loved and remembered for the good he'd done, but not Hercules.

And Theseus was due back. The streets were jam-packed, and most of those who did the jam-packing were preparing to greet their returning army. The mood was expectant. There'd be dancing in the streets, feasting for nights on end, torches flaming under the moon; there'd be games, sacrifices, plays, orgies.

So when word arrived that Theseus had been delayed by a pious pack of grieving women, diverted to castigate Creon and demolish Thebes, there was, understandably, some dejection. When word arrived that nonetheless *something* was approaching there was excitement tinged with suspicion. The People didn't intend to be fobbed off with a drab line of badly wounded

— 21 —

soldiers. They wanted something worth staring at, something to cheer. They wanted to let off steam.

'It's the Amazon Queen!' someone yelled.

'In chains!' Then, 'Under guard!' Then, most thrillingly, 'CAGED!'

There was no need for sobriety now. Most seemed to have heard that the warrior queen was to be the next wife of Theseus, but she might still be a wild animal. The marriage would be another proof of his control, not of her breeding. Most knew the names of several of his previous wives, too, and even of some of those girls he'd seduced and *not* married. Theseus had children scattered throughout the islands, and that was his business and part of his glamour. Marriage and progeny posed no threat to the Athenian People. A new wife was not a new leader; she would merely demonstrate again that Theseus could take what he wanted. And who would attack Athens when its ruler was so publicly powerful, so almighty, such a law unto himself?

None yet knew how the Scythian tribe had been beaten, though stories were already being born. None knew what Hippolyta would look like, but all had fantasies which the one word 'Caged!' set fire to. All wanted to get a good look at her; some to throw rotten oranges. No one felt any need to be awed and silent as she passed.

'They're coming!'

The People crowded and crammed and shoved to get the first glimpse. First there came several fine young knights on horseback, shining spears and polished shields in their hands because that sort of show was expected and appreciated. They came into the city quietly enough, and behind them trundled several wagons heavy with supplies, weapons and booty, and then there, in the rising reddish clouds of dust, was the cage – a big, four-wheeled wagon drawn by six horses and guarded by horsemen on every side, these horsemen grimmer than the leading knights, their visors down impersonally, their short swords drawn, their lives forfeit if the seething queen were killed before she was imprisoned in the palace.

The bars of the cage were of stout bamboo, and there was nothing regal inside but a base of scattered straw, with a heap of straw in one corner, just as you'd expect in a cage holding a lion, only in place of an exotic snarling beast this cage held the queen of the Amazon women, lately beaten into abject surrender by the great lord of Athens.

In fact there were two creatures in the cage. One was full-grown, the other a sort of cub-child, a sulking sullen thing that crept apart in a corner and tried to cover itself with straw. It had on a kind of clothing, a brownish, filthy, coarse material that covered its back but left bare its terracotta arms and legs and dirty, but surprisingly fair, almost white hair. And it had anklets and amulets of gold that gleamed dully while sparks from fragmenting straw flickered down inside the cage.

The adult specimen was almost terrifying to behold, scarcely clothed at all, it seemed, though none could be sure what was actually exposed to a public gaze. Undeniably there was a strong impression of nakedness and raw energy, and this some found glamorous, others repulsive. Later some would insist that this crazy-seeming woman, this spirited animal queen, had not only shaken the bars and growled and hurled little straw spearlets in her impotent rage, but that like a monkey she had clambered about and climbed the bars, and that she'd flexed her legs hanging up there above the crowd, swaying her backside down against the bars, and that then she had urinated at the gazing men and women. Some would swear she had four breasts, each emerging pendulous and purple from the deep red fur of her body. She chattered in a strange, comic tongue, not a real language. She had thighs and biceps like Hercules. She was wholly naked, or dressed in rags which she tore at and chewed at. She had hooves.

One thing was sure, that while the cowering timid creature was fair, this queen was dark – a mane, a virtual Minotaur's head, black, thick, impenetrable, yes, probably horned, probably concealing a black dribbling snout – was that a ring through her nose? She was wild all right, as fierce as Phea the formidable sow of Crommyon, whom Theseus had sought out especially to slay

— 23 —

when he was young and still had to prove his manhood. Phea hadn't gone for him but had terrorised many, and by seeking her out Theseus had early shown himself a true defender of the weak and oppressed. Perhaps Phea hadn't been a sow but a woman with sow-like manners. This Hippolyta was no normal woman either. She screamed and spat through the late afternoon sun, whose red glows pierced the tumbling clouds of shifting dust and motes of sparkling straw and allowed only glimpses of something far from regal, lacking the finesse of majesty, but something wildly wonderful, awesome in the prospect it suggested even to slow-moving minds of the new battle awaiting Theseus. What a task he'd set himself! To tame and teach and bring to heel, to bed and to respectability a creature so far from grace as this barely human Hippolyta! No, impossible – if he married her he'd have to build a maze to keep her in, for she could never be transformed into a proper Athenian lady!

So the People were pleased after all, those who had seen for a second, or nearly seen this queen, and those who shortly afterwards listened to the wondrously woven accounts of the spectacle. Some even threatened their children that night with this new horror, by now enthroned or entrapped in the palace: a warrior like that could easily break out and scavenge the city for naughty wide-awake infants, and gobble them up after skewering them with arrows.

So gradually the dust settled and the evening curled along the passages, separating sounds into isolated screeches of laughter and song, little flurries of running fights, and the sober commands of the nightwatch. And later, peacocks could be heard crying like disconsolate spoilt children, and from further afield, way beyond the city, the curlew and the owl.

Strange, then, that when this Hippolyta, guarded by a circle of soldiers unsure whether to face inwards or outwards, had been ushered up the steps into the Great Hall, strange indeed that her bearing and manner should undergo such a drastic and immediate change. For she stood upright, looked about imperiously, and said to the nearest shaking servants, 'Hot water and your best quality soap – at once! My sister and I will bathe before we dine. Bring a selection of our robes from the large chests that are being brought in now. And have any gentlewomen resident here come to us in the baths so that we may learn a little of Athenian custom and enjoy decent conversation after our ordeal. And bring to us wine and cakes, and ladies who can sweetly sing the songs of your history. Be quick, or be dismissed from our house!'

The small fair child took hold of her regal sister's hand and tugged for attention, then complained, 'Sister, I don't like it here – the men eye us like meat and the women are feeble. I want to go home where we are loved.'

'We can't go home, kid,' Hippolyta whispered. 'Brazen it out.'

V

WARM CLEAR NIGHT, deep blue with far-off ochreous hues in the stilled turbulence of the clouds. Below, some of the men were exercising, oiled bodies wrestling, some practising swordplay or spearing stooks of hay, others carousing near the blazing fires which sent up billows of smoke and flaming shreds of bark. Much laughter and light-hearted chatter passed back and fore all over the camp, gently binding the men to a common purpose.

Theseus and some of the nobles with whom he planned his campaigns and discoursed on statecraft and love sat under a large oak. Occasionally Theseus would break off to let out a long sigh of unrestrained pleasure which made his companions a mite envious, for Demetrius was massaging his tired shoulders.

'I hope,' he said, returning to his theme again, 'that my old friend Perotheus is not with Creon.'

There were sombre murmurings, for most had friends in Thebes, some were Thebans by birth, and the men they knew meant more to them than the grieving widows who had redirected them.

'Honour is a hard thing,' Theseus ruminated gravely. 'Yet, as we know, it is ranked higher than friendship and often calls us where we would not go if we served our individual interests. Your friend is yours alone, but your honour reflects all that men should aspire to.'

The nobles nodded. Only the youthful, favoured Demetrius was foolhardy enough to treat the sober pep-talk as a debatable issue rather than a grim article of faith for real men to bite on.

'It seems to me,' he said, wringing his hands, 'that we could find ourselves slaves to an abstract tyrant worse than Creon if we didn't first honour our friends and loves. Friendship is sacrosanct, my lord. Where I place my friend's fortune above my own, honour becomes mine.'

This sort of talk was no booster of morale, no consolation to men who might be hacking old pals to pieces in the morning.

'To sacrifice yourself for your friend may in some places be a noble act,' Theseus countered quickly, 'without ceasing to be a stupid one. Our friendship would certainly ennoble a worthless friend, but should we then destroy ourself for him our action would not have served the State and would most certainly have taken away the only part of him that had merit.'

'Is the State then the better arbiter of honour than a man's conscience?'

'It is more than a friendship, since all friendships exist within it.'

'Humbly, I hope I may differ, my lord,' Demetrius said, flushed with what he took to be the success of his argument thus far.

'No, Demetrius, you may not differ. We have many friends in Thebes who may die tomorrow, and that's the way of it. Leave off now until you've learned the way – you have displeased me.' Theseus was stern, but he didn't want to sound petulant, and deep down he wanted to retain Demetrius. 'Well,' he added less magisterially, 'who is this particular friend? Who is it that gives you your honour?'

'Why, Lysander,' he threw out, trying to copy the easy grace he'd had until a few seconds back, when it seemed a defence of friendship would work better. 'We are like brothers.'

'You have the valour,' Theseus conceded. 'What has he?'

'Lysander is valiant too, my lord, and would have been with us . . .'

— 27 —

'But?'

'Could not. A personal matter, sir, an embarrassment that should not . . .'

'Come, come, man, out with it!'

'A carbuncle. Lysander could not sit at ease on a cushion, let alone a horse.'

The nobles laughed vigorously and so did Theseus. Demetrius winced.

Theseus saw another lesson. 'Don't think our laughter mocks your friendship. We laugh at what is absurd, knowing that of such absurdities are our destinies governed. A carbuncular bum is a painful humiliation, petty, but not even Hercules could have ridden one out. Our bodies like to trick us when we're strong and even I don't understand the principles by which our gods rule. They allow these things while teaching us to aspire to a dignity above beasts – the paradox exercises me continually. Let's hope Lysander is well seated on our return. If not we shall see to it his carbuncle is lanced for friendship – we must at times be cruel to be kind. Pain and pleasure, my friends, pleasure and pain, they are at us daily.'

'Shall we think of Creon as a great carbuncle?'

'Tomorrow he will bleed, to be sure. And then the widows will get their bones.'

Silently Demetrius resumed his position and placed his hands on his master's shoulders. The muscles did not repel him. Gently he pushed his finger-ends towards the still sensitive places, and to his gratification Theseus eased his shoulder to follow the soothing rhythm and sighed as the knots unravelled. The nobles under the oak smiled now that sententiousness had given way to serenity, but in a moment came a new distraction, sounds of disturbance in the camp, sights of men moving fast towards one spot. A stranger had intruded.

Theseus commanded him to be brought up to the oak for questioning and this was done at once, the sturdy young alien insisting on leading his laden donkey.

'What are you, man?' Theseus demanded.

— 28 —

'A man, sir, right enough.'

'What are you in addition?'

'A weaver, sir.'

'What way do you weave so late into the night?'

'I go to Thebes, sir, by your leave.'

'Or bypassing my leave, since you did not seek me out to gain it.'

'I beg pardon, sir, you have lost me.'

'I am not sure we can afford to lose any worthy man. But I am not steeped in textorial habits – tell me, how often do you visit Thebes? And for what purpose? Before you answer, let me explain, in case you are as simple as you appear: we wish to determine one thing – are you what you claim, or could you be a spy in our camp?'

'No spy I, sir!' Bottom protested indignantly. 'A weaver is all I pretend to be, and, begging your pardon again, but if you want proof you should ask questions pertaining to the intricacies of my trade which none but a true weaver could answer.'

'Very fair. But how could anyone but another weaver pose such questions?'

'I know you could, being Theseus and all. You might ask me to name the parts of my loom, reveal the secrets of my dyes – my dyeing is much in demand and I shouldn't risk to tell you, neither, only I believe I could trust to your discretion, sir, to keep the secret.'

'You must be a very unpopular fellow, if all clamour for your dying.'

'Not so, I am well enough liked by my friends, though they do sometimes find me as irksome as I find them tedious. For all that we get along, and would as soon die for each other as for anyone else.'

'Dying again – and yet outwardly you are cheery. What ails you?'

'Any ale that's going suits me fine, thank you kindly.'

'Fellow,' said Theseus, 'either you're too dull to parry, or the subtlest fool I've found in three long voyages – I suspect the former. One further question, then we may give you ale and let you pass: Are you an Athenian?'

'Always proud to be adopted, sir, though I must live outside your city, it being the nature of my trade to require a good flow of pure water and a ready supply of those barks and leaves and juices that enable me to dye to such good effect.'

'So you are more dyer than weaver, and live near a stream and near a wood?'

'I do.'

'And dye there?'

'Frequently.'

'Well, such jests must be tiresome to you for they begin to pall with us already. But you have borne them well and given us a pleasant interlude. Do you, by chance, live in a palace made of stones?'

'That sounds too clever for the likes of me – a right riddler of a question. I'm a straightforward man who weaves and dyes.'

In truth, Bottom was nonplussed, and also rather frightened. Dewdrop's ears had pricked up and the donkey had snorted a warning. The collapse of the stone stable preceding this acute and only slightly misdirected line of questioning carried coincidence uncomfortably close to calamity. Fortunately Theseus decided he was satisfied – more than satisfied, pleased – and he told the textor that in return for entertaining the noblemen he might ask a favour.

Bottom thought hard. Or looked as if the process of thinking was hard. He knew at once what he wanted and simply had to find the words.

'Well now then,' he mumbled, 'it happened that I was with some chums this afternoon, and to be honest that's why I'm travelling to Thebes tonight, for our business in Athens was abandoned when we heard you were on the road home, so I come to Thebes to sell my wares in the morning and not lose out.' He hesitated, seeing he was losing everyone's attention. 'Well now then,' this more rapidly, 'we are in our spare time actors, as good as you could hope to find, and hoped if you met us on the road you might permit us to perform a play before you at the palace, sir, so that we too, being ordinary folk, might share in the celebration of your new engagement with the wild lady.'

'Mmm,' said Theseus dubiously. 'This favour requires some thought. A bad performance would be insulting to my bride and offensive to me – that would bring you no luck whatever. Tell me, how may I ascertain your acting skills? I should be loath to punish a man who'd done his very best, but incompetence demands punishment as merit demands reward. For your sake, how may I test you?'

'Allow me to declaim, sir. I have several speeches wrote out and ready to be read, if you'll let me unpack my pack from the back of my faithful friend here.'

'Ah, so *that's* why you wouldn't be parted from the beast! An accomplished thespian, eh? This takes us back to our suspicions!'

'Safest to kill him now,' one knight said distinctly, for he was bored, tired, and disliked the rough wit of artisans. 'See if he's as smart a dyer as he boasts!'

'Murder the donkey,' suggested another. 'He'll confess all then.'

'I think I have a part you can play in the morning,' Theseus said, a merry twinkle in his eye that the weaver shivered to see. 'You will sleep in our camp tonight, for if we let you on to Thebes where you might sell a few rags at first light your profits will be short-lived, our plain intention being to destroy that unkind city.'

'Then I thank Your Highness for preserving me. And do you have the lines wrote out for me to learn, sir? I should enjoy time to rehearse and adopt the most fitting character.'

'I will lend you a script tomorrow and you may read from it directly. If you acquit yourself honourably, or at all, then we shall invite your guild to perform at our feasting.'

Several knights were smirking and nudging each other. Nick Bottom touched his forehead apprehensively and crept away towards a fire's embers.

— 31 —

'You've done it again,' Dewdrop said when, half an hour later, they were settling down under the cold stars.

'You talked!' Bottom cried gladly, and kissed his donkey's nose.

'I won't have time to make a habit of it, Nick,' the dour friend returned. 'My bet is we shall both be dead meat by noon, and the dogs of Thebes will be your last critics.'

VI

PANIC IN THE palace!

There were gentlewomen, but the matronly didn't think it proper to meet Hippolyta before Theseus made them. Also, they rather thought they'd despise her and were reluctant to start off seeming to fawn. So they told their daughters to go and their daughters giggled and hid and got in such states of nerves that they just *couldn't* be first, they'd *die* – and so there was great bustle and foolishness in the corridors outside the chamber where Hippolyta and Emily waited impatiently.

Servants attended them. Servants had bathed them, robed them, and now chatted while serving wine and cake, and the regal couple were sufficiently amused. The servants were not so silly as their mistresses.

'And have your mistresses no minds of their own?' Hippolyta asked.

'Put it this way, Ma'am: they heard all about Scythia and your life, and urged their husbands to exterminate the lot of you. "Stamp 'em out," they said. "Stamp 'em out before they get a hold on our girls."'

'I see. They fear themselves.'

'Their husbands more, I reckon. And no wonder. If your husband takes against you he can throw you over and you'll be alone with nothing to show for all your years of service.'

'And did you urge *your* men to stamp us out?'

— 33 —

'Bless you, miss, no – or, if we did, only because it was expected, not with conviction. Some of us have long dreamt of running off to join you, if you want to know.'

'Ah, dreams,' Hippolyta chided the maid gently. 'If we had no dreams we'd live out petty days with hopes expiring at our feet!'

'You what?'

'I say we should not call up dreams for excuses. Had you truly wanted to join us nothing need have stopped you. To have a translatable dream yet not enact it is to accept your servitude, to embrace it.'

'If it comes to that a servant here would be a servant there, I reckon. Didn't you depend on servants, maids like me to clean your toes and shine your nails and empty your pots and run errands? And it *is* comfortable here, and for all our admiration we feared your example. Did you sleep in caves with kind and know no men save those you ate?'

'Is that how it goes? No wonder your mistresses shun us! Why have you so little faith in the hearts and minds of your sex? Look at my precious sister – isn't she the very picture of seemliness? Emily is as chaste as a May morning. Are we not perfect simulacra of fine ladies?'

'Oh, *yes*, Ma'am, but . . . don't you eat men at *all*?'

'Perhaps a nibble here and there, now and then,' she said naughtily, taking with dainty fingers another mint.

'Hippolyta!' Emily complained.

'My sister has never tasted man, and still prays that love will never weaken her. Or waken her, perhaps. She is a moral child and quite properly reminds me I am crude. Being a servant you are also crude, I dare say, though you haven't been ravished by Hercules as I have, the most bestial, rough and foul-smelling man in the whole world, so you don't have my excuse. Nonetheless, you must promise not to be vulgar before our Emily. We must comport ourselves like votaries of Diana in her presence. And please, don't make the mistake of assuming I jest. I am serious. Emily's virtue matters.'

—— 34 ——

'Thank you,' Emily said with smug graciousness, and Hippolyta nodded but without the smugness.

Emily's long fair hair had been combed and braided and it was no longer conceivable she had led any sort of primitive wilderness life. Hippolyta, however, could not so thoroughly disguise her unusual self. She looked exciting where Emily looked nice. Hippolyta was a new kind of queen, unpredictable. Queens were generally more like adult versions of Emily. They fitted easily into place, polished pieces of the palace. Their men could idolise and rule them because they hadn't the sense to be surprising. But how would Theseus rule Hippolyta? She might spit in his eye. Laugh at his more pompous pronouncements. Fail to tremble at his wrath. She might yawn and scratch her thighs in public. Surely she wouldn't last out their nuptials!

'Ma'am?'

'Yes, dear, what's on your mind?'

'My mind? Why, nothing, of course. It's one of our young ladies, Ma'am, who would be honoured if you'd receive her.'

'Aha! They begin to pluck up courage – curiosity kills discretion and disdain, Emily, remember that. Show her in at once. And then, girls, you'd better leave us awhile, for the poor thing will fear to demean herself and fear to offend me and fear to forget whatever she's been commanded to ask. And I don't *really* want to sabotage the Court, you know!'

So the maids, who'd never been spoken to so candidly except by children, withdrew with awkward half-bows and glassy smiles and general consternation.

'How d'you think they take us?' Hippolyta whispered to Emily.

'The servants? How should I know? Why should we care?'

'I'm sure we've made a hit. They seem confused – I dare say they've never been treated like human beings till now.'

'How does one treat servants like human beings? By saying thank you when a tray is brought? Encouraging them to betray the confidences of families they've served for years? Making suggestive remarks?'

— 35 —

'Oh, Emily, you're a gruesome little prude at times – I do wish puberty would up-end you before you turn us all into saints and hypocrites. I rather hoped that applying the dye and squatting in the cage with me would loosen you up – didn't you enjoy that a bit?'

'How could you even ask!' Emily cried, the outrage returning vividly to mind. She touched her clean arm and felt her clean robe for comfort. 'I've never been so wretched. And don't think I didn't see you either, or that I wouldn't tell Mother if she were alive. You peed in that poor man's face deliberately, and shrieked with glee like an animal, except I can't imagine an animal that would behave that way to its own kind!'

'You know as little of animals as you do of life. Oh, Emily, we have to play our parts, child.'

'Don't condescend. One doesn't have to play with such gusto!'

'The fellow was straining to see up my legs, his tongue hanging out like sad sex, a common, impudent rascal whose wife beats him. And I needed to go in any case. What does it matter? In all that dust. Tomorrow there'll be a dozen stories of my tearing at the bars, firing arrows at the populace; in this world nobody believes what simply happens, and those of us whose purpose is to be emulated by the world, we may do whatever we wish, knowing it will be subject to a hundred interpretations. We are legend. I was raped by Hercules. Who cares for the details? My disgust, his stinking feebleness. It was Hercules and therefore epic, Herculean, in fact. Does it interest anyone that he was so drunk he used the neck of a pot?'

'Please! There's no need for such coarseness, despite your ordeals. *All* men are beastly, *I* see that clearly enough, yet you, after the dreadful things they've done, go on admiring them! I think you're appalling in this mood. You should drink no more wine this week. You embarrass me.'

'Any more of that and I'll send you straight to bed. Watch me, and learn to be a queen!'

'As if the Queen ever lived with her nose beneath a man's navel!'

'You think I'm kidding? The first lesson is to survive. You'll notice we *are* alive, and neither of us in the donjon we saw coming in? By your indomitable virtue, do you think? Has your chastity protected you as well as you protect it? Or could it be my adaptability? Think on your feet, kid, and learn from your big sister.'

Hippolyta would have said more, but for the arrival of an Athenian girl with supplicatory eyes and a deceptively humble manner who cleared her throat politely and no more noisily than a sparrow. Emily turned and, seeing someone not vastly older than herself, though clearly, in her largely transparent dress, more maturely developed, smiled eagerly.

'Oh, I'm not to be alone!' she exclaimed softly. 'Oh, goody! Please tell me what is your name and house, and which deities you worship, and how often are there days of prayer and abstinence in this Athens?'

'Wrap up, Em,' said Hippolyta curtly, and to the astonished visitor, 'Come, girl, pour some of this wine for me and tell us what a marvellous lord my abductor is.'

Without batting an eyelid Hermia poured the wine and refrained from filling an empty glass for herself. The last thing she wanted was to cause offence. That was why she'd come before the new Queen all but naked, to be seen guileless with large unused breasts and rather broad hips (she was fond of burgers and onions, with ketchup, sold at a stall on the market square). Hermia hadn't come at the behest of a disdainful mother but to further a cause of her own, and she wanted Hippolyta on her side. She was young enough to believe a sincere plea could shift a mountain, in this case her father.

'*Is* Theseus your abductor, my lady?' she managed to ask in just the right tone of respectful but not ingratiating interest. 'Is he no more to you than a captor?'

'I cannot without absurdity claim to have captured *him*, but he may be more than my captor if I can make him my prey.'

'But no one is guarding you, and we have been warned to treat you as his wife. Didn't he win you legitimately, in fair fight? Am I impertinent?'

'Fine word, legitimately! To the victor the despoiled! Well, sister, you may speak here – was it a legitimate conquest?'

'What stories have reached Athens?' Emily asked.

'Too few, but we hear your women fought bravely until the inevitable weight of our soldiery bore down, and that in his mercy Theseus deigned take you to wife, allowing you to bring your infant sister so you shouldn't feel bereft of all old contact.'

'There was no engagement,' Emily said haughtily, glancing to Hippolyta for permission to continue. 'We were prepared to fight if necessary, though we are not a warlike tribe unless assailed first. Our first approach, as ever, was to extend the hand of friendship. I do not speak for myself, but for my sisters the arrival of a male army occasioned fancies of love rather than belligerent chants. So a deputation of alluring ladies went to greet them with gifts before they disembarked.'

'I took Emily along to show we weren't a bunch of tramps,' Hippolyta interpolated, and gave a hiccup. 'Besides, I'd heard that Theseus has a penchant for young girls. Call me irresponsible, but if you're going to get it from some dick anyway, it might as well be a descendant of the gods, yeah? I mean, at least that way you'll be remembered. The whole world knows I was ravished by Hercules.'

'No,' Emily broke in hotly. 'All the ladies, including this great queen of ours, had great dignity. They were out to seduce these men, but thought elegance and breeding were the means. This evening my sister acts the part of a degraded captive as she thinks Athenians would wish it played. Sobriety and some promise of decent treatment from your devious brute of a lord would reveal her true splendour.'

'I don't know what to think,' was all Hermia could say.

'Well, regardless of that,' drawled Hippolyta, 'the fact is there was no engagement. We ladies were invited aboard – all hopeful smiles and leers – our gifts were accepted, our persons admired. Then, abandoning protocol, Theseus upped anchor, set sail and

— 38 —

had all my friends chucked overboard. Is this what you hereabout term legitimate? Seems like dirty dealing to me!'

Hermia frowned. Her hopes were dwindling, for she had assumed that Theseus and Hippolyta were in love.

'I came to ask if you would intercede in a matter of the gravest importance,' she said sorrowfully, 'but I see I should accept my doom as you are resigned to yours.'

'Explain, child.'

'My lady, I have no one on my side. You are to be Theseus's wife. If you have influence with him, I beg you to speak for me. Yours is not the sole impending marriage.'

'You are to be chained too?'

'And I do not love Demetrius, yet Father tells me I shall marry him or die.'

'Marry him, then. Life is always more interesting than death. I don't advise that, it's too unknown. I have been greatly abused in my time, and I think I am much broken up inside, yet still I do live, accepting the ignominies that lie ahead and waiting on those brief moments of control when I share peace with nature. Such moments come, so long as we have breath. For the rest, be brazen, survive.'

'But Hippolyta, sometimes death . . .'

'Quiet, pipsqueak, you haven't yet lived. You don't even know why your chastity has such charm, nor will you, till you've travelled as far from it as I.'

'Death doesn't appeal to me,' Hermia said earnestly. 'The thing is, I do know love. I am *in* love. There is a man who is the world to me, Lysander. My father won't acknowledge him, wants only the wealthy and warlike Demetrius.'

'Then you have a problem.'

'One I hoped you might solve.'

'Poor child, my only concern is to ensure my sister's future and then my own. To accomplish that I'll play whatever games Theseus desires. I was stolen from my people by a formidable man who can rule whatever he sees. I am a woman, but not indomitable. I'm not without sympathy for you, though your

— 39 —

notion of love is unreal, but expect no help. I am not your queen. I am nobody's queen. Dethroned and forgotten, I am nothing, until your lord either binds me or frees me.'

'Forgive me, Madam, I thought you were free.'

'We *were* free,' Emily murmured sadly, and touched Hermia's hand for pity while Hippolyta poured herself another glass of wine.

VII

ICK BOTTOM HAD played the hero's part before, and loved an expansive gesture, a rhythmic roll of words, a sound like ceaseless waves devouring rock. But this part Theseus had given him was different, dangerous and more demeaning than any part he'd tried. No hero, neither wave nor rock, Bottom felt like a piece of that bulbous jelly clinging between the two elements, disliked by both. He was a Messenger.

'This is not an audition,' Dewdrop pointed out, speaking out the corner of his mouth with a tough guy's shrewd cynicism. 'Messengers deliver messages. Fine so far. Messages delivered, messengers have no further use. Think on.'

The weaver sighed, unprotesting. There was not, after all, a thing he could do. If he'd thought Theseus and the nobles were grateful, or that his likely death might spring a few tears, then he could have borne himself with a kind of grandeur for the occasion, but the aggravating fact was that he'd left them laughing. Having a humble weaver for messenger was a neatly turned insult to Creon – and something of a relief, since no one wanted the job, least of all those who promptly volunteered after they'd heard it was Bottom's part. He sighed again, then looked about at the usual signs of unwitting nature peaceably preoccupied with growing and feeding and effortlessly looking good.

'A lovely morning, anyway,' he said, 'and a fine path with no

— 41 —

sharp stones to hurt your hoof. I'll say this much for Creon, he's built some fine roads!'

The walls of Thebes hadn't been so imposing, so forbidding before. They used to leave the gates open. Now he was so close Nick saw the mound which he'd taken for a pile of stones resolve into bones and some flesh. He closed his eyes, gulped to keep his stomach from wriggling, and made a short prayer for the souls of these deceased to be delivered. Then he placed a hand between his donkey's ears, which was a sign for Dewdrop to stop whenever this gentle man was too confused to trust in words.

'I know,' Dewdrop said, stopping as bidden. 'I wish I hadn't taken so much to drink last night as well.'

'It's not that. Don't you see those bodies?'

'I smell them. I hope they aren't friends of yours.'

'Not when they lived, but shortly, maybe, I shall be glad of their company. Listen, Dewdrop, you've been the truest companion a man could wish for. None of my little weavers and dyers from the forest has meant quite as much, though God knows I owe them more than my livelihood and have never known how to repay them.'

'They're fairies, and fairies are industrious when they're not bone idle or fornicating. Their payment is the work you permit them to do, which keeps them out of mischief. Mortals would ask more, but not they. You owe us nothing, Nick.'

'Even so, when I've delivered this message the rain may pierce your hide too, and there's no cause for you to die, old chum. I shall dismount here and walk the remainder. You go back.'

'You can tell me what to do, Nick, but you can't make me do it. That's the nature of the beast in me. And as your friend I'd rather die beside you than live without you. Could you go on if I had to die?'

'What a question! How unfair! I'm afraid the answer has to be yes, old chap, though I should never replace or forget you, but yes, because you are a donkey and I am a man.'

'Ah,' the donkey said gruffly. 'I put the question badly. Would you put your life at risk to save mine?'

— 42 —

'Obviously – you're my pal. That's different.'

'Let's not get sentimental, then. Come on, let's get it done. Your mortal knights are waiting, and I want to show their stuck-up horses that a donkey has some style.'

'You good old boy,' Nick muttered throatily, and patted Dewdrop so that he continued, swaying hindquarters from side to side insolently. 'And it *is* a pleasant morning, live or die. Hear the lark?'

'I thought it was a rusty wheel.'

They arrived, the light breeze fortunately touching them before it passed over the congealing remains; even so, Nick couldn't help glancing. There was no blood left, only whiteness and darkness. The heap was not neat. Bones lay scattered where filched, chewed and dropped. A few dogs were still engaged, though what they could worry out could hardly be worth the effort now. The weaver forced himself to look at the gates, then to gaze upwards. There he saw the little heads of living men, and the jarring points of spears. He felt more fellowship with those bleaching near him. He cleared his throat, pulled the scroll out of his jerkin and grandly unrolled it. But before starting he bent forward and whispered goodbye to his donkey.

'I am Nick Bottom, textor of Athens,' he started, discovering that his voice carried strongly despite quaking innards. It was good to have an audience, however predisposed to hostility, and Nick determined to make his last speech memorable. 'I have been empowered to deliver a message from Theseus, Commander of War and Guardian of the Law of Athens, which men everywhere ought to follow on account of its good sense. Theseus the aforesaid declares that since Thebes is no longer officially under siege her best knights may meet him in open combat and die as befits once-honourable men. Creon he very generously challenges man to man. Theseus declares that, his offer being refused, he will tear Thebes to the earth from which it sprang and kill all within as equal scum, sparing none but women, old men, children and their pets. But I am to repeat that those who wish to die as knights, stained only in their own brave blood, may now do so.

— 43 —

'Now, if you want to waste good spears on this poor messenger and his ass you may do so, but remember it will leave you weaponless against the mighty wrath of Theseus and his dreadful retribution and an army of such ferocity I'd cling to my spear with both hands if I were in your shoes. I had hoped to die an old weaver, but if the gods wish me to go out a messenger I'll take my leave.

'Wait!' he cried as he saw spears being angled and aimed. 'I have more!'

'Cut the crap, Nick! This is Bad News City,' Dewdrop said, and at the same moment charged aside and found the shelter of the dead as the first rain thudded into the path. More spears and crossbow darts clattered in the bones. And then the sport of killing the messenger was forgotten. The gates groaned and shuddered. Knights rode out. None so much as glanced right or left, and from his grisly position Nick Bottom safely watched the rapid engagement. He thought the Theban knights terrifying enough as they galloped down, but the knights awaiting them were even more horrific, not galloping, not moving at all, but waiting in their ranks just beyond the field of combat, all dark and shining in the sun, like death.

Soon there were poor horses dying, the dying men smaller, their last movements less easy to see and suffer with. The noises of bodies crashing together eddied up the hill. Nick winced, as he did to see soaring spears finding their staggering targets. He shrank in fear and swore not to look or listen, then had to, as if to check it was no nightmare but the reality behind the glorious tales of victory that had moved him to pride more than once. In ten minutes the Thebans were bloodily vanquished. Next the winning side came thundering up in a formation similar to that in which the enemy had descended, and with a deadly intention still, for the coward tyrant had not emerged to salvage any nobility for himself.

Theseus commanded his men to stop, and the weaver had his first chance to examine the stained, determined faces of men who'd laughed at him not long ago. He was profoundly glad not

— 44 —

to be a warrior, for all the faces were identical and without decency. They were become a beast of prey, with Theseus the head. If honour had brought him to this place, murder was what kept him.

Slowly Theseus turned his awful visage towards Nick Bottom, who wanted to roll over grovelling for having remained alive when the world was death. But Theseus was not concerned with a messenger. His eyes were on the heaped dead and he stared until his fixity softened, though without loss of fortitude. It seemed he had located a justification for the slaughter and that he rose up spiritually, yet visibly to all. 'These bodies must suffer no further indignities. They shall not be moved from here. Ten of you, take axes to the gates to lay as tinder for their pyre. Twenty, go, bring me Creon. Kill any that stand in your way but bring Creon alive.'

Prudently the weaver retreated under the walls, well away from the bones. He watched the strong knights hacking into the city gates and marvelled at their strength and shivered to think that those axes had just been wielded into men and horses. He watched these powerful men carrying great timbers and placing them tenderly against the bony pile until the only thing to be seen was wood three times as broad as the mortal heap had been. Then he watched as twenty knights returned with the fat tyrant, who was dropping as if his legs were snapped and begging mercy as he came.

Theseus hadn't dismounted, nor had his horse made the slightest move in all this time, despite surges of activity on all sides. Creon was brought up under the horse and left to stand or fall alone. Amazingly, he stood. 'For your crimes, Creon, I have this morning killed the greatest knights of Thebes. The flower of your chivalry is gone. Now Thebes will burn. How can I make you suffer enough for what you have done?'

Creon listened abjectly, but then a strange thing happened: an ugly grin formed on his face. Not courage, he was well past that, a dead man's grin, maddening to behold. He spoke in a girlish, quavering voice. 'Antigone disobeyed me when she buried her

— 45 —

brother, so I was within the law when I imprisoned her. My son, Haemon, loved Antigone, and killed himself to die with her. And I live on. You have had many children, Theseus, but you've loved none. One day you will. I hope that then your son will die at a judgement from you, so that then you too will know suffering. I am a wretch. I couldn't match you in combat. You're the greatest warrior our world has seen, except for my son-in-law, Hercules. When he hears how you have killed me the world may discover which of you is the greater. But I care not; I am nothing, a piece of dung, not worthy of your wrath. Killing me you dishonour yourself. Do so, I urge you.'

'I wish I could understand you, Creon. Why flout every law?'

'I am a man. You have godliness. I have none.'

'That's no explanation. You are no man!'

Evidently he felt it profitless to question Creon further. He commanded that the pyre be lit, and that brands be taken from it to illuminate Thebes. Knights spurred their horses into the city and its dwellings flamed. Theseus gave another order that every cur should be speared and added to the pyre, for the dogs had supped on dead nobles.

Through all this destruction Theseus did not move. He didn't see the smoke-black sky or hear the cracking of collapsing buildings or the screams of the dispossessed. Nothing of lust or malice could be read from his impassive, noble face. All this was chivalry, pure and impersonal as winter. 'You see what you have caused, Creon. How do you speak now?'

'I only wish I had your vision, Theseus,' Creon said slyly, grimacing and satiated.

'Enough! Your day is done. Demetrius – his tongue – remove it. His eyes – pop them next. If he faints, revive him. He will be admitted to death only as we are removing his skin. Creon, your head will be spiked to appear sightless above the walls. Your skin will be spread upon your bed and your bed plunged into the midden. Your flesh and bones will rot here in the dirt and feed fat flies. If your soul reaches the gods they will torment it further. The brief moments of your agony here will extend through realms of time we cannot dream of, and every instant will bring renewed pain eternally.'

'You are too kind,' Creon managed to say with pallid bravado, just before Demetrius, whose supple hands could be so soothing, grabbed his head and wrenched his jaws apart.

Nick Bottom threw up against the wall. Dewdrop averted his big eyes for shame.

'This is no place for us,' Nick whispered, wiping his mouth. 'Come, let's creep away from such wicked lessons.'

He hadn't the strength to mount but with wobbly legs led his donkey down the grassy hill away from the burning city. Unfortunately he had strayed from the path and soon found himself picking a route around hideously wounded horses and the hacked remains of knights.

'Honour is a more dreadful word than I'd supposed,' Dewdrop said, treading daintily. 'It must be hard to be Theseus. If he is a man he must be like you, and you couldn't do what he's done. There must be that in him which is as simple as you, and that which sees the need for all this in order to protect your simplicity for all men.'

'You are very charitable.'

'I'm trying to keep my faith in you, Nick, for you are a man and these are men, and today I fear you.'

'I have no weapons, and I don't know what honour is. I reject it.'

'That's a comfort. Hey, some of your fellow men are not dead.'

Nick wanted to get well away and never return, yet he couldn't abandon injured men. He waved and shouted towards the smouldering fires and regathering army. Presently a rider came, who examined the two knights who had moved and rode up the hill again to report. Then several came galloping and Nick shut his eyes in case they dealt with wounded men by trampling.

'Theban knights,' one muttered admiringly. 'See how they've fallen together – from their colours they're of the same house. How bravely they must have fought, side by side until both were felled.'

Demetrius rode down and he too admired them. 'Theseus shows mercy,' he said. 'We will imprison them.'

The weaver felt a little better as he quietly left the scene. He had been ill used to start the battle, but saving two dying knights had been his own free choice.

An hour later he was overtaken by a rider. 'Are you the weaver who delivered our message? Theseus thanks you and grants your request. You and your troupe of clowns will perform before him at the palace. Fortune has smiled on you, rogue!'

Nick continued for a long while in thoughtful silence. It struck him that Fortune's smile had a distinctly cold aspect, but he didn't want to be ungrateful. He had requested a performance, had been cruelly auditioned, and was now granted his request. 'I should be gleeful,' he muttered. 'Only I am not such a fool.'

'That's not what Puck will say when you describe today's events,' Dewdrop told him glumly. 'He holds that all men are fools. This won't dissuade him.'

Nick allowed himself a brief grin. At least, he thought, in his own cottage in the forest there was another world of company far from the humours of his fellow men, and there he could hope to distance his tattered mind from the dreadful education Theseus had given it.

The two knights whose miserable lives he had saved had names. They were called Palamon and Arcite. Fortune determined that Nick would meet them again, in circumstances not much happier. But would they remember his crucial part in their story? You may well ask.

— 48 —

VIII

THESEUS TOOK HIMSELF to his private baths and soaked for a couple of hours, alone but for the girls who scrubbed his weary body and anointed him with oils to remove the smell of smoke. With the wise reflection that there was nothing so pleasant as a hot bath, Theseus fell asleep. No one dared disturb him and afternoon steamed on into early evening.

Hippolyta, who had been waiting nervously to be summoned, had changed her robe and jewellery three times before anticipation gave way to irritation. He was not God, after all, and she was not a simpering girl.

At seven she called for her sister. 'The bugger's forgotten I exist,' she complained recklessly.

'Shush!'

'But what should I do? Take myself off to prison? Get drunk?'

'Wait. And hope not to be noticed till he's ready to notice you.'

'And if he really has simply forgotten, won't he fear his lapse will be seen as a weakness; won't he have to conceal a weakness? He may feel obliged to treat me unkindly, then where shall we be? Men are vain, Emily, they can't bear to lose the upper hand, and the greater the man the more monstrous his vanity. Why, Hercules tried to kill me when he'd done, for fear I might spread the word about his incapacity. If a greedy servant hadn't emptied

— 49 —

my goblet the wretched death she imbibed would have been mine. All for vanity.'

'Calm yourself, sister. Theseus was courteous enough on the voyage, and the women here speak well of him – he hasn't assaulted any, as far as we know, so he's not to be feared like Hercules. Why not send someone to ask if he'll permit you an audience? That approach would impute no loss of memory.'

'Not bad, Em – good. But even better, yes, I'll go to him myself.'

'Oh, no!'

Hippolyta was not to be dissuaded, and straight away sent girls to discover the great man's whereabouts. She expected him to be in his study by now, catching up on State business, and was delighted to hear he'd only dropped off in the bath.

'He's not as young as he was,' she deduced. 'But I'll tread warily. An old boar is a dangerous boar.'

She let herself into the bath-house silently. A few girls stood to attention but Hippolyta smiled and motioned them to leave. The main bath was large enough for a dozen men to swim in, and Theseus lay at the shallow end, head and shoulders out of water, head back over the lip of the pool and resting on a red cushion. He was snoring like a pig after truffles. Realising her own finery might disadvantage him, Hippolyta disrobed and then eased herself into the warm steamy water. It was barely deep enough to cover her knees. She dropped forward on to her hands and made her way towards her groom on all fours, belly grazing the surface. Still he slept.

'Good evening, my lord,' Hippolyta said in her soft deep voice, after she had poured wine from the trays beside his head.

Theseus made a vague nod and accepted a goblet, evidently half-sleeping still. She shuffled back on her knees until she was at his feet, crouching submissively so her nipples appeared and disappeared. Theseus studied her slowly. Hippolyta felt as a slave at auction might feel, a disconcertingly erotic sensation, she thought – he seemed too sleepy a potentate to want to kill her this evening.

—— 50 ——

'Well,' he said after another languid examination of the somewhat scarred but nonetheless firm and vibrantly full form, 'Hippolyta.'

'Well,' she copied carefully, 'Theseus.'

'Home at last!'

'So you are.'

'So you shall be. How does my palace please you?'

'I cannot tell, sir, until I know my position in it.'

He pondered that, chuckling and sipping his wine rather delicately. Then other thoughts darkened his brow and he looked as if he might choose sleep again.

'Sir, I do not know if I am to be paraded about the city and set in the stocks, installed as your legitimate wife, given the freedom of a courtesan, or kept in a box. It seems to me that the noble women here are of less use than servants. They chatter and look pretty and have no power.'

'I wonder if you're going to be troublesome, chuck?'

'I'm going to be whatever you desire. I have no choice.'

'What if I *give* you choice?'

'And I chose to return to my people after denouncing you for that cowardly abduction? Giving me choice is beyond your powers, sir, unless you are so mighty you heed nothing your people say.'

'I wouldn't let you return to Scythia, that's true enough. I captured you and you belong here.'

'Then I'll be whatever you desire, sir.'

'What I desire is that you choose to serve me.'

'Then I do.'

'That easily?'

'I have no choice.'

'Damnation! There was a time when women were honoured to have their fate in my hands. Ariadne doted on me. Even the girls I took before their time . . .'

'And where are they now?'

'Past – they have their place in history. Which is more than they would have had. Hippolyta, I want you to lighten my long

— 51 —

evenings. You have a certain reputation which makes me hope you will prove a suitable mate. We've both knocked about a good deal, and now I want you to be . . . I don't know exactly.'

'Available?'

'Enchanting, maybe. Companionable. A friend. Able to surprise me, liven me up when my thoughts are ponderous.'

'A clowning whore for you and a paragon for the world?'

'Frankly, I'm beginning to feel old and philosophical, but I don't want to lose all touch with exuberance. Nor do I fancy being a brutal tyrant, vicious in loneliness. Ruling is hard. I need my lighter moments, and I'd like some of them to be with a woman of some spirit. Would you turn around, please, so that I may address myself to your buttocks?'

'You desire to rape me, sir? As you wish,' she said disdainfully.

She hoped her comment might put him off, her submission might make him feel shame. No such luck, but at least he wasn't rough about it, but tired and workmanlike. Afterwards he flopped back with a great splash. Hippolyta remained stolidly in position until he told her she could relax. He laughed loudly to persuade himself he'd had a good time, but he was touched with confusion, almost with shame. He put it down to dejection from the previous day's destruction. His instincts were a trouble, though. He wanted to have better control over them, was tempted even to apologise to Hippolyta, but what was the point of apologising for being prey to a sudden impulse? Besides, she hadn't earned that degree of intimate confession yet.

'We'll eat,' he said. 'You'll eat beside me. Have no fears, you need want for nothing as my wife. I took you because I needed the release, and because I want you to know who's who, but I shall be more tender and consoling a lover in future, now you've learnt that I'm not just a sentimental dotard.'

'You are my master, sir; there's no getting around that.'

'And you'll be my mistress, as near my equal as any woman could hope to be. I'll try to give you more power than you ever knew as Queen of Scythia. Come, we must dress and look dignified. The custom on my homecoming is for me to hear plans and adjudicate in family disputes while I eat. It will give you an opportunity to see how fine and just Athenian life is. Let your sister be seated beside us too.'

Hippolyta acquiesced without a word, but her thoughts were not on how best to serve her lord. He was more subtle in approach than Hercules, but that only meant more confused. He thought he was a new kind of man with a new kind of greatness. Hippolyta thought he was an old kind of prat with the usual delusions.

IX

OBSERVING THE REFINED table manners of Hippolyta and her sister Theseus experienced a lightness of heart not felt for years, a thrill of anticipation of quiet domestic pleasures to come. This time home really would be home, somewhere to stay and enjoy the peace and plenty he had almost unwittingly been working towards. He smiled a rich, satisfied smile and patted the back of Hippolyta's hand, apologising absent-mindedly when he saw it was actually Emily's hand, then patting it again more paternally.

'Child,' he murmured, 'you're the most exquisite thing I ever looked upon.'

'And I thought you had looked upon my sister the Queen,' Emily replied tartly.

'Ah, and you shall have claws! Don't excite yourself, little one, my days of delighting foolish girls are gone behind me now. You are perfect, being untouched, a creature not quite of nature, an odd thing, an artificial, spiritual, Court-bred thing, sophisticate yet all unknowing. Don't agitate yourself with the thought that an admirer of your strangeness is about to seduce you. I had your sister not two hours since and she is a woman more mysterious than you'll ever be.' Abruptly he dropped the hand he'd been stroking. 'Bring in those who are less fortunate than ourselves!'

There was some shuffling now outside the tall doors, as those who had already been queuing for several hours suddenly forgot

— 54 —

their impatience and jostled to find somewhere less immediate in the confrontation line. Theseus was well used to awe and waited, smiling in a fatherly way as much as to say, My people are timid souls, grateful for leadership. But as he smiled that message a striding figure emerged, closely followed by three much smaller and far less confident ones. The strider was a man of considerable stature, a bearded man as big as Theseus. And there was no timidity in *his* soul!

'Perotheus!' Theseus stood in astonishment and stretched across the table, scattering carcasses and drinks, to greet his friend. 'But if you're here you should have dined with us. Only yesterday my heart was heavy with the fear you might be home in Thebes.'

'Aye, it would have grieved me to have killed you, my friend.'

'No more than it would have grieved me to have killed you.'

'Yes, we'd have had no choice, such is honour. So perhaps there's that much good fortune in the matter that's pulled me here. And you will understand, Theseus, that while I love a feast and you, I could not join this, the destruction of my beloved city being one of its happiest elements.'

'Not so! But let us say that the Theban part of the feasting is done, and from now on we celebrate marriage only. Our revels will be complete with your presence.'

'You may not believe that for long, I'm afraid. I'll waste no time. Sir, my daughter was brought here as soon as it became clear you were making Athens the city where she'd get good education and learn true obedience. I impute no failure to your State, but this daughter has grieved me; she goes quite against my will, is ungrateful, selfish, shrewish, overweight, independent-minded and in plain has staggered me by her deceit and utter disregard for every form her training has equipped her to appreciate and meekly follow.'

'What are her crimes?'

'She will not marry Demetrius.'

'What! Demetrius, don't sulk there behind Perotheus, man! I took you for a shrimp. What am I hearing? Is this the girl you spoke of?'

— 55 —

'It is, sir. This is Hermia – my love!'

'And she will not marry with you?'

'She tells me I love another.'

'Helena, whom you once favoured?'

'Exactly. And whom I look upon as fondly as she were a dead horse.'

'Is Hermia hiding too? Perotheus, you must stand aside to let these children be seen. Hermia? Peep forth, girl.'

Hermia, blushing at this condescending introduction, stood out as firmly as she dared and overcame her stock of diffidence in anger. 'Demetrius loves Helena, who loves him back,' she said petulantly. 'He is childish to persist with me, for I love him not. He loves my father and my father him – let him marry with my father, then, for I'll have none of him!'

'Demetrius, this is a very forward girl – can you be serious in your suit? Better perhaps a dead horse than a live scorpion!'

'I love Lysander!' Hermia declared more loudly than necessary. 'Lysander is no less than Demetrius and I love him and he loves me and Father is spiteful to stand in our way and you are a great lord and have the power to make all Athenians happy and treat all justly, including women.'

'Peace! Silence! Where do you think you are, girl?'

'In Scythia, maybe,' Hippolyta whispered loudly enough to create an awkward pause.

Theseus chose to ignore it. He bore down on Hermia, who was already short of stature and now, with two imposing, disapproving middle-aged men staring at her, wilted.

'Your father made you,' Theseus thundered, and the old line was so familiar it needed no embroidery but he worked on anyway. 'Your father made you and should be as a god to you. You are his creation, to dispose of as he chooses. That is the law and I wouldn't intercede if I could because it's a good law, a universally observable and applicable law, which works well, as all that is natural and comes from the gods works well. A father's word is a final word.

'Besides, isn't it true that this boy Lysander remained behind in Athens while Demetrius accompanied us to war? Isn't it true that this same boy Lysander took the advantage of his friend's absence to seduce your affections from their approved course? I am not sure but that this Lysander should be punished as a backdoor man, for I smell dirty work here.'

'No!' cried Hermia.

'I say,' said Demetrius confusedly. 'May I speak? You remember, my lord, how I claimed Lysander as my best friend? So he has been. I would not have him punished any further than so: that he abandon his claim to my beloved. It seems to me, after all, that in love any man is apt to lose sight of what is honourable. Many wars have started from such causes and I find it hard to blame my friend for falling in love with so lovely a girl as Hermia – who would not?'

'You're right that love can undermine the strongest state and lay waste the careful works of man.' Theseus leaned forward, perplexed, struggling with his instinct to vent his anger. 'You're a curious young man. If anyone trifled with a woman of mine I'd slay the fool, yet you appear to believe there are no effective laws where love is concerned. Perotheus, old friend, I begin to share your anguish: the younger generation is turning weird. Perhaps we've made life too easy.'

'As you say,' Perotheus nodded unhappily. 'They've too much ease and with time on their hands think life is theirs in any way they can have it. We should have left more chaos in the world and kept them clinging to some dream of order. The thing itself makes them rebel.'

'What says my Hippolyta?' Theseus asked unexpectedly.

'I think I must follow your thoughts, my lord.'

'A good answer,' Theseus beamed proudly. 'What use could there be in the thoughts of an unguided woman? But supposing for the moment you knew enough to have thoughts of your own, where would they lead you? I'm curious.'

'It does occur to me that if Lysander has equal merit, loves and is loved by Hermia, he should have a distinct advantage in this case.'

— 57 —

'No, no, weren't you attending? Hermia's father affects Demetrius. Shouldn't a daughter honour her father above all else? Or is it Amazon custom to spit on true authority and praise anarchy?'

'It is our custom to be impartial in judgement, sir. We recognise as an absolute truth that every child has a father, but add that fathers are men and men may be good or bad. A bad man will sire bad children, should they follow him in every thing. Amazon women believe goodness is not consonant with meek and thoughtless submission. A daughter should honour her father if he is right.'

'Unconditionally! Hippolyta, you are new to our State, but you must know I am not a cruel man. My desire is to make all happy. How, then, shall I make grief as small a portion of life as possible? Clearly we must have general rules all can recognise and abide by. In this a law is like a god, above each one of us and not to be shaken down at whim. Accept law, as you would a god, and you may know where you are free and where you cannot aspire. Such restrictions are not there to harm, but to guide everyone in the right path.'

'How can a right path tie me to a man I do not love?' Hermia protested bleakly.

'Hold your tongue, girl!' said her father. 'Know your place – that is all Theseus is saying, and sadly you demonstrate again your ineptitude. She is as unlike her quiet mother as fire is unlike snow.'

'Yes,' mused Theseus, 'and yet a woman's passion is pleasant enough, kept within honest bounds. God forbid I should deny passion any expression; only in its uncontrolled form when it is so destructive would I take and mould the stuff for safer use.'

'We all have the beast within,' Perotheus conceded. 'Women have it in a greater degree, lacking, as they must, our higher virtues.'

'Lysander, you haven't spoken and that isn't noted in your favour. Another silent man is the nightworking thief. Have you nothing to say? Are you caught out, and does it not concern you?'

— 58 —

'I am not an Athenian of long standing, sir, but I have upheld your laws, for they are just and work to the advantage of the whole. I would not thwart Demetrius for all the world. And yet I love Hermia even more than I love the world, and had we to settle this in combat I should kill Demetrius for her sake. Even Perotheus, and knowing I should lose. I would fight you, my lord. I am not foolhardy, I wish to live, but I am beloved.'

'And you illustrate the issue nicely! Love cannot be granted so much misrule. Good God, man, the city would be decimated if love gained a hold! What a wicked thing it is that seems so kind then makes a man take up sword against the world! We must abide by law. Law gives Perotheus power of life or death over Hermia. We may help to this extent: Hermia, if you refuse to marry Demetrius you may choose death or exile to some chaste island, never to see a man's face again. That's three options you have. I call that lenient.'

'Athens is less advanced than our teachers say, for if the law always devolves from fathers it always offers only half-justice. Our mothers are creators too, yet where are they consulted in law?'

'Perotheus, tell your daughter to stop. She speaks close to treason and invites summary execution, which would sour these festivities. Women are vessels, men begin as their passengers and become their helmsmen. What destructive power would follow if women were granted equal status in the legislature? Does a ship plot and sail its own course?'

'Crazy child!' spat one of the queens at the table in horror. 'Witch! Execute her! Burn her!'

And so on. Hippolyta sat silent.

'Very well,' Hermia allowed, 'I've gone too far towards reason and I withdraw. I cannot choose death because Lysander would suffer so. I shall live chaste, far from the corrupting influence of men, and pray continually to Diana for strength.'

'I find that sad, when you could have chosen happiness, but so be it. The matter is decided. Are you satisfied, Perotheus?'

'I am. Chastity is a longer lesson than death.'

'Well, that's certainly something – *one* of you is satisfied!'

—— 59 ——

'I'd have made the same choice,' Emily piped up. 'Men are beasts.'

'And there's always your dead horse, Demetrius,' Theseus added.

Along near the end of the table a man coughed, an elderly, thin man with a white beard and no courage. His name, which most forgot, was Nedar. 'I must . . .' he started, and mopped his mouth before correcting his unprecedented interruption. 'May I cavil? I mean, I am Helena's father. Demetrius has eaten with me, and gave me understanding that his intentions were honourable. I do not like to hear Helena thrown down in such ugly words.'

'I agree,' Hermia said spiritedly. 'Helena is my best friend, a better friend to me than this two-faced Demetrius is to my Lysander. She is lovely and deserving and shouldn't be called a dead horse by anyone, least of all a braggart who thinks himself another Hercules!'

'We will arrange your passage in the morning,' Theseus said coldly. 'The quicker you find the remote company of like-minded maids the better!'

'I meant Demetrius,' Hermia stuttered.

Theseus sat with finality and clicked his fingers for his glass to be filled. The four made their formal thanks and withdrew stormily.

'What do you think of our law so far?' Theseus asked Hippolyta confidentially.

'It craps on those it should serve,' Hippolyta answered bravely. 'The girl should marry the boy she loves. It's no bad thing to have women supporting you, since they can influence the men whose support you may one day need.'

'Wise – only Perotheus is not a man I care to cross. He and I have fought together. He's saved my life. It's a shame he's not as enlightened as I, but there we are. Besides, Demetrius is valiant and Lysander strikes me as effeminate. God, your eyes have a look in them! I'm tempted to clear the room and have you again on the table – what do you think to that?'

—— 60 ——

'I don't doubt the risen impulse, sir, but I doubt I started it. It's Hermia you'd like to have. Her fiery defence aroused you. You may think to shock me with your unconventional table manners, but it's prompted by something all too common: you'd have me while having Hermia in your brains.'

'Not bad,' Theseus said, with no sign of offence, 'but I'm afraid it doesn't displease me when you tack that way. Except – why imagine I could only have one other woman in my mind, eh?'

'Oh, very vigorous! That's one for your drunken chums!'

'Hippolyta, I have greater strength and greater everything than you. You are a woman and I won't pretend to offer an equality you haven't earned.'

'Then I predict a rather static affair for us.'

'I say not.'

The evening wore on pleasantly. More complaints were heard and adjudicated, more wine consumed.

At last a very nervous fellow whose face was rigid with fear approached the great table and stood, head downcast, unable to speak his name without a prompt. 'P – P – P – Peter Quince, Your Worship, at your service, sir, and humbly beg to take my leave of you.'

'Wince, did you say? Come, speak clearly, friend, have no fear here. Every man in Athens has an equal right to be heard at this table. How may we serve you?'

'I am a carpenter by trade, Your Majesty.'

'And that's a fine trade, too. Where would we be without carpenters, eh? Without a leg to sit on!' Theseus had developed a very agreeable mood. Hippolyta evidently appealed to an unexplored side of his nature.

Peter Quince, however, was too nervous to catch the reference to furniture. 'Only a carpenter, Your Grace,' he insisted modestly. 'I make stools and such.'

'We all make stools,' quipped Theseus merrily. Perhaps it was the wine as much as Hippolyta, for generally he wasn't a vulgar lord.

'It is my craft, sir, I have a certain skill in doing it.'

— 61 —

'You remind me of a fellow who claims to die with some frequency.'

'Tables, too, and have been known on doors and rafters. Your basic house is much within my scope.'

'Right, Peter Quince, we know what you do. Now, what are you doing here? Have you a competitor in the wooden way? Think you the palace needs your handiwork?'

'My name is Peter Quince, my trade, carpenter, by way of introduction. I know who you are, sir. My request is more in line with your wondrous celebrities.' Here he dried up, anxiously fingering the sleeve where a note was secreted, but not daring to get it. Instead he dropped dramatically to his knees, clasped his hands and launched into an appalling wailing speech which at last turned into an attempt at acting. Concluding the lament to a stunned silence, Quince found his feet once more. 'That's nobbut a sample, sir. We do tragedy, juggling with fruit, choral effects, anything you request admirably, and you would be honoured to appear before us.'

'After so compelling an extract it saddens me to tell you you've come too late, Peter. We've booked our players. But on your way out collect sixpence for your pain.'

'Much in your debt, lord, Peter Quince, ever to be disposed, hereby takes his leave. Oh, and wishes seasonable greetings from Snug the joiner, Francis Flute, Tom Snout, Robin Starveling and Nick Bottom the weaver.'

'Take two pennies for each of your friends, but that last named – I recommend you visit him this very night. If I am not mistaken, he will give *you* something!'

He had half-expected not to get out alive, but now had coins and a story to tell. More, he'd managed to look at the Amazon woman, as refined as a wife of Theseus ought to be. She bore no resemblance to the caged woman, who must have been a vile beast after all. No mortal woman, he was glad to reassure himself, would have stuck out such a hideous long red tongue with such animosity. Or pissed in his face.

— 62 —

X

MONGST THE POPLARS and cool stones of the cemetery Lysander breathed the fumes of the night and sighed. The dark air was like a stream at dawn. The sky glistened, the piercing stars and bright full moon gleamed on grey specks of cloud and amongst the graves sombre shadows were laid out, still as death. This was the secret meeting place.

'Hermia,' Lysander called softly, and two doves in a dark tree shuffled at the mild disturbance.

Hermia detached herself from the pale stonework of a family tomb and seemed to float towards him over the dark grass. But as soon as she clutched her lover he knew she was no spirit, and also that she was as deeply troubled as he.

'What are we to do?' he asked hopelessly.

'Submit,' Hermia replied plaintively with tears more bitter than his own.

'I know we must, and yet, what life remains then? I'd die in a moment if it meant that you could live, but that's the only separation I can take willingly. And Theseus says you go tomorrow! Hermia, let me touch your hands, look at your fingers, your cheek, the rounding of your face, let me see your neck once more and touch . . . oh, Hermia, to think that by morning we'll nevermore be together!'

'What are we to do?' Hermia pleaded.

'Submit!' Lysander said vehemently. 'By Jove, I'd defy the law if I knew a way through to happiness!'

— 63 —

'The Amazon woman said life is always better than death, but these will be our only living seconds. What consolation can there be after the loss of life's only meaning?' She squeezed his hands and searched his eyes. 'Lysander, do you understand me?'

'Yes,' he answered solemnly, 'and you're right. We are at least together tonight, and in time perhaps you will bear our child, and . . .'

'Hush, darling, I didn't mean that. I mean we should die together. You have your sword.'

Lysander was appalled. Hermia looked so cool and fresh, and felt so delicately warm, such sensitive tingling life coursed through her! Yet she was earnest. 'Yes,' he reflected carefully. 'There's no better way. And the gods will lift us at once and we shall love for ever in Elysium. But let's make love here on earth first.'

'Do you think that proper?'

'As pure as the death that must follow. Let's die glad in our own knowledge, Hermia, in the grip of our innocent ecstasy – does it matter how they find our abandoned bodies? What? You hesitate? Mistrust me already, dearest?'

'No. No I don't. I can face dying for love more readily than offering my virgin patent to you whom I love enough to die with. Don't think me coy, but I hadn't thought to attain this state this soon. I had hoped our marriage would be solemnised alongside Theseus's, with all Athens out to wish us well.'

'Let the moon be our priest and the stars our witnesses, and let our lovemaking be our holy rite and death our door to a heavenlier estate than even Theseus can attain.'

'Yes,' Hermia decided clearly. 'Come, then, walk me down this leafy aisle.'

In slow procession the doomed lovers walked the grassy slope towards two stately poplars, beneath which the grass was soft and cold. Hermia turned away chastely while Lysander removed his sword and tunic. She disrobed. Both turned again to gaze for the first dazzling time on a nakedness vulnerable and mysterious, awesome and desirable. Hermia bent to arrange her thin dress as a sheet, and then lay down, nervous but determined.

'This is not a moment to hurry,' Lysander murmured as he stretched out next to his almost wife. 'We should have the whole night ahead, and know the hope of every night beyond this. We should have musicians in an anteroom making soft music to please us as we sleeping wake for an instant before embracing and slumbering once more. Come, let's embrace for the warmth of our bodies and not fear what should follow. Perhaps it isn't important that we make love, for your body is so lovely I don't know if I can bear a greater pleasure than this bliss of holding you near and knowing nothing lies between us.'

He was neither as old nor as powerful as Theseus, yet Lysander could control the urges Theseus thought fit to abandon himself to at once. Even the prospect of imminent suicide hadn't defused his passion, because he was coming to believe it apt and beautiful. What to Theseus would have been an immediate expression of feeling was impossible for Lysander because he loved Hermia, and could not leave her out of account, could not just take what he thought his without losing it. So, tenderly, they hugged and almost swooned out of time altogether, and gradually, without thought or worry, the moment began to grow towards fruition.

Then, with a strange angry grunt Lysander slackened his hold.

'What, love? Did you hear someone?'

'Only my conscience, damn it! Oh, Hermia, I've had a thought I'd rather have kept to myself another hour – we need not die! I know of one who will help us; it's possible we might escape. You are to be banished from Athens, and Athens is nothing to me without you, so what law forces us to yield? What does it matter where we go so long as we go together?'

'Who do you know? Wait. Let me dress. And clothe yourself!'

'Oh, but now we have come so close, what harm if . . .'

'No, Lysander.' She was firm, yet flung herself at him, kissing his head all over. 'You are more than ever the best man in the world, the most honourable, most decent and, though I cannot say from experience, I've no doubt having looked on you, the best endowed of men – oh, Lysander, your body is *wonderful*, and I can hardly wait till we can make love all night, every night, and have a wealth of time to delight in legally.'

'Not under Athenian law.'

'We'll find a better, and a proper time for this. It's no small thing to do what we have nearly done, and to go on now . . . no, but it *will* come soon, and we have it to spur us on still. Who can help us?'

Before the noble Lysander could answer, however, there came a sound of a tactfully singing female voice, close by, and a moment later the fair child Emily appeared. 'Ah,' she said, failing to convey great amazement. 'I came looking for you, Hermia, and guessed that if *I* only had one night *I* should pray amongst my ancestors too.' She clapped her pious little hands gleefully. 'We are of like mind.'

'Are you planning to betray us?' Lysander asked, reaching unobtrusively for his sword and assessing the child's height so one quick swipe would behead her before she could scream murder. It was nothing personal. Emily was no more significant than a dandelion whose globe one might scatter carelessly simply by strolling past to admire the daisies.

'Why, no,' Emily said vaguely, since their intrigue meant nothing to her either. 'I seek your help. I have a letter which I implore you to deliver. It must go to Scythia.'

'But we may not pass near that country.'

'Don't worry,' Lysander came back abruptly, 'we'll see it's delivered for you. You miss your home so much already?'

Emily stared at him as if he were simple-minded, then handed the precious letter to Hermia and pressed her hands and exhorted her not to read the thing. After that she was lighter-hearted and slipped away softly, hurrying to confide what a brave thing she'd done to Hippolyta. Emily did not write with the confident grace of an educated adult, for all her airs. This was her letter:

Cum quik. You now we were captured now we are being rapped every nite and beaten by the wikid men. Athens wud be easy to distroy coz they eat all nite and drink themselfs

— 66 —

silly. Save me quik. We are helpless and rather die than this.
Hoping this finds you well, best regards Emily.

But Hermia didn't read it.

'Come,' said Lysander, 'we must get to the forest.'

'No one lives there! Can't I at least go and change, and pack a few things for the journey? And I must tell Helena.'

'No chance! She'll tell Demetrius and he'll tell your father – they'd have us before morning. Don't worry, it won't get much colder tonight!'

Hermia had always wanted adventures – it seemed unfair that only men had them – but this was sudden. Half the pleasure of an adventure was in anticipating everyone's responses, but this way no one would know what had befallen her. Plus her dress was short and very thin. Back home she had some super travelling clothes, including a black leather jacket which looked great over her short white dress. A lot of shoes, too. On the other hand, Lysander was being impetuous and masterful for her, and such flattering gallantry was seductive.

After they had left the cemetery another figure emerged from the leathery-leaved rhododendrons: Helena, with a mischievous expression. She gathered up her skirts and raced lickety-split back to the palace.

I'll tell Demetrius, she thought, I'll tell him there's no time to rouse Perotheus and he has to act immediately. He'll dash off in pursuit. I'll dash after him. I must remember to pick up a few things for Hermia so she'll know I'm on her side. When I catch Demetrius in the forest he may recall how he used to fondle me and how I'd let him touch me to the quick and how hot he came. He doesn't really love Hermia, it's just a pash.

Puck, whom we haven't met yet and can't see even now, observed the entire chapter from the top of a tomb. He rubbed his hands together as if he were crushing petals in his palms, invisibly, of course, then sped like a lightning bolt to the forest to relay his gossip to Oberon.

XI

'OH, *LYSANDER*! WE'RE going nowhere after all!'
'That's not exactly true – we've nearly reached the forest – no, all right, sorry – but even though I've never met the old fellow I *know* he'll help us once we find him. Do listen.'

'What are we going to do? Live on nuts in the forest? Have fish for friends and drink from old tree stumps? Will you lace flowers in my hair and have me dress in grass and leaves?'

'There's a sarcastic side to your nature, isn't there?'

Hermia aimed a kick between her lover's legs, but he side-stepped, caught her ankle and lifted her deftly as she fell. He had powerful arms and was as quick as a young nobleman needed to be. 'I'm going to tell you the whole story, and you're going to be my wife, and we're going to live on Naxos.'

'They haven't even got hot water on Naxos! And you come from Crete.'

'I may have implied so, but I never stated it. Hermia, my mother is Ariadne.'

'Then you're the son of Dionysius – that's marvellous!'

'No, think back further, to when my mother lived on Crete. Every year fourteen Athenians, seven boys and seven virgin girls, were shipped to Crete and delivered up to the Minotaur, who ate them.'

'That's one of our earliest lessons. Pasiphae, Ariadne's mother, had intercourse with a bull, whose name I don't know, and gave birth to the monster. In spite, Minos compelled the annual sacrifice.'

'Your history is censored. Minos and Pasiphae had a fine son called Androgeus, a great athlete. He entered the Panathenian games and won every event. It was such a blow to Athenian pride that Egeus had poor Androgeus killed. That was why Minos exacted the sacrifice.'

'And the practice continued until Theseus, against his father's wishes, chose to be one of the seven. Yes, I do know the story. Ariadne fell in love with him and gave him a sword and a thread. He beheaded the Minotaur and found his way out of the labyrinth with the thread. And he gave Ariadne two sons for her help, Oeonopion and Staphylus.'

'History is not truth, but for the moment just consider that thread. It had to be incredibly long, because no one knew how many false ways Daedalus had built into the labyrinth; then, because such length would make the ball of thread too huge to carry, she had to find the finest thread ever made; finally, the thread had to be uncommonly strong, for there were sharp corners. So Ariadne sought the help of Titania.'

'The Fairy Queen! Oh, Lysander, I believed you for a minute!'

'Theseus tells you there are no fairies, and no one dares see them any more. He robs you of your imagination and gives you reason, which you already had; nature falls out of sympathy with you. You believe in the gods whom you never see, and dismiss the fairies you might see!'

'Have *you* ever seen them?'

'On a night like this, well away from the city, we *could* see them, if we were quiet and trusting enough. It was Titania who brought my mother to this forest, where she met and lay with the old weaver who spun for her the famous thread. She told me so. He is the man we must seek. He knew no other woman than Ariadne and will most surely help when he knows I am her son. I'll tell you more shortly, but we're not out of danger yet. Come.'

The next disappointment was finding the hovels on the edge

— 69 —

of the forbidding treeline empty; they hadn't been used for years, except by a few incontinent sheep. But Lysander could see a dim light in the forest and so, with some trepidation and a gasp at the hoot of an owl, the two left the kind moonlight for the crackling shades of a world where nothing human ventured or stirred. The dim light was an unexpected clearing, wide enough to have remained open to the sky. It was the friendly moon that bathed them once more.

'That's it,' Hermia declared. 'No further. No one would live in a place like this, not even a robber. This is nowhere, and I won't take another step till morning. Sit! And keep your distance as you would if my father was watching. Tell me the rest. Back! Tell me from where you are.'

'I never moved a muscle! You could run a chariot between us!'

'And it would crush your hand. If you must recline, pray do so in a direction other than between my feet, sir!'

'I can't say I admire this new strain of coquettishness, Hermia.'

'Then tell me the remainder of your yarn and maybe I'll let you kiss me goodnight.'

'Mmm – or, of course, I could throw you over my knee and spank you. But I won't. I suppose you were taught how Theseus came to Athens in the first place? Or do they still say he's Neptune's son?'

'He is Egeus's son, silly, which was proved by the sword and sandals Egeus had left for him. Egeus didn't have any children by Medea, so when Theseus turned up she was jealous and plotted to poison him at the banquet before Egeus knew the truth. The poisoned wine was before Theseus when the meat was served. He drew his sword to cut the meat, hoping Egeus would see it and recognise him through it. Theseus raised the poisoned wine to his lips . . .'

'And Egeus recognised the sword and dashed the goblet from his hands and embraced his long-lost son. Yes, I guess that's how it was – but bear in mind how nearly Theseus was killed. The son of a great ruler is never safe. Now, my mother had four sons in all, as far as I know. Oberon took one from her in infancy, to be brought up by his real father – so I've never traced that brother of mine. But Theseus wasn't the father, and by then he loved her sister, my aunt Phaedra.'

'Too many names, I'm getting lost!'

'Well, when Theseus abandoned my mother on Naxos she was pregnant again, by him, with me! I came to Athens to declare myself, but soon realised how foolhardy that scheme was. Even if Theseus acknowledged me, there are many who still dispute his legitimacy – the fifty sons of Pallas, for starters. So you are the only Athens I claim, and to claim more would endanger your life and the lives of our children. I'd rather see my children grow in decent obscurity than put the curse of greatness on them.'

These were stirring words, and although Hermia had hitherto found little romance in history lessons, although a forest clearing on a night of flight was not the most propitious setting, she felt a heightening in her blood, a shimmering thunder in her pulse. For Lysander to be the secret son of Theseus was awesome. The nobility of his restraint impressed her anew. He seemed to glow in the moonlight, gathering an aura from those superhuman legends that still shot through the plain fabric of history lessons. She was torn between a desire to prostrate herself and an urge to race home to her father. She elected the Athenian way, of rational thought. 'It's true Theseus hasn't acknowledged any of the children he got in his wanderings, and that their mothers are all abandoned or dead. I suppose he hopes to get some fresh ones by Hippolyta, and as she is to be his wife in Athens it's reasonable to infer that her children will be his successors. So you're right to be prudent.'

'Not too prudent – we are on the run, and unless we make good our escape I've no doubt the reward for our love will be summary execution.'

'I fear nothing with you beside me.'

'Then come, let's find the old man while the moon guides us.'

Hermia jumped up, not noticing that the letter which Emily

— 71 —

had entrusted to her had slipped from her keeping. Lysander drew his sword and led her off bravely into the dark.

Back at the palace two things were happening. Helena was trying to see Demetrius, who was doing his utmost to avoid her; Theseus was issuing orders which, on the face of it, were bizarre. He wanted several dozen soldiers to march out and surround the forest, to stand guard there and see to it no one entered. The explanation was simple: Theseus planned an intimate game for himself and Hippolyta. A clearing had already been prepared. Behind trees at opposite sides were disguises for them to assume. The clearing was a stage where they would indulge themselves in play. Naturally it wouldn't do for anyone to catch them.

And one thing was happening outside the palace. Peter Quince was performing his audience with Theseus to his goggle-eyed friends. At length he recalled his lord's odd concluding remark and suggested that the intoxicated group should head out to Nick's cottage forthwith.

The cornered Demetrius listened, fingering the soft leather of the jacket folded in Helena's arms. He'd seen Hermia in that and loved her at once; something about black on white, a virgin sheathed in leather, appealed to both the warrior and lover in him. 'My best friend!' he spluttered. 'Wait till I tell Perotheus! Hermia, beloved, hold on, I'm coming!'

He shouted this ridiculous rescue bid as he broke from Helena and ran down the great echoing corridor. Helena had with some difficulty told him that her friend seemed frightened by Lysander's bullish demeanour. Demetrius's cry cut deep, for all she longed for was to hear him cry like that for her. But the forest was dark, and anything could happen under cover of darkness. Clutching the clothes and shoes she'd gathered for Hermia, Helena sprinted after her distracted man.

XII

ROM OUTSIDE YOU couldn't tell where forest paused and cottage started, though inside all was cosy and workmanlike. Nick lit a fire when he needed one. He lay on a bed when he needed rest, lit candles when he needed light. It was not his activity that would have surprised a visitor so much as the activity around his tables and looms.

At first sight it appeared an invasion of humming insects which had settled everywhere in a seething coat that mimicked the forms of chairs and bowls and bolts of cloth. Nick was not in the least perturbed by all this buzzing itchy life. On closer inspection you could see why.

These were not massed insects carrying wicked stings and lingering sicknesses after all, but an industrious tribe of fairies forever spinning, weaving, dyeing and generally performing the myriad tasks that made Nick Bottom's workmanship a byword for quality merchandise. They seemed to work unceasingly, but fairies are quite unlike ants: individuals will co-operate on a particular job, then knock off and be replaced while they chase one another off the table, sing, drink, practise mid-flight fornication, or any of the hundred and one things that off-duty fairies delight in.

Usually a number would be chatting to Nick Bottom, eager for any crumb about life amongst the giants; they had no conception of trivia, regarding the slightest operations of any

— 73 —

mortal's life as profoundly appealing fragments from the great puzzle of existence. It didn't seem to them that fairies had all the charm, or even that their longevity was enviable. On the contrary, the uncertain duration of a mortal's life was the key to its exciting beauty. The fairies didn't take umbrage when men stopped believing in them, but they felt shamed and they hid. They clung to Nick because he believed in them and didn't belittle them. They'd have done anything for him.

And they saw that he was melancholy.

He refused to distress them or himself by telling what he'd seen men do at Thebes. But something was gone since his return, some of his exuberance, something of innocence.

Puck conferred with Oberon and Titania: mortals were coming to the forest – perhaps they could be used to cheer Nick? Perhaps. Oberon wondered what would bring the weaver back from despondency.

'Ariadne gave his father some spring for his last winters,' Titania offered helpfully.

'But we can't use her – she's far too old now. Besides, she's his mother, and mortals have some curious taboos about love.'

'Silly! I was thinking of the girl, Hermia – she might do.'

'I don't know if Nick's ready yet, he's been so content till now. His father, remember, had used sixty years and he was only just able to cope with a woman then. He said it was like all his birthdays came at once, and he shook like the pond when a chill wind passes. The *good* mortals have appetites so unlike ours that however we try to emulate them we can never achieve such beautiful chastity without devastating our race. Moderation for us means missing an afternoon of love – very occasionally!'

'Other mortals are less like Nick, though. We have him in the prime state. I've often observed Theseus, and his habits are nearer animals' and ours, and to other mortals Theseus is more the man than Nick. And as for Hercules!'

'Their ways are mysterous and certainly inconsistent,' Oberon laughed, 'but at least we can't doubt their existence. Still, we

— 74 —

mustn't debate these great imponderables now. We must help Nick tonight. Come, we'll find these young Athenians and guide them here and give them sleep.'

At this point it's useful to know how fairies get about, and to know that you really need to know about size and substance. The first glimpse, of fairies swarming in a countless mass, has perhaps suggested delicate creatures, thinner than pencils, thin as wires, and anything from half a centimetre to – if you happened to imagine dragonflies – a few inches from head to toe. Well, that's not inaccurate as far as it goes, only the chances are you wouldn't *see* them at all.

They move. They can shift into the future and back again whenever they've a mind to. Titania spends much of her time in Hollywood in our 1950s; Oberon likes to sit on a hot-water tap and watch women bathing while he smokes a pipe (he'd prefer to follow heroes, and revisits the Risorgimento from time to time, but there haven't been many men to interest him of late); Puck – well, no, we'll leave Puck out of it, since his predilections, perfectly innocuous to his kind, might be unnerving to anyone unfamiliar with the ways of creatures that lack our curious sets of proprieties.

In space, too, they have considerable latitude. No one has ever weighed a fairy successfully. At the still variable insect size they look pretty substantial, you can make out features, clothes, and all of that – but if the light hits them at a certain angle you'll discern that they're not solid forms; it's rather a pretty effect, like catching colours in a bevelled glass. Nick has seen them tiny as pinheads, and then through his magnifying glass has found their flesh-tones only slightly darker, which means they can get smaller yet before becoming solid through and through.

Now, when they are tiny they can whiz along, but apparently they can't get through really solid objects without risking harm to their wings. So whenever they want to travel immense distances fast, either around the globe or forward in time, what they

— 75 —

generally do is enlarge. If you think of the larger mammals – your dinosaur or whale – increased speed hardly seems concomitant with girth. Which brings us back to substance. When fairies enlarge they don't put on weight, quite the reverse. Their minuscule kernel of substance spreads ever thinner, and well before they reach a man's size they're invisible – you could walk through one without noticing and without disturbing it (indeed, you must have done so many times). Fairies become so fine that the wind cannot ruffle them, finer than air, and thus, you see, released from earthbound constraints.

They do this mainly for ease of movement but also, I'm afraid, to hide from us. *They* know they exist, but you can imagine the blow to anyone's self-esteem if its simple being is flatly denied by those who seem to have ultimate authority. They hide so as not to confuse us, guessing our reactions would only hurt them more on the rebound.

The sword of Lysander stripped leaves off branches, severed branches from trees and mortally wounded several young ash, birch and sycamore. He was trying to find ways where there were no ways, and the trees repulsed him and the forest darkened appreciably and glowered angrily.

Poor Hermia, following behind, a hand in his, was aware of the grasping, cutting, tearing of the forest at her dress; the night yapped at her ankles like a pack of hounds, leapt to her arms and back, snaked round her legs, snapped and scrammed her thighs, clawed her hair like falcons.

Lysander fought on, abstractly determined and unaware of the enemy gathering and snatching reprisals against his beloved.

'What on earth is he doing?' Titania cried out. 'Why is he slaying so many of our friends?'

'These humans are altogether extraordinary. We must stop him, at any rate, for his own sake. In a moment that branch he is tearing will disembowel the young lady, and beyond those berries he is scattering are ranged the thorns that will prick his angry eyes which see so little of life. Puck – stop him before his sword completes its arc!'

Hermia bumped abruptly into Lysander and muttered a cry, which modulated into protest as he tumbled over and sank senseless to the ground. She felt around, her soft white hands reaching into the black gap where he had been, reaching and twisting in a blind girl's ballet as she stooped and finally found his prostrate form at the ends of her fingers, her knee on his head, hands interpreting the inverted ribcage. She adjusted her position, moving her hands till they told the position of his head, and then bent her ear towards his mouth. But he made neither groans nor words, even his breath was as far as the sigh of winter across the sea. But Hermia was too plucky to collapse in useless tears or run off. She obeyed her first impulse, which was to save Lysander, and grabbed his arms and began dragging him in the direction she thought they'd come from.

'Oh,' exclaimed Titania sentimentally, 'look how she cares! Aid her, all of you.' And at once teams of fairies descended and lined up either side of the dreaming body, and at once Hermia found the going easier.

Back in the clearing she propped Lysander against a fallen tree and looked at him. No tension remained in his face, only a half-smile; he looked a little absurd smiling in his sleep and holding tightly to his sword. Hermia pinched his cheek. No effect. Kicked the soles of his sandals. No change. Pouted, kissed his cheeks, his nose, his mouth. Nothing.

Hermia took stock. Lost, alone, hampered, and punishment surely not far behind. She gazed up at the moon for inspiration. Gazed at her torn, flimsy dress. Gazed at Lysander's irritatingly happy expression. Reflected that but for his bright idea the pair of them would by now have known the two ecstasies of love and death. She wondered if the gods were tormenting her on purpose.

Oberon and Titania studied the girl, nodding and sighing together as her beauty and dignity of spirit impressed them; even her torn apparel could not reduce her loveliness.

'Surely she will bring our friend out of his despondency!'

— 77 —

Oberon said with keen approval. 'This girl is without blemish and as full as a peach.'

'Nick will soon be as glad as he was wont to be, as happy as his father when Ariadne closed his life with meaning more than he had sought. But Oberon, how are we to make her love him willingly? Ariadne, you'll recall, had experience enough to know what she was doing.'

'It would be a cheap deceit to put it in her mind that to save her lover's life she has to go with our weaver. She must be almost as innocent as Nick Bottom, so she should go dreamingly and have no memory of the event. She'll meet no harm, for Nick is the gentlest of mortals and can only add lustre to her virtue, exchanging her maidenhead for a loving disposition.'

'Puck,' Titania said softly, 'you hear your master, and be sure you obey him with care, for as I love Nick Bottom, so have I taken to this maiden, and I'll have none of your nightmares fed to her.'

If the gods *are* tormenting me on purpose it could be because I've gone against my father's will; it could also be to make me understand how grave a step elopement is; happiness may be the outcome, then, so long as I don't show faint heart.

This optimistic thought commandeered the clearing and transported Hermia into a kind of waking sleep; without being aware of time passing or any physical exertion such as walking would involve she found herself inside a plain, pleasant cottage, facing a young fellow whose head was down and whose demeanour suggested dejection. 'Excuse me, sir, for intruding,' Hermia heard herself saying quietly.

Like Dewdrop, Nick believed he was a man the same as other men, and what one man did all men might do. The cracking of Creon's jaws! The satisfaction on the knights' stern faces, their ability not to flinch! Frightened so much of what must be hidden in himself Nick Bottom had lost his appetite for acting. His heroic style, now he'd seen heroes in action, was risible, all

— 78 —

rolling words and haughty gestures – and yet to achieve the truthful reproduction he would have to nurture that in himself which he was desperate not to uncover; then, even if he sacrificed himself to achieve it, what good would be done? Audiences would be sick and would lose heart, and the proud city would be proud no more. Such a true performance would bring the world to ruinous despair, but it would not be acting then; it would be a transformation, a new reality.

These things he pondered in his armchair, together with the implication that his innocent life had been all unreal, and so deep in gloomy thoughts had he been that he didn't notice the commotion when most of his fairy friends disappeared. He did realise that someone new had arrived now, though without hearing any words, noticing a sweet scent. He lifted his head as if to sniff a subtle breeze and saw Hermia.

But he saw not the seemliness Hermia affected despite a ripped and smudged dress, rather, a languorous, dreamingly sensual vision of willing, submissive beauty. As she stood before him her fine dress very gradually began to slip of its own accord from her shoulders, at the same time rising like stage curtains at the hem. She neither aided nor hindered the movement, yet seemed aware and happy enough to be revealed to the simple man.

The promised, awaited vision, Nick thought.

Yet it was not as he had often imagined it would be. There were strains of melancholy in the air, some from his own thoughts and some emanating from the silent girl. As the descending and ascending parts gathered under her breasts the gossamer fabric floated all of a piece to his earthen floor and she stepped towards him. Nick had looked on statues – every time he set up his stall he studied the great Caryatides of the Erechtheum – but their colouring was never so delicately ripe as this vibrant reality. Clearly she was no dream and no stone but a comely and aroused girl. It should have been easy, unavoidable, to take her and make himself a man in the sense he knew of well enough. She strolled provocatively near and then rested against the table in the most welcoming manner, her arms reaching back for support, her

— 79 —

belly pushing towards him. Nick had the capacity and vigour for the part, and saw her tongue moistening her parted lips, and yet he could make no move: her eyes were on his, yet she saw someone further away.

'My friends,' Nick said sadly. 'I know this is your doing and that you wish to cheer me, and I'm in your debt for entrancing this moment, but I can't act the part of god, bull or man with her, not now. Friends, you yourselves must have sensed that she's troubled. I don't reject your kindness but ask you simply to restore her to her modest waking sense, so I may have the pleasure of helping her, and none of the shame of taking advantage.'

At this several dozen fairies appeared, all giggling naughtily, at least until Titania hushed them. Puck continued to look disgruntled, for he loved to watch the wild antics of copulating couples in their first embarrassing engagements; these to him were funnier than the most energetically earnest battles of civilised armies.

'We learn from your sensitivity, Nick,' Oberon said with admiration. 'I've heard your Lord Theseus speak impressively of dignity and respect, yet he can't master his own passions, while you, without ever having unleashed them, restrain yours and halt your thrusting instinct at the behest of a more devotedly human instinct. What says my wife?'

'I had reservations,' Titania answered softly, 'for this maid's sake, and although I'd have enjoyed the scene of Nick's tender discovery I'm glad to see it postponed. You are a sweet man, Nick Bottom. We will restore this girl to her troubled senses and depart now.'

'Excuse me, sir, for intruding,' Hermia said very quietly. 'The truth is I'm not sure how I've found you, for I am absolutely lost.'

Nick looked up and saw a beautiful, plump Athenian girl whose torn dress echoed her evident distress. He rose courteously. 'Don't say you're lost, miss, for you've found my house and I can take you wherever you must go. How can I serve you?'

— 80 —

'Are you a gentleman, sir?'

'I fancy not, being nothing but a weaver, Nick Bottom by name. But sit – my chairs are as clean as marble – and I'll brew up some tea and victuals while you rest yourself.'

'You are kind, and if you were old I should know you as the man I'm looking for. But you are as young as Lysander. How old are you?'

'Well, I've been here all my life, and that seems a longish patch of time. But I am a slow fellow so in truth it may be precious little time spun out thin in my solitariness. However, if you seek a man in these woods I am likely him.'

'This man is a weaver, but he was old twenty years ago.'

'Then you seek my dear father, who is dead.'

Nick worked a poker under the log fire to bring up a blaze and heat the water pot. He sprinkled various leaves into the water for flavour. Hermia watched him. This, she thought, was an attractive specimen of raw young manhood, as tall and broad as Lysander, almost as gentle of manner, yet for all that a man of the common type, normally invisible to well-bred girls. She felt that she could talk to him, and she did, and Nick listened carefully. 'So you see,' Hermia ended candidly, 'if you helped us in our flight you'd fall foul of Athenian law too. Even sheltering me and offering meat and drink to a fugitive you risk imprisonment, even death.'

'As for that,' Nick could say without hesitation, 'I don't hope to control the laws that govern me, nor disobey them so long as they make sense, but I'd give a supper to any weary traveller without calling myself brave or foolish – I'd be no man at all to do less, that's all. Now if I'm to be punished for boiling water and flavouring and giving it, which has cost me nothing, then the punishment you mention is so far beyond my poor comprehension it concerns me not.'

'It would concern you most directly if your body was hanged. You're very fatalistic, Mr Bottom.'

'Am I so? Being cleverer I might want to comprehend all I'm ignorant of, but that wouldn't make the punishment more

— 81 —

agreeable. Sit tight, now, while I go find your Lysander and bring him to you. I've been pondering awhile and it seems to me that your Lysander is by happy chance a relative of mine – yes, miss, it's astonishing and most unlikely, I grant you, for until tonight I never knew my mother's name, but you have provided it.' His hands were trembling and Hermia feared she might need to defend herself against a madman, though his energy didn't seem directed destructively at her. 'I am almost of the gods in my descent!' he exclaimed, wonderingly. 'That's a bruiser of a thought that takes a bit of beating in! But don't fret, Miss Hermia, I shall cope.' As he spoke the weaver stood taller than usual and thrust his chest out. He didn't just walk now, he strutted, like a local monarch with a new mirror.

Oberon glanced at Titania and then at Puck. All three tut-tutted and bit their little lips in general consternation. This was not the boost they had meant to give their friend at all. Before their eyes he was transforming into a monstrous pompous stranger who might have no more use for them.

'He is becoming an Athenian!' Titania cried in pain.

'It's fatal for a man to start believing in gods. Right away he wants to be a descendant. The imagination rots. Poor Nick! How can we get this madness from his brains?'

'We're helpless,' Titania said. 'We'll have to let the law get to him – let him be punished as Athenians are – let his recent dejection be the foretaste of disillusion; we cannot save him now!'

— 82 —

XIII

'WHY HAVE YOU given me a mount that could leave yours standing?' Hippolyta enquired suspiciously.

Theseus straightened his back and laughed amiably. 'I thought you'd look fine on her and you do. This stumpy old soldier of mine lacks grace, but he suits me, being heavy and reliable.'

'Are you tempting me to escape?'

Theseus laughed. 'No, chuck, I haven't underestimated your intelligence. That mare couldn't grow sails to speed you across the sea, and if my country is your prison there's no place worth galloping to.'

'So you aren't taunting me?'

'On the contrary, I'm hoping to win your love with gifts.'

'Now you sound like a senile man.'

'I talk as I find myself. You're more mistrustful than you need be.'

'Really? Everyone says you're another Hercules, and he, after slaughtering most of my women, left me for dead as well. There was no refinement in Hercules, the model all men follow.'

'The latest I have heard of Hercules,' Theseus said with distaste, 'is that he dresses as a woman and performs a housewife's duties. Some penance for murdering more of his children, I dare say, unless his mind has gone – what there was of a mind! He tarts himself up to milk cows, and shakes his tail like your mare

— 83 —

at every gentleman he passes. Men run from him now in greater fear than when he wielded his club. Don't measure me beside that blood-brain. To tell the truth, Hippolyta, I've been having second thoughts about many of my famous exploits. At times I am so divorced from my younger self I cannot bear to acknowledge him. Still, I don't want to cloud our night with my perplexities. Tonight we aren't constrained to act ourselves; instead we shall inhabit the freedom of other beings. Once in my forest I'll don the garb of King of Fairies, and you'll be my dreamy Queen, Titania.'

'What a strange conceit – you've outlawed the existence of the simple folk! Vanquished them quite from people's minds!'

'*Our* minds are strong enough to distinguish harmless fantasy from dangerous superstition. As Oberon I command all nature's realm and may bring thunder, rain, flashing light – or mild summer zephyrs scented with pollen. As my Titania you're no slave, no abducted queen of the frustrate women, but a full sharer in that realm of mine. Perhaps you will learn tonight that I intend you no harm, but hope to train you in companionship.'

'Perhaps, then, you will learn that the dispensations you're willing to concede will not match true equality.'

'But the best of it is to be away from the Court where everyone hangs on my words and forces me to be serious.'

'So you seek privacy in a forest?'

'It is my forest.'

'Ah, everything is yours, my lord,' Hippolyta jeered, injecting the plain fact with a strong dose of protest, though the injection had no effect on the inebriated man's robust constitution.

'Everything is far from being mine,' he groaned selfishly. 'Time eludes me, and the inner thoughts of men. Even my own – I can't always say what prompts them. On the inspiration of a moment I do things that wouldn't have my own approval. Everyone sees Theseus in my actions, and I become a man I don't know intimately. I want to plan ahead and see my plans come to fruit; I have a vision of good government; but I am not a god. When I took you in my bath . . . Well, no matter. Thought

— 84 —

is slow, you see, and makes a man virtuous and old.' He grunted and adjusted himself on his horse. He thought Hippolyta needed to be made jealous. 'Take your sister, now,' he said abruptly. 'Don't you think she overdoes virginity, using it to tempt a man? I think so. I felt it tonight, at dinner; those little passionate vibrations from her pallid hand. I believe the child desires me.'

'Emily!' Hippolyta had been distracted almost to sleep by his tedious monologue – for a legendary man of action he was disappointing, the most boring old fart she'd met in years – but this startling vanity aroused condescending mirth. 'No, Theseus, that's your dream of younger days. At the moment Emily is only attracted to pretty young women who dare to answer back.'

'Ah, but Hermia too – in the directness of her gaze I read a kind of anguish that she could not be mine.'

'Well' – Hippolyta refused to play jealous when she didn't care where his fantasies went – 'you could have taken her – who'd stand in the way? Her father is your old friend and as used to grabbing what he wants as you. Hermia herself couldn't beat you away. But if you hanker after these children why have you ridden out with me?'

'Girls are easy, and their charm is all gone in surfaces. I've simply been testing your feelings; I detect some defensive aggression, I think. Flippancy doesn't fool me.'

He smiled and led the way down to the mouth of the forest, where a captain of guard stepped up to steady the horses. Theseus dismounted and stamped his feet. He let Hippolyta get off in her own time, meanwhile calling for torches and reminding the captain that no one was to enter the forest until he and Hippolyta emerged.

He handed a brand to her and she followed him, supposing him to be as mad as most great men. Power had that effect. She wasn't a bit surprised to learn about Hercules; he'd worn lipstick when he raped her and made her sprawl back on top of him so he could play his hands over her body as if his own were transformed. So much had to be left for the gods to explain, and the gods never did explain anything – you just had to trust their

— 85 —

knowing what it was all about. If they didn't exist either then the passage through life was all waste anyway, so you couldn't afford to doubt them – for sanity you had to believe that *someone* saw the point!

Theseus liked striding jauntily through the forest, torch in one hand, economy-size club in the other. Night made him a brave man even when he was unlikely to touch danger. At one time the forest had been truly wild, but the bears and boars had been speared and clubbed for sport, the remaining deer ran and hid from happy hunters. The forest was tamed, yet it could still chill the flesh and make the thud of blood come clouding fast – and drink helped that too. Blood bumped around his body and thudded into his forehead. If Hippolyta hadn't been keeping up so well he'd have sat and rested.

'Do you get the feeling we're not alone?' she said.

'I'm glad you noticed – my soldiers encircle us. The creatures are therefore clumsier than usual, that's all, I think.'

'Are you well, Theseus? Your brow glistens.'

'My active imagination,' he said, shifting the torchlight. 'Come, if you're not too weary, the clearing is near. Are you ready to be chased, or to give chase, or to stand and fight me? How will it be?'

'I could outrun you if I wished, but you remind me that your soldiers guard the trees.'

'We can hide and seek a couple of hours, if that's the game to warm your blood, but I will have you before dawn, Titania, and we'll return to Athens as lovers, not captor and captive.'

So saying Theseus plunged his torch into a stream, then Hippolyta's. They were in a broad grassy space which undulated into banks and moon-shadowed hollows. Theseus directed Hippolyta to her oak tree, then walked slowly towards his own. Despite his determination, the wild and jolly night he'd planned seemed unlikely to reach earlier expectations. Behind her ironies, he feared, lay more dislike than admiration, and that bothered him, which in turn made him feel old. Why did she keep mentioning Hercules? he wondered. Did she *love* the brute?

— 86 —

I'll give her till morning, he thought grumpily, and if she doesn't see my way by then I'll have her tortured for being a renegade to sense. No I won't, he admitted as the tonic fancy worked, at least, not just because she plays hard to get.

A leader had to be capable of impartiality, and there was a distinction between private and public affairs. Men of the old school carried on like that, but Theseus was training himself towards appropriate conduct. Ages to come would revere him for throwing in his mighty lot with the fates of nobles and artisans.

He unhooked his antlers and fixed them to his head, then took the great swan-wings and strapped them to his back. His costume was based on the common notions that fairies could fly and that they hung around in forests, like stags. The tickle of feathers almost revived him. 'I am Oberon,' he said aloud, and glanced down to see if he had an erection. But he was a tired Oberon who needed a few minutes' rest before finding and ravishing his Titania.

'Bloody nerve!' Puck muttered, and caused the man who slew the Minotaur to snore like a baby.

XIV

YOU WOULDN'T EXPECT a man with Demetrius's advantages to get upset by a trifling poke in his vanity, but even the most valiant have their weak spots. The fact that Lysander openly loved Hermia was not in itself unbearable; it became so because in consequence Theseus must slacken his regard for Demetrius. A favourite shouldn't be gullible in his choice of chums. This elopement just carried the thing a twinge further, from humiliation to the destruction of his credibility at Court. Demetrius imagined himself the laughing-stock of Athens. His name would be the standard for absurd loyalty. Theseus would drop him.

He was out to get Lysander. And force Hermia to her senses, of course, though she didn't fully enter into this. He'd asked Lysander to look after her. What a way to repay friendship! Lysander came from Crete with only the scantiest letters of introduction, yet he'd reached down and helped him to his elevation. Such altruism deserved a better upshot. True, other Athenians of his age shunned Demetrius, saying he was arrogant – they envied his closeness to Theseus – and true, Lysander just accepted him as a friend straight off, but . . .

He thought to confront the escaping pair, talk sense into them and get them back before anyone else found out. He had a vague idea that Helena would be placated if Lysander was offered as an alternative. He planned to be magnanimous to Lysander, so that Hermia would fling herself at his feet and beg to be reconsidered. Graciously, he intended to take her back, and he could imagine how his graciousness would affect the prostrate but attentive Lysander. In future years Lysander would visit often and play with the kids, and the two men would get drunk together and grow old together. Everything would be swell, if he could arrest their crazy flight.

He flew past the soldiers, who were marching at a regular pace. Several called out sarcastically, 'Where's the fire?' and, 'Look at him go!' When Helena followed soon after they jeered and made the sorts of uncouth jokes that soldiers are famed for. Demetrius heard and knew Helena was closing, so he put on an extra spurt, reaching the road above the forest in a state of collapse.

He was flat on his back when Helena sprinted up and tripped over an outstretched arm, flinging Hermia's trousseau into the air. 'Have I hurt you?' she cried, smudging the blood from her nose with the palm of her grazed hand. 'Speak to me, Demetrius!'

'Get lost,' he said surlily, then remembered he was a gentleman and added, 'if you will.'

'I *am* lost if I'm not with you,' she countered ardently, scrambling towards him on her knees and collecting dresses, pants, shoes and jackets.

'Then *be* lost, but leave me be! I have told you, I love Hermia. I dare say your old father loves you. I dare say your dog and parrot love you. Be content. I love you not.'

Although his lungs ached and his calves were wobbly, Demetrius heaved himself up and continued his journey. Helena caught up easily, which was galling, for although she was clad in a light summer dress and was long-legged and weighed next to nothing, she was carrying a big load.

'The forest is below, Demetrius – why are you still going ahead?'

'If you want the forest go to it. I have no interest in the forest, only in Lysander. Hermia, I mean. They'll come out, if they have brains, at its farthest end, not where they went in. I'll be there first.'

'You're so intelligent! What a mind! And what a body! What a waste, that you've neglected me!'

'I plan to neglect you to the end of my days, so drop away while your disappointment is a relatively private matter.'

'I'll never leave you. Spurn me and I love you more!'

'This fawning revolts me. You leech. You clinging vine. You cloth-ears. You're less to me than the chair I chuck my clothes on at night.'

'Let me be the square of carpet you tread before launching into bed. Let me be your quilt, or the pillow you punch into shape. Treat me as your spaniel. Kennel me outside. Teach me tricks. I beg already, that's one. I'll go through hoops for you. I'll lick your hand, your foot, any part that likes my licking tongue and total devotion.'

'Peace! Can't you hear how each word reduces you further? A sow has more eloquence, a bitch in heat more decorum! A decent girl does not chase a man like this; you're as suggestive as the most vulgar soldier in the ranks. Helena, no man could love a girl driven to such debased extremity by misplaced lust!'

'Loving *you* brings me to this extremity. I am your creation. I'll do anything you ask except desert you.'

'You're mad. Theseus is so right to speak of the evil in love. But you're not fit to hear the word. Get gone, you wretched pseudo-whore! Oh, that I was as fleet-footed as you! I'd use my speed to catch Hermia, and then you'd see who I love!'

'Hermia loves Lysander.'

'Your jealousy won't confuse me. You're Hermia's friend, you should be concerned for her happiness.'

'She doesn't want you, and I'm after you more earnestly than you are after her.'

'Helena, this has gone far enough! Be warned, I no longer answer for your safety. If you obstruct me in the wood your life is forfeit.'

'Kill me if you wish, or ravish me, slake your lusty thirst

— 90 —

here – I know your threats, they aren't real – you'll never harm me.'

'A man in love is bound by no law, as Lysander has demonstrated, damn him! Don't imagine that because I was gentle with you once I cannot be rough.'

'Gentle you were when you knew yourself, and warm, and hard where warmth and gentleness are forged. Have pity on me, because I do not govern myself. Before your touch I was as demure as any maid of good family, but you felt the spot. There is a natural progression, but you, having started my eyes half from my head, left me wildly awakened and in desperate need – an unnatural move, Demetrius. If I am mad it is a power you set in motion – do you fear the passionate motor you have started? You have a manly duty towards me; don't run away, be natural!'

Demetrius stopped running. He was above the place where he meant to enter and hide. Exasperated and short of breath he faced Helena, who showed no sign of tiring. She didn't even sweat, but gazed back with preternaturally eager eyes, making him feel guilty for corrupting them.

'Understand this, lady,' he said, and punched her beneath her bundle.

Poor Helena staggered, crumpled, and fell under Hermia's things. Demetrius knew decisive action was the best way out of a tricky situation. He staggered down into the trees. Helena curled around her pain and cried at being served so brutally. Wow, she groaned, totalled by the guy I love! Some arrow, Cupid! Thanks a bunch!

After rolling and groaning some more she persuaded herself that this proved Hermia had blinded poor Demetrius. She recalled the delicacy of his hands in earlier days. Soon he'll hate himself and remorse will overwhelm him. I must find him and be ready at hand, to forgive.

Puck had been fascinated by the comic running dispute and had watched its savage conclusion with admiration. 'I'll help you find him, miss,' he whispered, thinking it would be instructive to observe more of this affair. This fine Athenian maid had

— 91 —

needed no fairy interference to rob her of her rational mind. Love alone had made a slavering lap-dog of her, and she'd be bound to pursue her quarry until, cornered, he turned and destroyed her.

Puck chuckled: would she pant her devoted gratitude even as Demetrius battered the wiry life from her unloved body? What sport they were!

XV

ETER QUINCE LED the way, holding aloft a lantern. The joiner, Snug, was next, his right hand clutching the tail of Peter's shirt, his left holding Robin Starveling's hand, whose other shivered in the prayerful paws of Francis Flute. The tinker, Tom Snout, brought up the rear and had his own hands encumbered with a leaky kettle, a sieve, and various clanking ornaments of his trade, which he always intended to mend at any spare moment, or to sell should any late-night housewife be come across. He was joined to the file of timid men by his teeth, which gripped the woolly ends of Flute's long scarf. Now and then he would sneeze and either let go the scarf or half-strangle the bellows-mender. There would follow a sudden tinny clattering, a halt for hushed abuses to be hurled back, and then Peter Quince would lead on again.

They were in the wood, but walking in circles. They knew no other way to locate Nick Bottom, who usually intercepted them after they'd tramped about for half an hour calling his name.

'I think, Peter Quince, that it grows very late into the night,' ventured Snug the joiner in a quaking voice.

'Perhaps Nick is trading elsewhere,' Francis Flute piped up. 'We may as easily return tomorrow by day.'

'I don't like dark woods,' came Snug again. 'Dark deeds get done in them, which none can see till it be too late.'

'Aye,' agreed Tom Snout. 'It *is* too late.' And then, realising

— 93 —

the freedom of his teeth and the blackness on all sides, and especially in front of him, 'Hey! Chums! Stop! Stop!'

Then Quince's lantern died and all were in the dark. After a few panicky moments spent blinking and flailing their arms and struggling not to scream or race off in every direction at once, their eyes adjusted and they saw that they could see, and what they could see was a moonlit clearing, to whose pale glow they fled like bumping moths.

Nick Bottom had propped Lysander so that his head caught some moonbeams, and there studied him until he fancied he saw significant resemblances between them. After a while he convinced himself that a stranger would hardly determine any differences, except in the superficial matter of attire: they were brothers, nearly.

'Heave-ho!' Nick muttered as he hoisted Lysander over his shoulder. 'Heigh-ho,' he added as he began walking towards the cottage. Belatedly it crossed his mind to call Oberon and seek a second chance with Hermia, whose sumptuous nakedness now boiled his brains. Lysander's weight put those thoughts to him, for Lysander would have her and Lysander was his kinsman. But he remembered Oberon's touching reaction to his decency. 'Ho-hum,' Nick continued, smacking Lysander's backside and shrugging him higher on his shoulder. 'This is what men call desire, I guess – fretting what could have been with what cannot be. Now I think Hermia's body was shaped expressly for clasping into mine, but there it goes, and I expect I'll live single like my father till I'm too old to sustain much interest in female matters. My word, it's a close night!'

Nick was about midway through the winding brake that formed part of his cottage wall when he heard the commotion caused by the guttering lantern. He stopped to consider Hermia. 'Rest you here, brother,' he sighed, knowing she'd come to no harm, and he slipped Lysander carefully to a mossy bank. 'I must join my pals before they scare the squirrels with their ruckus.'

Peter Quince, however, had already restored a semblance of

calm by launching yet again into his intimate exchanges with Theseus. He was not so much a barefaced liar as a man whose very dryness of approach, however speculative, suggested that nothing better than plain truth could reside in him. Bluntly, the man was short in the imaginative colouring department, so if he implied that Theseus had found his conversation tasty the others believed it so. By nature Peter was more gimcrack philosopher or cavilling critic than actor; his treatment was strictly imitative in the somewhat reductive sense of being largely unconscious, and of adding little to his own stature and providing no insight into the workings of those whom he copied. Whatever role he traduced you knew it was Peter Quince in his own dull voice. There was a charm in that, too, a kind of integrity, or reliability.

Now, he'd come out to meet Nick Bottom at the curious urging of Theseus, but there was also a competitive motive. He and Nick were friendly rivals, and Peter was more frequently piqued because Nick had the best tales, as well as the trick of telling them. Peter, when all was said and done, was accepted as the intellectual in their group. Without him nothing would get accomplished. But they brightened up at Nick's improbable schemes, and Peter had often wanted a thing to come off that would prove his leadership to be more fun than Nick's happy disorder. This audience with Theseus was promising to be that thing, and Peter wanted the weaver to know it and submit.

'Thought I heard you, chums,' Nick said casually, strolling into the clearing with his hands in his pockets as if nothing had happened since he saw them last. 'What brings you so far at this hour?'

Peter Quince grinned – as near a grin as he ever got. Nothing altered in his eyes but his mouth twitched and his head wobbled with preparatory zeal as if the stew of words inside was lifting his lid as it bubbled up. 'There is an *excellent* reason, a cause for celebration . . .'

'And you thought to include me! That's mighty staunch, friends, and I'm mighty moved, indeed I am. But sadly I've none left of the vintage we enjoyed the last time you came by, so unless

—— 95 ——

you've carried some liquor from sweet Margery's I fear the celebration will be eked out in honest moonshine.'

'Have you moonshine, Nick?' Francis Flute peeped hopefully.

'I dare say, perhaps, if sufficient reason be given, I may . . .'

'A jug to pass about! You're all heart, Nick!'

'One moment,' interrupted Quince, fearing the loss of his moment. 'Nick, before you uncork let me give you good cause. Guess what: I spoke with Theseus this evening! Aye, in very truth I did, as close as I stand to you I stood, and he spoke as natural as any one of us, man to man to me! "Peter Quince," says he, "you are as fine a carpenter as can be found in Attica. We need the honest work you are famous for." I tell you, Nick, so fulsome were his praises I had to block the man or he'd have had me rebuilding his palace. "Ahem," says I. "Ahem, Theseus, I'm proud my work comes before me, sir, but tonight I have another matter to put." You see where I was leading him? At this point I fell to my knees, like so, and clasped my hands, like so, and gave him extempore as great a speech . . . well, some, I noticed, were driven to tears in the force of it. I surpassed myself before that auspicious audience. Theseus confessed he was astounded, and paid me sixpence for two minutes' drama. There is more. It grieved him that not knowing of my coming he had already booked his players aforehand, and being a man of honour couldn't go back on his word to them. *But*, he begged the names of my actors and gave, gratis, twopence apiece in addition to my sixpence. Here is two for you, as evidence that I, Peter Quince, had the ear of the greatest man that ever lived. Count on it, the very next time he needs players, Peter Quince will be called for, and Peter Quince's men! I have done.'

'But in addition,' Robin Starveling recalled, 'didn't he single out Nick by name and tell you to visit Nick tonight?'

'Some such,' Peter grudgingly agreed. 'Yet not quite as you sound it. *I* named you all, Nick at the conclusion of the list, and on reflection it seems to me that what he was saying was that we

— 96 —

should all get together tonight, our Bully Bottom included, none left out, you see, to talk over this great change in probable circumstances.'

Nick nodded as he took all this in, and smiled affectionately at his friends, who were so shaken with Peter's undoubted courage and tenacity on their behalf. He didn't want to lessen the impact of Peter's story, but had to tell his part to complete it. 'I thank you for this twopence, Peter Quince, and even more for the story that engendered it, for it's the most heartening I've ever heard, don't you agree, chums? We owe you a debt beyond money, Peter. I know *I'd* never have mounted the long steps, however ardent I was. You make me feel better, after letting you down so badly the day Theseus rode home to a diversion.'

'That was no fault of yours, Nick. The idea was good, if only he'd kept to the path.'

'Thank you kindly. But listen, lads, for we've had another happy accident. I take no credit, but I happened to be over Thebes way when this knight came riding by and asked me if I knew of any players. He'd been scouring the country lucklessly. To cut the matter short, I was able to collect my wits and suggest us. At once we were engaged. Peter, you see how well it falls out? Theseus wanted you, but had already engaged you without knowing it!'

This brought several exclamations of wonder. Peter Quince rubbed his chin and grumbled inaudibly instead of cheering.

'But I don't get this,' he said. 'Weren't you so much as auditioned?'

By now Nick had his inspiration, for with a single untruth he could avoid all reference to the horrific ordeal and its sickening aftermath. 'No,' he said gladly. 'Uncommon good fortune, wouldn't you say, for I was not as ready as you to be called upon.'

'Mmm,' Quince ruminated, walking aside to mull it over.

'Well, lads, it *is* late after all, and we've much on tomorrow, so if you'll excuse me . . . thanking you once again for these tidings.'

'Hold on, Nick,' Peter Quince returned. 'We can't leave off all our rehearsals. We must cast parts, and we can run through the script by here – I've brought several copies.'

He whipped out the papers and distributed them. Nick was trapped. Somehow he had to help Hermia and Lysander escape before daybreak, but he couldn't let the company down either. Peter jammed a scrap of paper into his hand and Nick cast his eye over it, not reading a line. But the others were reading, and making heavy weather of it. Snug, usually such a slow scholar, was the first to get through the laborious title, and he repeated it questioningly, '*The Most Lamentable Comedy And Most Cruel Death of Pyramus And Thisby?* What is this, Peter, laughing matter or stuff for tears?'

'Whichever,' Francis Flute was quick to complain. 'It's more than we may cope with of a sudden, like. Give us lines we know, Peter.'

'Aye,' added Robin, 'give us a Hercules one, and let Nick be Hercules as he always is, and have him tear at his lines as he always does. I get goose-pimples whenever I hear Nick's Hercules!'

'No, no,' Nick broke in with unexpected fervour, 'I have no stomach for Hercules. I think I've always given the tyrant wrong. He needs no words, it's all in the stance and eyes, and I should need others to be the horrid corpses so all would see how strong men have a habit of anointing their feet with blood. In short, I can no longer give the part of Hercules, since to play it true would upset the audience and give us only nightmares to talk of in prison.'

'This is strange speaking from you, Nick,' Peter Quince said with genuine consternation.

'I'm sorry for it, but play-acting ain't all artifice; it needs grounding in a kind of verisimilitude that we are too innocent to accomplish fairly. So let's go at this new play, making clear it's only a coarse fabrication, not a deep-felt truth.'

'This too is strange talk. Do you mean to produce my play an' all?'

— 98 —

'Save us, no, Peter! I couldn't do your job! Come, how d'you want me? Shall I be Thisby? I can thpeak lithpingly thoft, like tho, "Thithne, Thithne – ah, Pyramuth, my lover dear, thy Thithne dear, and lady dear, and dear oh me, dear Pyramuth, what thall become of uth?" Eh?'

'*Francis* is marked for Thisby, for he may also *look* the part.'

'What? I have a beard coming, very nearly!'

'THISBY!'

'Very well, under protest. I shall not easily be the part, though I may become it by actorly skills alone. I am a man.'

'Nick Bottom – Pyramus. A lover that kills himself most gallant.'

'Well enough, I can do him. What are the other parts?'

Quince tried to summarise and assign them simply, and after a half hour or so a first reading commenced, and Nick saw the only chance he was likely to get for escaping, when he had to be off-stage for a scene.

He rushed to Lysander and hurriedly exchanged clothes, for a Lysander dressed as an artisan would pass through the country unchallenged. Then he lifted Lysander on to his back, hoping to reunite the lovers before completing his performance. But already his friends were shouting with dreary sarcasm: he was past his cue. 'What can I do?' he mused.

'Tell me your line,' came a familiar voice in the darkness.

'Dewdrop! Am I glad to see you – or hear you at least! Where've you been? I'm in a dreadful fix.'

'Yeah, I've been watching. Danger's nearer than you imagine. The Athenian guard surrounds the forest. Theseus sleeps where you might tread on him. But I can create a diversion. Tell me Pyramus's line.'

'"If I were, fair Pyramus, I were only thine."'

'Who wrote that crap? It doesn't make sense!'

'Do you want to say it, or review it?'

'I'd like a bit I could get my teeth into. Never mind, you hurry on, while I scatter your friends so they won't come looking for you. I'll rejoin you shortly and get you to a port.'

— 99 —

Bottom leant forward to kiss Dewdrop's wet nose, but caught only the flick of his tail.

'Pyramus!' Quince was calling. 'Your cue is past!'

'"O,"' Francis Flute said again, straining for a scale almost beyond belief in a young man. '"As true as truest horse, that yet would NEVER TIRE!"'

At that moment he turned and beheld, strutting on hind legs, Dewdrop, who declaimed his line as beautifully as it could be done, without a comma. The company shrieked, dropped scripts, threw up hands and ran, sharing the same panic and bringing it to many blind collisions. Dewdrop snorted and resumed his customary posture. He was proud of himself.

Snug, who had been given the lion's part on account of his stammer, was first to break out from the trees. Two soldiers bore down and without challenging the startled man ran him through, two spears at once. Then they lopped off his head for good measure. Proud of their skills they winked, nudged each other and resumed their posts. Peter Quince saw it happen and fainted.

'Well, I reckon we'll be made men for this night's work,' the one soldier called to his accomplice.

'Aye, quick and bravely done. The first moment as he broke from cover I thought him a great beast. Lucky fear transfixed the fellow! Sixpence a day for life, I reckon, or preferment – he must have been a dangerous spy or an assassin.'

The other actors were still hopelessly lost and banging into trees, but as they grew aware of their separation their noise gave way to silent terror. Even as they blundered on they tried to creep, and the slightest noise made them freeze and shut their eyes like children believing themselves invisible. All the superstitions that life in Athens had calmed were roused once more; they were acutely aware that unpredictable, possibly malevolent spirits crowded every inch of space outside the ordered society they had so foolishly departed from. They were truly lost, for they believed in what was there yet had no contact any more, no harmony but the flat orderliness of Athenian society.

— 100 —

XVI

THESEUS, WAKING FIT as a flea, found Hermia and thought Hippolyta had excelled herself in disguise: a Titania after his heart. No good Hermia protesting that her name was Hermia. She was able to see through the antlers and the white wings. She saw Theseus, all-powerful and, quite evidently, insane. The confused protests she dared make were interpreted as Hippolyta's enthusiastic acting. Fortunately Theseus was poleaxed by Oberon before he'd ruined the girl.

Ten minutes later he rediscovered Titania, this time disguised all over again as a thinner, shriller, but still fairly mouth-watering maid called Helena. He hadn't dreamt Hippolyta would enter into the spirit of the game so perceptively. But, before his playful lust was indulged, poor old Theseus was attacked from behind with a blow between the antlers that put him right back to sleep.

Demetrius had thought he was saving Hermia from a vile monster. Double despair when he saw it was only his clinging Helena he had saved, and that the monster he had saved her from was his beloved master!

Helena managed to stop him running himself through on the spot by pointing out that Theseus never knew what hit him, and *need* never know. Assuring the chastened Demetrius that she wouldn't betray him even if he kept after Hermia, Helena showed a loving nobility of spirit which obliged the young man to admit

— 101 —

he hadn't considered love seriously until then. When the chips were down Helena was a good sort, loyal as a brother. 'I've misjudged you,' he said humbly.

'And misjudged yourself,' Helena replied with verve.

'But what shall we do about Theseus?'

'Run away.'

And so they did, but not far because the forest was sealed. Far enough to locate a secluded clearing of their own, where Demetrius could be astonished and elated to begin seeing himself through Helena's doting eyes. He had to agree with her that he was gentle and perceptive as well as immensely strong. She was, he began to realise, neither plain nor unintelligent, but one whose judgement obviously counted. We'll leave the pair without examining their love too closely.

What of Lysander? Dressed as a nondescript weaver he was lost for some hours, though at one point several wild men ran towards him shrieking incomprehensibly. He went for his sword and remembered that it was being worn by Nick Bottom. He was just getting to the notion that these crying men weren't vagabondish assailants after all, only frightened artisans who had raced forward expecting help – perhaps mistaking him for someone they knew – when they all took on a look of horror as they peered into his face. Yelling with renewed conviction they ploughed back into the night. This upset Lysander's balanced mind and he wasted the best part of another hour creeping ahead silently instead of shouting Hermia's name.

Eventually he found her crying inconsolably. She refused to say why because Lysander would attack anyone who had assaulted her, and he wouldn't have much luck against Theseus. Privately she wished they'd gone ahead with their suicide pact back in the cemetery; everything would have been grand then. Lysander hugged his trembling pathetic love and swore he'd never lose sight of her again and cried helplessly with her.

Meanwhile the fairies had seen their chance to help Nick Bottom out, only this time not with Hermia. Oberon separated him from Lysander, while Titania whispered a thought to

Hippolyta and Puck tickled Nick's genitals with a damp thistle. The scene that ensued was of such erotic intensity that its most enthusiastic observer, Puck, who had seen women in deep mud fellating water buffalo, and was not easily aroused, forgot all about his study of Demetrius and Helena and instead zoomed off to copulate with three hundred and twenty-seven fairies in quick succession. Most were female, many close relatives.

In short there was considerable activity in the forest throughout that night, so much confusion that a dozen interpretations could be made and none be faulted. It was mild enough for all to dance naked if any so desired, and the fairies, lined like shining silver along branches or thrumming about prismatically in high excitement made colourful music the whole night long. It was lovely. Except that some of the mortals had a terrible time. The trouble was they couldn't stand outside their events and see the loveliness-in-transience of moments which, far from being heavy with corporeality, were light and fleeting as the breeze a butterfly makes. Think how much better fun they'd have had if, instead of scurrying about in fear of their lives, they could have watched and laughed at their own silly antics from a position of safety such as readers inhabit. Only time and distance separate the suffering participant from the smiling spectator; only a simple act of willed imagination is needed and anyone may move mentally aside from a frightening involvement, to reflect on the brevity of life and the pointlessness of limiting himself to one perspective on it. As if your suffering or mine ever made a hiccup in the steady breath of Time! We come and go in an instant, yet we divide and subdivide that instant, and lament and lengthen out bits as if that made the whole multiply its dimensions. What folly! Even fairies only achieve longevity at the expense of size and substance. Their freedom is a prison. They'd rather have our constraints if they could become the same size without becoming invisible. It's not easy being a fairy. Even if they gain some pleasure from copulation there's a practical necessity for it: they don't reproduce easily. Here it's more useful to imagine wind dispersal than animal fornication. Imagine dandelion globes

— 103 —

getting a little tweak of pleasure and you'll be on the right track. By going at it like Puck an infant might arrive in five years, but it wouldn't be considered unusual if a few hundred went by before they struck lucky – and then, of course, no one would know who the father had been. The concept of the father is one of the things they envy humans for possessing, since it makes possible the small family unit and consequent rapidity of character development and identity. Most fairies don't know who they are. A fairy takes on average twelve hundred years to gain a name, and that's roughly a third of its lifespan. So getting named is its purpose in life. We mortals get that before we even know it. For the most part being a fairy means living a seeming eternity and having no recollection of it. They do have long lives, but even they can be cut off short. Fire does it. There's an audible crack as they burst, often accompanied by a swift flash of white flame. The phenomenon is observable, and mortals generally take it as a cue for a remark like, That log's spitting – get the guard! Well, fairies think we're gods, practically. Because they idolise us it embarrasses them to see us using our power and beauty so casually. Titania and her train wept acorn cups to see Hermia so hurt and withdrawn, but they didn't know *why* she'd changed because she was clearly a virtuous soul and therefore unassailable, essentially. It was as if she didn't know the value of her soul, that she took on so when only her pretty body was threatened against her wishes, and that would be gone before she knew it anyway.

'I have it,' Titania said quietly, wiping her eyes, 'Hermia weeps for Theseus! She must think he too had a soul as unblemished as her own! So she weeps at the wrong he did himself, the aeons of torment his soul might endure!'

'Can sorrow for another soul intercede on its behalf?'

'How, Peaseblossom? With whom? Where is the court of souls?'

'Mortals speak of creatures above, in Elysium, who control them.'

'I can't imagine that mortals' souls are so remarkably different from the rest of nature. Which of us has ever seen a god in her travels? Why are you crying now, Mustardseed?'

'Because,' Mustardseed sniffled, 'Theseus tries to help his people. His soul shouldn't suffer so long.'

'There must be pride in his soul for him to want to help before he knows more. Let's go wake the man, anyway. I want to know if Oberon cries for Theseus as we've cried for Hermia.'

When Theseus did come to he wasn't alone. Hippolyta had joined him. Tactfully she'd removed his silly wings and antlers and dressed him as Theseus once more, but she fastened the antlers to her own head and he, not having any clear or happy recollections of the night, supposed from her cute appearance it hadn't been as miserable as blank misgivings told him. So he tried to be jolly, but the bump on his head, the dizziness, and a general weariness and stiffness in the joints all undermined good cheer to make him thoughtful and restrained.

Detecting this, Hippolyta refrained from needling him and fell in behind as if the last thing she wanted was to disturb her master. This was not how the submissive movement was framed in her mind. In the arms of Nick Bottom Hippolyta had experienced a kind of revelation. Now Hippolyta had had more men than most men had had women. Like Theseus she had availed herself from the earliest opportunity of every potential partner who stumbled into view. A novice she was not. Her quarrel with Theseus wasn't about his physical power and brutally unfair treatment of her – that was something she despised but understood; great men were that way. What she couldn't accept was his extraordinary ambition to use that power in the same old way while at the same time hoping to conquer her free soul. The jerk really believed he could give Hippolyta her freedom and gain it for his own use, without for a second relinquishing his enforced hold. That was asking too much. Nothing had changed that. The difference was that now she was willing to allow him to be wrong, just as she would allow Emily or any woman to be wrong, and not to bridle at the error. He was mistaken if he thought he could demand that she love him, but the mistake at least suggested a

latent interest in her feelings. That it also suggested total ignorance of her feelings was another matter. He expected fealty, but
needed more. He knew he was not absolute.

Now Hippolyta herself had sometimes wondered if there was
more to life than evading traps, arranging ambushes, accumulat-
ing wealth and status, getting drunk and getting laid, but her
wondering never got beyond the disappointingly nugatory
negative. Thoughts of staying alive were usually paramount.

Nick Bottom's forthright lovemaking, his puppyish earnest-
ness, his sheer joy at eventual success, his whoops of amazed
delight and his wondering, if polite, reprises through the night,
all reminded Hippolyta of a primal innocence that not even
Emily possessed, since her innocent little sister was merely
inexperienced sexually, and childish to boot; in other ways she
had the shrewd sophistication, and dogmatism, that went with
being spoilt rotten since birth. But the honest weaver had retained
a touching human quality given out liberally at birth and forgotten immediately afterwards by most. Hippolyta, generous and
sentimental, supposed that Theseus, gnarled and perplexed
though he was, retained elements of this hopeful stuffing somewhere within his lumbering frame. So she fell in mutely behind
him, and Theseus thought it a blessing that she wasn't inclined
to enrage him with taunts this misty morning.

He almost wanted to put his arm around her so they could
emerge together like young brave lovers, to adulatory applause
from the loyal soldiers. But he didn't feel like a young lover, or
even an old one. The gods, he thought, reconsidering his several
interrupted visions, wanted to teach him something important
by bashing him on the head whenever he got excited. Was it that
he should ban sex? No, on practical grounds it couldn't be
anything so wholesale. Just sex with women? No, for then men
would die out.

What was I doing that was wrong? Theseus asked as he found
a tree in his way. He frowned as though the tree had no right to
block him, but decided against head-butting it and looked instead
for the trail his feet had misled.

— 106 —

Was it the impersonation that was wrong? But then why bump *me* on the bonce? It was Hippolyta's idea to be those juicy girls. We played together. Surely there's nothing against shared fancies?

'Why was I bludgeoned unconscious?' he demanded suddenly.

Hippolyta could think of no quicker reply than a surprised, 'Don't you know?' which only made him defensive.

'Of course I know – I just wondered what *you* knew. Yes, the gods are so swift and sure! What an example, eh!'

But if I can't fathom my own activities, by whose authority have I upheld Athens's laws? I must know myself better, and when I do be sure not to endorse all I've done. This thud on the thinking cap was as much as to say, Here you go wrong, m'lad – go no further! Yes, I'm proud I can admit that even I may make mistakes. I proceed thus: a mistake is a Wrong Thing, and implies a Right Thing not done. Very well. Right and Wrong are established. But now two supplementaries emerge, viz., when I say Right and Wrong, do I mean absolutely, for universal application? And, granted a mistake is Wrong, is it necessarily undesirable? Recognition of Wrong may lead to a Right Act. So should Wrong Doings be punished, or merely defined? A law against so-and-so may stop that Wrong Doing and, for want of the example of mistake, it may stop Right Doing too. For surely we can't call Right that which men conform to merely, that's just dull habit. Right and Wrong are products of Experience and Understanding. 'Struth, this is alarming stuff! 'Hippolyta,' he asked bluntly, 'have I done Wrong?'

'You are Theseus, so your arbitration carries the day, as we saw when you adjudicated in the matter of Hermia who asked for love and was given her father's peace of mind.'

'Ah yes, the *actual* Hermia! Mmm, could be the lesson lies off in that direction. Thank you, sweet.'

'I am not sweet.'

'I meant it endearingly.'

'But spoke it casually. I am no confection.'

'I'll try to remember.'

An outright prohibition on Wrong Doing will reduce that uncertain testing of life which is fundamental to education. Deny that and a man will not earnestly yearn to identify with the quest for Right. The merit of one depends upon a crushing understanding of the demerit of the other. I begin to suspect a female touch in this throbbing lesson. The clout was as much as to say, If this were the *actual* Hermia it would be Wrong to take her in this wise. I feel I agree with that, yet where was the harm?

'Hippolyta, answer this plainly: in an ideal society, should a girl have the right to refuse a lord's advances?'

'In some cases, certainly.'

'You honestly believe that would benefit and not shatter society?'

'If a girl knows her own mind.'

'Though the principle would in effect put a mere girl on equal footing with a man, as if her worth was demonstrably equivalent, which in most cases it palpably is not. Your tribe apart, where do women bear arms in defence of their lands, or bring booty home to add to the general wealth? Where do women participate in good government? As they do so little, how can they be granted so much?'

'That's easy: grant more, then they can do more.'

'Yet you resist what I would grant you.'

'A good trick! Very well. Hermia claimed to love Lysander. The law forces a choice, but what harm would there be in allowing her the man she loves, so long as he loves her?'

'We must tread the right path here – I'm loath to tread a path that places Love above Law.'

'Then modify the law so a case like this can fall out happily within it.'

'I have it! I will offer Perotheus the city of Thebes, to rebuild and rule in amity with us, so long as he withdraws his stricture. I'll offer Demetrius the second-best ruin in Thebes, if he will assist Perotheus and take the other girl to wife. Then I'll tell Hermia her petition has touched me, since it coincided with our nuptials, and that on this day every year I'll allow maids of good

— 108 —

family to marry the man they love, even against their fathers'
wishes. How does that sound?'

'You are a statesman, lord.'

'Then let's emerge arm in arm, like man and mate.'

And so they did, coming into the damp yellow morning light
just where they'd gone in under crisp moonbeams. They looked
good, the grizzled veteran and the sultry, springy Amazonian
sheltering against her master like a fawn with a lion.

The soldiers had been waiting, cold, hungry and disappointed.
The nightwatch had been unrelieved tedium, except for two of
them. Some excitement had been generated by the arrival of
Nedar and Perotheus with a posse of tough gents. Nedar, always
frail, looked worse than ever after the hot ride, and just sat on
his nag weeping silently. Perotheus, however, conferred angrily
with the captain and glared impatiently into the mouth of the
forest.

About time too, he seemed to be saying when Theseus finally
appeared, raising an arm to meet the customary rousing cheer and
turning the redundant gesture into a greeting. 'What – Perotheus?'

'Aye, Theseus.'

'And you, old fellow? Out of bed so early?'

Nedar nodded, too overcome for words.

'They've skipped,' Perotheus explained curtly, almost as if he
blamed Theseus. 'Done a bunk! I want that bastard's balls! As
for Hermia – chuck the ungrateful bitch from the highest cliff
and you'll go some way to finding favour with me! Oh, and this
fellow's kid ran off with your protégé.'

'You are intemperate, friend,' Theseus said in a tone worth
more attention than Perotheus gave.

'Intemperate be damned! The slut's betrayed me! What
good's a daughter, except to look after her father when he's senile
and incontinent? Do you see Hermia so dutiful? No chance!
She's scampered off, a bitch in heat, after that craven dog
Lysander. Bind 'em together if they won't be parted, bind 'em
and kick 'em off a cliff top!'

'I will remind you,' Theseus said icily, and not at all cryptically

— 109 —

to those who knew what he was getting at, 'that my father who lived is now dead, with a sea to his name.'

Anyone who didn't know what he was getting at would have found the effect of these words remarkable. Perotheus, as massive, gnarled and dangerous a man as Theseus, blanched. Then reddened. Then stammered without articulating a single word. Then fell to his knees in supplication. 'Forgive my unfortunate outburst. I meant you no offence. Rage spoke through me, drowning out tact. Blame my wretched daughter.'

'No.'

The soldiers nudged and closed in hopefully, thinking: How is he going to do this? He doesn't have his club! But most knew Theseus didn't need a club – he could twist the other fellow's head off, or catch his sword in mid-flight and snap it, then hurl him up and over the trees. Theseus had never been beaten in any form of combat. What! He even had this wild woman eating from his hand – there was a man!

Wearily, beaten before he started, Perotheus pushed himself to his feet and sighed. But Theseus did not engage him. No. Theseus made an announcement. 'We'll find these elopers in my forest.'

The soldiers were astonished, because no one ever got by *them*! They were also stupid and forgot that Demetrius and Helena had passed them on the road.

'We'll go in now,' Theseus said, 'and when we've found them we'll listen to what they have to say. Be warned, Perotheus – I want happiness, not blood!'

The clearings where the lovers lay were soon located. All four were scared out of their wits at first, for a variety of reasons, but gradually they realised that the night had worked subtle changes and, hesitantly, they sorted themselves out: Hermia loved Lysander, who loved Hermia; Helena loved Demetrius, who understood her obsession and liked her for it; Demetrius still loved Lysander; Lysander regarded Demetrius as a bit of a jerk, but was fond of him in a way. Everybody was happy. At least, jovial laughter echoed through the trees and reassured the timid

— 110 —

fairies. Perotheus was grumpy but obliged to accept the soft option Theseus had taken. Nedar gazed at Helena as if she was a heap of May blossom, and wept some more. No one noticed Peter Quince and his remaining friends making their getaway.

On the whole it presented a very satisfactory conclusion. The sun was over the rise shining brightly between the boughs on smiling faces and steaming clothes. A good day was beginning, and love was in the air. The story of the two pairs of young Athenian lovers had come to its happy end, with only marriage and families ahead of them.

One warning note, though, a note which none picked up because it had been noticed already: our happy weaver, presently contentedly dreaming, had, on passing through the clearing shortly after losing Hermia and Lysander, picked up and pocketed unread a paper, which he took to be one of Peter Quince's playscripts. It was a small piece, so he thought it contained simple lines for Snug to learn. Snug was always losing his place. But Snug's lines were not on that piece of paper. Emily's letter was.

Nick Bottom dreamt a good man's dream. His vision had come, surpassing expectation. Even in sleep he was a different man now. There was much he might forget of his innocence, but also, there were things he could now bear to remember. He remembered the hideous battlefield. He remembered that he had saved the lives of two Theban knights. He dreamt he was a hero, but he didn't dream that because of the unread piece of paper he would soon meet those forgotten knights, far from his home in the forest, far from all friendship.

— 111 —

XVII

THE JUGGLERS WERE good. One kept four clubs spinning while he balanced on a big red ball and made it inch up the incline of a plank. The plank see-sawed over a log, so as the juggler progressed the incline changed gradually into a line of descent. Loud and prolonged applause greeted his success, and no one asked why he had perfected so perfectly useless a skill. Some took it as a metaphor for Life, and said the juggler was a great philosopher. Next came bull-leaping and he was forgotten. Nobles gasped at the agility with which these lithe naked Minoans – every one a prince or princess! – somersaulted over a horn-hooking bull. The bull was slaughtered afterwards to even greater squeals of delight, its head adorning the great table in tribute to Theseus's prowess in the bull-slaying field.

Then came exotic dancing boys, then wrestlers. Clowns and fire-eaters punctuated the main acts and helped clear away the rubbish and injured. Quince's troupe weren't able to find a quiet spot to rehearse because they were continually on stand-by and then stand-down. The feasting was prodigious. The wine bill alone could have financed a small aggressive expedition, or rebuilt a city. Yet the effect of this lavish expenditure was to make the audience progressively less attentive, more critical, until acts that would earlier have won plaudits for skill received catcalls. A young fellow was badly gored, the horn hooking in above his

— 112 —

knee and shredding his leg to the ankle, much as you might split a log lengthways, only with more copious and brilliant sap. The audience gasped, applauded, and laughed at the clowns who hurried in to carry the fellow away and skidded in his blood.

Peter Quince peered around the drapes and withdrew, shaking his head. This was not the occasion he'd dreamt of gracing for so many years.

'How goes it, Peter?' Tom Snout asked, looking as though he wanted to be lied to.

'If we forget our lines they won't notice, and if we do them right they'll find fault.'

'Then let's do as I said before,' Francis Flute suggested again, 'and explain we lack our complement and beg to be relieved of our duty.'

Peter considered this solemnly and some signs of his agitation became apparent. 'I'm sorry, Francis – lads – but I just don't know who to approach.'

'*Theseus*, Peter, the man himself, he has your ear!'

'If only Bully Bottom was here!' Robin Starveling sighed. 'Then we could at least go on with most of it in good repair. Snug, when all's said, hadn't an important part.'

'Even so, we should have gone back this afternoon and found him. You were wrong, Peter, to say he'd find his own way home. Snug's direction was ever a tortuous matter.'

'Aye,' Peter Quince sighed miserably, 'I'm much in error, lads, more than you suspect.' Some idea of saving the performance had kept him from sharing the weight of Snug's murder, but the man had been his friend from boyhood and shouldn't have been so easy to put aside. Snug was not rich, but he wasn't a worthless commodity either, he was a man and deserved a proper pause between acts.

'Ready yourselves,' called the toothless fire-eater who'd taken charge of the sequence of performances and was doing the job officiously, if ineptly. 'You're on next.'

'We . . . we're not all accounted for,' Peter protested humbly.

'No one'll notice, mate, just stand tight-packed and speak fast.

— 113 —

Have you anyone who can fall over? They're in a nice mood for antics, though I don't recommend another juggling.'

'We are actors,' Tom Snout declared, nose in the air.

'I'd try summat else if I were you. Come on, get up by the curtain here and put a smile on ready.'

'Don't rush us,' Peter Quince said with dignity and bad nerves. 'We are actors, not cattle!'

'There's brave! I'll get more for what I scrape off the floors than you lot would fetch at auction!'

'I repeat, we are actors – but – we shall not act!' Peter Quince made this announcement with a mad bright resolve that had the fire-eater sucking his lips down his throat, and put his friends in a turmoil.

'What shall we do, Peter? What else *can* we do?'

'I have my lines by heart, nearly. I'm close.'

'Peter, if we don't act we must surely die, for to fail in this duty is as much as to rebel, when men's distinguishing organs are soaked in so much wine!'

'Friends, I have some poor news for you . . .'

'Partners!' Nick Bottom boomed as he pushed past some drunks. 'I overslept all day. Have I missed it? How was it? Who took me?'

'We're about to go on this instant, Nick,' Francis Flute said. 'You're in the nick of time – I thought of that long ago, but only now married the inspiration to its opportunity. We lack Snug, but now the main thrust is in and I fancy we can kill 'em with our conviction after all.' He turned hopefully to Quince. 'We'll act now, shan't we, Peter?'

'I believe I have Snug's lines about me somewhere,' Nick put in helpfully. 'I'll double him easy enough – none will notice, I dare say, for I can throw my voice undetectably.'

'I lied to you all,' Peter Quince confessed in a low arid monotone. 'That's why we won't act. Snug was ever my best friend and in a second was speared by two spears at once in the ribs. I saw it happen and could do nothing. Snug is not late, friends, nor lost, but killed. At first I didn't know what to do.

—— 114 ——

It's come to me now. You keep safely here, or go to your homes. I propose to fashion a speech in defence of Snug, to replace our play. I'll say what manner of man he was, and how little he deserved a beheading in his prime of life, for they cut off his head with one stroke, and then I fainted.'

He was very frightened, and too certain of what he had to do to conceal his fear. Robin and Francis were shivering. Tom and Nick stared at each other with what looked like stony indifference until they both declared in unison that they would go out with Peter and stand by him.

'It needn't go too badly with us,' Tom Snout reckoned. 'Theseus is reputed honest and just, and the joiner did no wrong I know of, except in one piece of work he did for me, but then he came back and fixed it at no extra charge, so I support him as a blameless citizen.'

'I hope you're right,' Robin Starveling said, 'but if it's all the same to you I'll take Peter's first advice, for I have no guts.'

'Me neither.'

'Very well, Francis, and Robin. And be sure to lock your doors and say nothing, however it falls out with us. Good fortune to you both!'

'And you, Peter.'

All passed around closely shaking hands, then the two younger men left and the three older men braced themselves.

Easy to imagine the attention span of the Athenian gentry by the time Peter, Nick and Tom made their way past greasy athletes and over heaps of bullshit, the stench of smoke in their noses, eyes smarting: the gentry were full of fine food and afloat with wine. A tragedy, however brilliantly executed, was not what they wanted, and they took it for granted that Theseus had booked these uncouth players as butts for befuddled wit.

With Nick Bottom and Tom Snout one step behind him Peter Quince cleared his throat, glanced once with a severe frown at the less than ready audience, and then studied his feet in fear of losing his nerve. 'If we offend, it is with our good will,' he said, taking his opening from the prologue he'd written to the play.

— 115 —

'Speak up!' someone mocked, banging his sword on the table.

'Just say it as you would to anyone,' Nick whispered supportively. 'Take no notice of hecklers, Peter – Snug do notice nothing now!'

'Justice is the word,' Peter continued quietly. 'In Athens we are taught that every man may expect justice, that justice is what puts a shape to life. Our play was to have illustrated love, and a tragical error causing death, but I am here to protest humbly that Snug should not have died by the spear in the night. He leaves a wife and children with no provider and it is not justice to be cut off without apology . . .'

'This is the silliest stuff I ever heard,' Hippolyta told her husband. 'The man's bumbling beyond sense. His lines must be his own sad invention.'

'Let him be,' Theseus admonished her gently. 'He's the fellow we saw before, such a bag of nerves you wanted to shake him out and stamp on him. These ordinary chaps are intimidated by us, they mean no offence, as he said. Let him ramble a bit, I want to hear what there is of justice and error in his play. The brawny fellow on his left did us some service at Thebes, I believe. I'm curious to discover his part in this as well.'

'. . . if only you, Lord Governor Theseus, would say so, then all would be put to rights, widows and orphans gratified, and meaning replaced . . .'

'This is a new kind of play,' Lysander quipped to Hermia. 'You see, the ambitious fellow is trying to get Theseus to join him on stage!'

'To me he looks in real distress,' Hermia said. 'I don't believe this is a play at all – he means what he says. The man has suffered some injury and seeks redress. If his feelings were words I think we should cry. And Lysander, don't you recognise the man on his left? Isn't he the weaver who promised to help us? Is it possible?'

Demetrius threw the carcase of a suckling pig at Peter Quince, who had ceased his peroration and stood panting and dejected, awaiting some verdict.

— 116 —

'I second that,' Nick Bottom suddenly said, stepping bravely into the silence. 'Snug the joiner was a simple honest rogue like us, and hurt no one in his short life. It would have been an honour to perform our play for you tonight. I was to be Pyramus. My Thisby is in bed by now. Snug had little to say, but I crave your indulgence, kind sirs and ladies, for I will read out the lines we set aside for the sorry man and let you judge yourselves what it is to miss a friend, however slim his part may be.'

Hippolyta leaned forward and stared hard at the weaver. A pleasurable sensation coursed through her body, followed by a fearful wave. This was certainly the innocent, the very grateful, comfortable, gentle man with whom she had lain – did Theseus know? Had he even planned her encounter? He said the man had served at Thebes, so was all this a trap, this feasting for the marriage a teasing game to end abruptly in accusation?

'Cum quik,' Nick began haltingly, for the words were hard to decipher. He had not said more than a dozen before a shriek pierced the drowsy chamber.

'Treason! Arrest that man!'

Nick stopped, petrified. But it wasn't the frightened child who froze him with her wild command. Beside her, resplendent and ravishing, was his forest enchantress. Was she now his doom? If so, it was all so far above his comprehension that he could only accept it as his due.

Everyone else had stretched to look at Emily. She, her even tan turning coppery red, was on her feet, pointing her finger straight at Nick and not daring to think out what she was doing.

'What gives?' Hippolyta demanded urgently. 'Emily, are you drunk?'

'I have a premonition,' she cried, almost without faltering. 'This is a dangerous, subversive man. Don't let him escape. He will destroy Athens – I see death!'

'Extraordinary!' Theseus exclaimed. 'I had similar suspicions when we camped out before taking Thebes, yet I spoke not one syllable to this child. Is she gifted with foreknowledge, Hippolyta?'

'If she were we could have eluded you at Scythia.'

'You underestimate her. You are jealous, perhaps?'

'Protectively, not otherwise.'

'Theseus!' Demetrius hissed urgently along the table. 'I recognise him now – he was an intruder in our camp.'

'Well observed, my boy. I noted that the moment I saw him. You, fellow! Weaver! Step up, let us examine you closer. We know who you are. What do you mean here?'

'Only to complain, sir, of the manner in which my friend was murdered last night.'

'Which friend?'

'The joiner, sir, in the forest. For his honour . . .'

'The spy!' Demetrius cried triumphantly. 'The men told me of this earlier, my lord – a spy was in your forest last night.'

'We need no more, I think,' Theseus said sternly. 'I don't know what you hoped to accomplish by this brazen act, but you've been found out before your mischief could bear its rotten fruit. Guard! To the tower with him – I won't have an execution on my nuptials, but imprison him against my pleasure. As for the other two scoundrels . . . are you this man's accomplices? Do you plot against me too?'

'We know no plots, sir,' Tom Snout murmured, and Peter Quince agreed from an open but silent mouth. 'We are honest Athenians, sometime actors, and very sorry men.'

'Well, that may be so. I am inclined to be lenient. My guards will accompany you to your homes. You will pack up tonight and vacate our city. Thebes is to be rebuilt. You, carpenter, may find honest work there – I advise you to give up acting and give your life to wooden work. Demetrius, they will report to you periodically, and if they don't come up to the mark deal harshly with them.' He paused to gaze admiringly at Emily before nodding at the disappearing and uncomplaining figure of the bemused weaver. 'I almost liked that chap, you know. I had him down an innocent that I might even cultivate; I have too trusting a nature for my own good. We mustn't take people at face value, Hippolyta.'

—— 118 ——

'I never did.'

'Ah, well . . . a sobering end to our festive night, but let it be. Lovers, to bed, 'tis almost fairy time . . .'

'It certainly is, jerks!' Puck muttered angrily, having noted most of the proceedings from inside the suckling pig that Demetrius had aimed at Peter Quince. 'And if you think we fairies are going to tidy up this mess after what you've done to Nick Bottom, you're in for a big surprise, Buster!'

He flew out immediately to report back to Oberon. Ordinary mortal scrubbers came in later with pails and mops and set to work happily enough, seeing leftovers which would bloat their stomachs for days to come.

Theseus and Hippolyta, Demetrius and Helena, Lysander and Hermia went drowsily but hopefully to their marriage beds.

Peter Quince and Tom Snout went gloomily to exile in the ruins of Thebes.

Nick Bottom went to a dark cell to await execution.

Emily offered a grateful prayer to Diana for giving her the wit to stop the weaver before he destroyed her. Then she scribbled another even more desperate note, telling her sisters of the horrors that had already occurred and urging them to deliver her before she shared Hippolyta's unimaginable fate.

XVIII

IN GOOD TIME another day of great celebration came to Athens, with a fair and many bands making music all over the city, dancers with tambourines threading sinuous lines down every street; bells rang out all day, and trumpets sounded as if heralding the arrival of a mighty king.

The Queen had given birth. This news passed from mouth to mouth in tones of awe. It was a familiar story that she had been so mistreated in the past that she'd never endure a full pregnancy. So how wonderful Theseus was! He took a woman broken and barren inside and nurtured her so skilfully that a bare nine months after he brought her to Athens she bore fruit. She must have conceived immediately, under the full moon more than likely. It was a wonder, a miracle. A son was born, and they called him Hippolytus.

A less important joy occurred at about the same time: Hermia gave birth to twins. Lysander fretted to see his beloved wife suddenly ashen and weak, but she assured him it was natural to fade as the glory of birth passed into two such bonny sons.

Demetrius had brought Helena from Thebes to be with her ailing friend, and although he didn't say much he was riven with jealousy. So far Helena had failed abjectly to be late for a single period. He suspected her of having periods more often than other women just to taunt him. He'd even taken to sleeping with his

— 120 —

wife's maids, but they seemed just as incompetent, as if in conspiracy.

'I don't think he can,' Helena confided to Hermia in an effort to put colour in her cheeks. 'I give him full marks for trying, but he hasn't got it in him. The girls are sweet and don't mock. They say he labours half the night and they do their utmost to get a babe for me, only he's of a waterish consistency. Something lacking. I wouldn't care, for truly I love Demetrius whatever he lacks, but I'd dearly love to give him a son and see his face light up again. You're lucky, Hermia, such bounty so happily come by! You'll be up and about again soon, won't you? May I hold one of them?'

'Of course. Listen, they're beginning to cry again – don't they sound like little lambs fields away from us? Lysander says soon their cries will stop us sleeping, but I don't sleep now. I'd hear if they were twenty fields from me. Lift them to me, Helena, gently. See how I feed them together?'

'Do they hurt?'

'Is this pain? Oh, I can't describe the feeling of my milk nourishing Lysander's sons – I feel such power, such gentle, marvellous power passing over!'

'I wonder if I should deceive Demetrius – take another man secretly, then say the son is my husband's.'

'Are you sure this isn't his suggestion?'

'Oh, never! He sleeps with my girls but that's another matter. He couldn't love as his own a son he hadn't got. It would be a lovingly-intentioned deceit, Hermia. He'd never know, and he'd be so glad!'

'Is there anyone in mind? How are the men of Thebes? I thought all the best had died at Demetrius's hand.'

'It would have to be an absolute stranger, almost encountered by chance, yet not a wicked man. I fear it's quite impossible.'

'Absolutely – such polite obliging strangers are only to be met in certain dreams. They can't exist in fact, and would be bound to disappoint us if they did; I imagine they'd have vile faces and awful breath, or be pot-bellied and have the wit of an ass! Though

I must tell you this: Gloria, my maid, is close to the Queen's girls and brings me delicious rumours from them. They say Hippolyta encountered such a man. They say he is the child's real father, not Theseus at all.'

'That's juicy!'

'Aye, and deadly to know, so never whisper to a soul.'

'Does Hippolyta tell servants her intimate secrets?'

'Oh, no, her sister only, who squirms and hates to hear, while the girls overhear, as everywhere.'

'So Theseus dotes on a bastard! Our greatest man a cuckold!'

'He'll never know it. What's more, I think I met the man they only weave gossip around. He languishes in jail.'

'Ah,' Helena sighed in mock yearning, 'if only I could have met that potent man the same night as Hippolyta, then Demetrius too would be the proud father today!'

They talked pleasantly and aimlessly for some time, despite Hermia's tiredness. When she'd finished feeding the babies she looked as if most of her life had been sucked from her. Helena was not insensitive, but knew no better remedy than the distractions of gossip.

Gloria brought in a tasty blood pudding that cook had prepared especially for her mistress, and Hermia managed a few bites but gave Helena most. The maid waited until at last Helena asked what she wanted.

'Please, mistress,' she curtsied, 'it's all the jollity. My friend Molly whose father keeps the jail has called to take me out. He's given her the afternoon to buy ribbons and sweets.'

'Yes, Gloria, go and enjoy yourself. I'll entertain Hermia.'

The girl beamed her thanks and hurried away, giving Helena fresh occasion to lament the surliness of some of her own girls, at least since Demetrius had accused them of scheming barrenness, and of life in Thebes generally. Perotheus was not as benevolent as Theseus; even Demetrius didn't approve of all he did, and they longed to live in Athens once more. Demetrius was with Lysander this afternoon, trying to win favour with Theseus, though unconvinced that he had ever given offence.

—— 122 ——

'But Theseus is changed,' Hermia said. 'Lysander tells me so. He has taken to Lysander in recent months. Life is strange.'

Here she trailed into some private distance where Helena couldn't follow. Now that Hippolyta had given birth it was out of the question for Lysander to declare his paternity, yet now Theseus loved him. Hermia could not forget being pinned against a tree. But for providence her very own babes might have been Theseus's too.

'Is it his Amazon who's changed him? Does she do much, as Queen?'

'She organises archery and gives lessons in hand-to-hand combat – some of the single girls flock to her. But it seems to me it's her sister, the obnoxious Emily, who has the finer intelligence and could actually gain for us a stronger footing in Athenian affairs. Only she's too young to achieve anything yet, and too remote to gain a following – and too disgusted by Theseus to use, or even notice, the power she has over him. He pretends to listen as though she were an oracle, but nothing changes. Emily has made us observe more dreary goddesses, we have a few more feast-days. No, the change in Theseus is hard to define – he sees the strength in gentleness, he says. He used to mock Lysander for being too much lover, too little fighter; now he praises him for following his precepts and not merely aping his heroic feats of yore.'

'So Demetrius has no chance of winning favour?'

'I can't say. Theseus claims he promotes love and peace, and Hippolyta complains because he sits up pondering the way of the world and rarely remembers to visit her. The servants giggle and say Theseus is no longer a man but has gone sublime, an unsexed god, beneficent to his people but lax in his duties to his amorous wife.'

Hermia sank down into her pillow, smiling feebly. Helena patted her folded hands and looked lovingly into her friend's eyes, but Hermia's lids were too weighty for her to return the look. In a moment Hermia was asleep under the fond gaze. At last Helena sighed and leaned back to watch the healthy sleeping twins who had absorbed Hermia's vitality, and pale, chubby little pods they were, poorly armed for life's long struggle. She wasn't sure she envied her friend, however greatly she desired a child. Death seemed a heavy price. Hermia looked serene enough to pay it gladly, but Helena hadn't reached that state. Quietly she left the bedroom and wandered to the kitchen. There she sat and sobbed until Gloria returned unexpectedly.

'Oops! Sorry, ma'am, I didn't mean to intrude.'

'Keep me company, Gloria, if you will. How is it in the sun?'

'Very exciting, miss, but Molly bought what she wanted in a hurry and said she had to go back. Although she hasn't quite said so, I know she has a feeling for one of the poor imprisoned men in that tower. She used to watch him when he had a stall in the market, and never dared speak with him. Now she brings him his food every day. Isn't it odd, miss, that although we see the tower daily we spare no thoughts for the forgotten men whose lives go by there in darkness?'

'Are they many? Yes, I suppose they *are* living men, with hopes and fears.'

'Oh, miss, I can't bear to see Hermia so sickly. She's so brave about it, but when she loves her man so hard . . .'

'I know. We've been close since we were children. It isn't such a lengthy time, I suppose, for we're still young, yet I've loved her all my life. Does she know, d'you think, how near Death is? I feel him in the room. He makes me shiver.'

'Don't talk so! What shall we do? She's been the kindest friend to me! Surely she can't die who was so full in life until the babies came!'

'It's terrible to think.'

'Yet she says death is necessary and not to be feared. Her husband sits up all night beside her – he's taken advice on every remedy and had experts from wherever they may be found. I never heard of another man taking it so hard when his wife is badly.'

'Lysander is a good gentleman, all right, but so is *my* husband,

Gloria. He may be brusque, yet Demetrius is about as tender as a man with State responsibilities ought to be.'

'I'm sure you're right – and he's a fine figure of a man, too!'

'Has he ventured a proposal? Tell me honestly, child, and you shan't suffer.'

'I don't like to say nothing. I'm such an unimportant person, quite without ambition, and it should be an honour to be complimented by a fine gentleman like your husband.'

'Then he has, obviously. Did he give you the explanation?'

'In a manner of speaking, besides which I couldn't avoid overhearing your talk with my mistress. Indeed, it could be that I have a method of helping you, other than giving up my virtue, which I'm reluctant to go for.'

'Speak on, then. Don't be nervous of me.'

'Well, what you were saying about men you wouldn't meet twice – it happens there's a fund of such men willing to perform the service – noble men, too, of good homes, and you need never see their faces nor any part of them, nor they yours.'

'This is intriguing. Surely not in Athens? Noble men who sell their favours?'

'*Give*, miss, and gladly, grateful for any kind word or deed. I speak of the forgotten men, lonesome and thoughtful as months wear out the years, gently appreciative of any kindly act. You need not fear them, they aren't brutes. If anything they will fear you, despite their tender gratitude, for if you should be offended and voice a complaint, that would remind Theseus of their existence, and they would die.'

'What can they live for, then, if they must keep so quiet?'

'I dare say they have forgotten. Some may hope to be ransomed, perhaps, or that one day Theseus may declare an amnesty – it would have been a kindness on such a happy day as this, but no word came from him. Maybe some now dream of escaping.'

'They sound like very sorry specimens. I doubt they'd make a success of the operation I have in mind. Still, I should think it over carefully. On the other hand, if I think too long I'll be too nervous, and Demetrius may want us to return to Thebes any moment. Could you take me there now, Gloria?'

'I daren't leave my mistress, but I'll give you a note to give Molly. If her father answers just say you want her alone, and he'll not disturb you. He leaves the daily work to Molly, for he has a small garden at the side of the donjon and is fonder of vegetables than poor gentlemen.'

'Quickly, then. I'll sit with Hermia while you write.'

Not fifteen minutes later Helena was walking in the sun, heart in her mouth, fearful that all her intentions were scribbled plainly on her face. But everyone was in noisy, cheery celebration and no one marked a long-legged girl striding along alone on such a day. As long as she didn't bump into Demetrius she'd be all right; even if they did meet he wouldn't be suspicious – no wife of his could look twice at another man, the very idea was too preposterous to entertain.

Dead ahead, the great round tower arose in magnificent disregard of maiden blushes, and Helena took in its girth and stature and marvelled at the powers that could keep a thing so straight and long. She gulped, hesitated, and finally mastered her febrile nerves and walked on, smiling inwardly. There was something stimulating, she imagined wickedly, about being bonked inside so blatant and public an erection; almost being on view to the entire city, after all, yet possessing her desired end in the rich darkness of the senses. The risqué glamour of the adventure gave her a sweet little shudder in anticipation. She marched boldly up to the big door and knocked firmly. She knew she had become someone else, no longer commanding her normal senses or the surrounding situation, instead abandoned to dreams of liquescent desire.

Molly was pretty and wholesome, and some of Helena's dizzying lust left her immediately – more when she saw how clean and neat was the interior. Nothing was frivolous or tawdry; everything had a simple charm, like a wayside temple to one of

— 126 —

the gentler deities. With some trepidation Helena gave the letter to the girl, ready to say she was only acting on a silly dare, but Molly read it respectfully enough. 'I understand,' she said kindly. 'You wish to have a child for your husband and be its loving mother – there's no sin in this.'

'None?' Helena sounded a trifle disappointed, yet why the word of a common jailor's daughter should influence her was beyond reason – the cheek of the girl!

'A marriage without children has no future,' Molly said. 'My mother's gone, and Father's old, but I mean to survive and remember them. It's no sin to create futures, so long as we love them and teach them true.'

'Who instructs you, child? You don't sound like a jailor's girl.'

'Isn't life walled around like this tower? Don't we all serve out our sentences?'

'Then must all our futures be prisoners likewise. I don't like that, it's pretentious. I prefer "Life is a game".'

'But you are sincere in this cause?'

'Absolutely. Only don't let me conceive in a holy-seeming place, lest it seem like blaspheming. I prefer shadows, where lecherous imaginings, though they come to me unnaturally, might flower.'

'Then it's a good job I'm only a simple girl and don't understand fine ladies, or I should say you were no better than a lickerish whore craving strange satisfactions, and I should call on my father to cast you into the street.'

'Please don't, my dear. I long for a child, and it's for my husband's happiness that I've come to this. To countenance it at all I'm having to make myself another kind of woman.'

'I think I appreciate the dilemma, ma'am.'

'Today there is great celebration in the city, with Hippolyta's son being announced. I beg to be allowed in, so that these good eddies of legitimate joy may wash me towards my own fulfilment.'

Molly nodded slowly at this, then, not wholly convinced, she bade Helena wait.

Some little time later they ascended the stone steps. The way

— 127 —

grew more drab, the air cooler but lacking freshness. Helena drew back her hand from contact with the wet outer wall; it was not hot blood that throbbed in this gigantic chimney, but the chilly stuff of illnesses and racking coughs, despite glimpses of open blue sky above.

'The cells are tidy and dry, ma'am, don't lose heart. I do all in my power to make my men comfortable in their confinement.'

'Everything?'

'In the way of providing food and clean water with no flies in, and stories from the outside. I'm a good girl, ma'am, and wouldn't do as you imply.'

'Or as I mean to do?'

'You're a married woman with a sad cause. I am a virgin. Though there is a fine, sorrowful young man I'd be happy to court, if only he would notice me.'

'Is he arrogant, then?'

'Oh, not at all – he's a quiet, courteous man, but locked into a dream that will not set him free. He used to breeze into Athens as happy as a lark, always singing and joking while he sold his wares. And now he's at the heart of the city and sits in gloom.'

'I hope this isn't the man you're leading me towards!'

Molly smiled. 'You wouldn't want him, ma'am, for he's an ordinary fellow. The man for you is a knight from a royal house. He's young and handsome as can be, and we're outside his door. I'll return to my chores below. Fear nothing, no one will disturb you and I'll never talk of this to anyone. Now knock, and enter.'

Molly withdrew and Helena waited till her steps devolved into the rounds of seeping silence. Then she offered a brief prayer to Venus, opened the door and met enclosed and stuffy darkness.

'Sir?' she heard herself asking plaintively, much like an infant begging forbearance. Heart thumping, Helena pressed her chest to control herself and resume in a more fitting tone. 'Is a gentleman within? Sir?'

She heard a slithering movement, not of chains, thank God, but maybe cloth and straw dragged underfoot. A window-slit allowed in some vague grey matter that must have been light,

— 128 —

though it failed to give shape to anything. Helena repeated her question and the thumping of her heart nudged her words.

'I am a gentleman,' came an uneasy though obviously well-bred voice. 'Who seeks me?'

'A stranger who wishes to remain unknown.'

'Are you to be my benefactress?'

'I pursue my own ends, sir, but you may regard me so when you discover them.'

'Are you licensed to gain my release?'

'Not from this place, but consider if you have more reasonable fancies while you endure this long darkness, and I will relate my story.'

Speaking to a darkness so great she couldn't be sure her own body was still with her, Helena felt a quiet reasonableness in her explanation and request – felt that she herself was removed, delivered into a limbo where nothing would ever happen, where the tang and savour of life would never be apprehended again.

Her confessor, for so he seemed, didn't speak or make any sign that he had listened, and Helena lingered in her peculiar suspended state awhile, disembodied, merely a heart beating distantly and a mind that formed no images, pursued no thoughts, yet was present and aware of the absolute absence of the world.

If it were possible to conceive without intercourse, Helena thought at last, I'd believe the dear gods have given me a holy child, for this must surely be one of those moments mystics relate of revelation – yet nothing is revealed, and I desire for nothing to be revealed, only the serenity of this darkness. I understand why Hermia awaits death with a tranquil heart.

'You have shared a moment in my long silence,' the gentleman said in tones so velvety there was no shock to the mood, 'and I have filled my side of it with the cadences of your voice. From these I have constructed you in my mind's eye. You are beautiful. I'm honoured to participate in your dream, but please under-stand, lady, that a man in my position loses something of spontaneity – it's no insult to your person if I seem inadequately

— 129 —

prepared. It is the casual punishment carelessly added to a prisoner's dull sentence.'

'You speak delicately enough, but now I am hesitant. It would shame me if we failed here. But . . . no, I am steady. I do not doubt you. Come, take my scent and see if that awakens memories of sweet courtships in sunny meadows.'

'I have a clean pallet, do not fear. Take my hand, then, and trust me. Ah, the touch of a hand in my hand! The scent of your neck and body! May I touch your hair? Let me guess its colour, length and weight as it falls about your shapely head. Yes. Yes – now I remember!'

'A girl?'

'All girls. Human fondness. It's a torment to see nothing beyond the veiled images our words half-fabricate, yet I fancy it's delicious in some way.'

'Yes, and that we'll remain strangers. I am virgin again, untouched and aching everywhere to be touched, and no touch defiles or disappoints. Your breath on my arm creates my arm anew, your warm hand on my cheek creates my features, and here, I reach out and build a man and breathe life out of darkness!'

'Wondrous! Here is my pallet. Let us ease down, our fingers now like sable brushes that must blend all lovely colouring for the inward eye. Here, I brush a white with the faintest pink to blush in it. I brush here, and here . . .'

'Oh, brush on, gently, lover, brush me here then, and here!'

And the awkward words passed back and forth in ever lower tones until they became a murmur of pleasure given and taken, and the pleasure became eloquent beyond language, celebrating the magic of tenderness, the liquefaction of solitary suffering, the restoration of the deepest memory that joined all lives to the one life freed from petty form and congruent with the rivers and the stars.

He must be Demetrius, Helena thought at one reminiscent touch, he knows me so well he cannot be a stranger; yet Demetrius wouldn't prolong a touch so thoughtfully – good grief, then he is Lysander! Oh, good, honest and gentle Lysander! Ah, now,

— 130 —

this is heavier, heavier – this is no man at all, he is a god! Zeus, Jupiter! Great God alive, I am visited by divine powers – he is two men! Oh, yes, oh, a groaning breaks from me, yes, yes, and now again so soft, relenting, persisting, so patient soft – no, no man, no god, he knows feminine caresses, he must be Venus, Aphrodite, Persephone now – no, better, let him be . . . yes, little Peneis, flowing daughter of the river god, oh, I like it thus, Peneis, my Peneis, so cool and with that waiting torrent ready to . . . Ah, now, male again, mine again! I know you now, Poseidon, my god of all the mighty sea and his ceaseless waves, Poseidon . . .

And then he seemed the great bull created by Poseidon out of the sea itself, that came ashore, that thundered in the rolling surfy waves amid the foam and fleecy onrush, that immensely potent bull charging in again, again, again, then turning in the foam, slowly resuming tender form, slowly becoming the erupted forgotten man in the forgotten confined space of a dark sad cell.

Unspeaking they lay exhausted some time, chewing silky wisps of straw from the fresh pallet, eyes open unseeing.

'I have conceived,' Helena told her lover proudly at last.

'I am your slave,' he replied.

'No, sir, we shall not meet again, or we'd meet every afternoon and I'd be ruined, and my husband would slay you.'

'Then may I ask one favour?'

'Anything, only not to know my name, see my face, or meet again.'

'If ever it's possible, without compromising yourself, to mention me as too long incarcerated a knight, there is one who might sue for my release, if he still lives. You may not know him, for though his daughter was tutored here in Athens he was a nobleman of Thebes. I, my lady, am a knight of the royal house of Thebes. Do people still speak of my city?'

'Yes, and live there,' Helena admitted warily. 'But I cannot see how I may help without knowing your name, and we must preserve anonymity.'

— 131 —

'Yours, unquestionably. Why mine? Do you know if Perotheus lives?'

'He governs the rebuilt city of Thebes.'

'I did him some service.'

'Hush, sir, there are difficulties in this already, that you do not know of. I'm afraid – and yet I long to help you.'

'By no means, if you endanger your name.'

'Tell me your name, gentle knight.'

'Arcite.'

'Then never despair, Arcite. For much more than your name will I remember you devotedly, and however long it takes, Perotheus will hear of your suffering.'

Before leaving the tower Helena gave money to Molly, which the honest girl refused as earnings then accepted on behalf of her charges. It was enough, she said, to give all new blankets and spoons.

Helena hurried to see Hermia, wishing she could share her rich experience yet knowing she dare not disclose it to anyone. Once she had gained the bedroom and looked again at the sunken eyes and grey complexion of Hermia, then at the twins who had caused her decline, Helena reprimanded herself – she should have checked with Arcite in case multiple births figured in his family! If she carried twins she might soon be at death's door too, and although her afternoon had been beyond value she knew that if Death came to collect his reward she'd still want to haggle. 'Come, Hermia,' she pleaded tearfully, 'you mustn't languish so! Death can learn patience if you prove you have a more pressing engagement with life! Don't leave us – live for us, who cannot bear you to go!'

'Helena,' Hermia smiled exhaustedly, 'how sweet you are, yet how perturbed – you seem different now. Your words are more troubled than before, but you are less – why, you are radiant!'

'I am?'

'Radiant, sister! Something is happening!'

Helena was struck by her friend's perspicacity and thought she'd have to confess, but in a moment she checked that eager

—— 132 ——

impulse, for Hermia's gaze slipped from an examination of her radiance to wander wonderingly and without focus.

'All is radiant,' she breathed. 'So much light, sister, and *such* a light!'

'No, Hermia! Oh, please . . .'

But to protest was as useless as to call back the setting sun. Even the bleating of the twins could not break the seal of that radiant light.

Where is justice? Helena cried as she held the cooling hand and searched her lost friend's eyes for an answer. Youth, virtue and honourable love meet untimely death. Where is the measure, then? Punish the unblemished, let sinners live, and there is no sin, no virtue, no mean.

'How is she?' Lysander, just home, was asking Gloria in the kitchen.

'Perhaps a touch stronger,' Gloria replied hopefully.

Helena arose and turned and stepped towards the quiet voices.

XIX

HERE'S NO REMEDY for a loss like Lysander's, and no point dwelling on unending suffering. Some say a bereavement purifies the soul and improves the character. That's true enough to go by, if we avoid the crippling impoverishment of Lysander's sense of the mild well-meaningness of life, and ignore that private bitterness which sometimes made him glare at his beloved children as if they were hateful to his sight. As they learned to walk and talk these twins never lacked their father's love and, though they weren't spoilt, never had any reasonable request denied. They were bright and thoughtful lads who understood Lysander's occasional sombre moods and pitiable silences. They laughed when he laughed. They remembered their mother when he fell silent.

He took to visiting the hospital and the prison, always with a food parcel or a pile of clothes or a bucket of leeches. Those he visited were worse off than he, and what was left of his generous heart went out to them. When he heard of a leper colony on one of the small islands he arranged for regular parcels to be sent there too. His wish was to keep his good deeds secret, for he believed they were essentially selfish; he hoped to ease his pain, easing the pains of others. Naturally, though, word got around, and eventually word reached Theseus and impressed him. He saw an aspect of society previously overlooked and ripe for good government. Theseus created a new post, making Lysander his

— 134 —

Minister of Health and Public Charity, and allocating a sizeable budget from the city's funds to continue the good work. Consequently the people found themselves taxed to give succour to subversives, cripples and assorted deadbeats, and Lysander found himself hated. He didn't get much spiritual comfort from disposing of other men's money, either. It seemed to Lysander that life was an absurd business that could only be endured grimly. 'It can't be helped,' became his response to every complaint.

After Hermia's funeral Helena and Demetrius had returned to Thebes, Helena not yet certain that her remedy had worked. Their household was unexpectedly abuzz with excitement, but she was pooped and went to bed without learning its cause. It was given to Demetrius – appropriately, he thought – to hear the tidings first.

In brief, the pretty serving girls with whom he had so earnestly laboured had taken his insecurity to heart. They had applied economics to it and found that by bearing Demetrius a son – any son – they would be assured a good pension. This enticing fact was communicated to various stalwart but impecunious sweethearts, who set to labouring with them in Demetrius's manner for the benefit of all.

'Wake up!' Demetrius cried to his wife, who hadn't even had the strength to take off her riding boots. 'We're to be parents!'

'How can you know?' Helena asked in alarm, sitting bolt upright.

'They're convinced. And *two* of them, Helena! Two of the choicest girls – I forget their names, but selected them for their resemblance to you. One has long legs, the other is short-sighted. Isn't this a great homecoming gift?'

'I'm overwhelmed.' And crestfallen, but she couldn't say that.

Helena thought fast and decided to gamble on a whim; Demetrius was a sucker for a ploy that would make his wife sound like a silly eccentric girl.

'Take me now,' she said ardently, 'and then we can say it was this night that brought us our children. And who knows, perhaps

— 135 —

we shall make a third child, and that the best and most legitimate!'

'Well, it's not exactly necessary now. I mean I've proved . . . and I thought you were tired? Besides . . . Oh, all right, if it makes you happy, you silly thing! Only don't be despondent if you fail me again. I shan't mind.' He was feeling excessively forgiving and Helena lifted her skirts hopefully. 'It's you I love,' he added, charged with the sentimental sincerity of the moment, 'not your blasted reproductive machinery!'

And so, a few weeks later, a shy triumphant Helena could give her husband yet another boost to his vanity. Now he regarded himself as far too potent to sleep around. He didn't relish the likely outcome – dozens of bastard boys growing up in competition then plotting against their father (he expected to be in an enviable position by the time they'd be old enough to kill him for it). So Demetrius became a good husband, hardly a Lysander, but at least in his way faithful. And his wife loved him as she had always loved him.

She also recalled her promise to the romantically obscure young knight. There were other matters to attend to and a long time passed before she thought of a way of bringing his lovely name to the attention of Perotheus. The way was simple: an anonymous letter. Even so, it couldn't be placed until the right occasion arose, until, that is, a number of visitors from Athens, any one of whom might have penned the thing, had stopped by. In the mean time Arcite served his sentence and Demetrius became the proud father of three men's sons.

XX

RCITE SHARED HIS cell with Palamon. Two nobler, braver, more pious adherents to the ethics of knighthood could not be found under the sun. As it happened, Arcite was very like Demetrius, while Palamon resembled the young Lysander. On the day of Helena's visit, Palamon said he'd go downstairs to the cell of the third prisoner. However, while he and Arcite were making the top room ready by stuffing blankets into the window slits to preserve the lady's integrity, Arcite, noticing how very dark the place had become, pointed out that his friend had as much right as he to this windfall. Both were, to put it mildly, frustrated, and ever-anxious to help a lady out of her distress. The important thing was that she shouldn't know just how popular she was about to be. After she had come and gone they didn't make crude jokes as some men would. They discussed her relationship with her husband, and concluded that she was honourable. Putting themselves in her husband's place they thought they'd be grateful for her discretion and initiative; they'd not be vindictive if ever they found out. On the contrary, they'd commend the knights involved and try to gain their release.

That was how Palamon and Arcite saw the thing, and it was swell for a while to see it like that, and then it was just another pipe-dream and it didn't matter whether or not Helena had served her husband as a loyal wife should, and no one came to free them.

—— 137 ——

'I wish one of you gentlemen would talk to my other gentle-man,' Molly said almost every time she brought them a meal.

'He isn't a gentleman,' Arcite invariably replied. And that was the end of it.

Palamon had been down a couple of times, prior to Helena's visit, but he hadn't been stimulated and was in no hurry to repeat the dull experience.

'He hardly says a word,' he told Molly this time.

'He doesn't hardly eat or drink, either,' she said, hoping to awaken some desire to aid a fellow man. 'I fear he's pining.'

'Come, come, girl,' Arcite broke in impatiently, 'don't inter-fere with our discourse. Who do you think you are, to speak so familiarly?'

'I reckon I'm a girl you shouldn't offend, sir, seeing as how you depend on me for your daily rations.'

'What manners to throw that in our faces! Lack of breeding always shows, I say. Go on then, starve us if it makes you feel better! See where that gets you, my girl!'

'It wouldn't get me nowhere, but it wouldn't matter to no one else if I did, neither. You should be grateful I take pity on you. I thought you knights were nice gentlemen.'

'I apologise,' Palamon said. 'You're very thoughtful. I'll talk to the fellow later, if it pleases you. Only you mustn't refer to him as a gentleman, d'you see – distinctions are terribly important to us, especially here.'

'Distinctions are the counters of meaning; unless you discrimi-nate you cannot evaluate. If you cannot evaluate, all experience reduces to the petty porridge of accumulated chance, without design, purpose, or any hope of destination.'

'So you distinction yourselves above human kindness, and distinction me to know my place, and still expect the distinction of being looked after, not by providence above you but by me below you! Where I come from that's called chancing your arm.'

'Your obvious feeling for this dismal mechanical downstairs is making you rebellious, child. Calm yourself. You can't hope to

— 138 —

understand the finer points of our code, which was formulated for devout sophisticates. That is the nature of a distinction: we know what we know, and you must accept it, because you cannot help but be ignorant.'

'I think I'd indeed be ignorant to accept what you know, sir.'

'Hah! The sharp tongue of the insolent is their defence against knowledge! What a rusty thing! You are rusty, madam, you squeak! Palamon has assured you he will visit your feeble charmer in due course. You should prostrate yourself, but I'd rather you just let us eat in peace.'

'I'll go, and good riddance!' Molly said furiously, and slammed their cell door. She could also have locked it, but it wasn't in her nature to hurt anyone unnecessarily. She couldn't do it. Escape was impossible anyway, because the lower doors were double-locked. So the prisoners had the run of the stairs and the opportunity to gaze through other window-slits at different prospects of the bright city.

'Within her limits a sensitive creature,' Palamon reflected as he mopped his gravy with a heel of rye bread. 'I listened as you did your valiant best to introduce her to some basic concepts, and I couldn't help noting sparks of intelligence in her responses. There was a kind of acuteness in the feeling I found some sympathy with.'

'My dear chap,' Arcite countered urbanely, 'take care! Would you compare a chit of a thing like that to the civilised specimen who honoured us before?'

'Obviously not. In the one, rawness of emotion has been governed and well seasoned with right reason; in the other, lack of proportion makes her a prey to every disorder of the flesh, every disease of the underused mind. I saw something touching there, but I won't promote exogamy!'

There followed a prolonged discussion of womanly virtue and what a loss to the world of women their imprisonment incurred. Conversation travelled late into the evening and Palamon felt a twinge of dishonour when he recalled his promise. Arcite insisted

— 139 —

that a promise to Molly was inconsequential, but he continued to feel a bit mean, and suffered a fitful night. He was young, and should have been courting the girl of his dreams by now, and he only had Arcite for company. So Palamon was wide-awake well before dawn, pacing sadly. As the wan light began to filter through the depressingly familiar room he sighed loudly, shook his head, and left to call upon the other inmate, the once-cheerful weaver.

'Good morrow, sir,' Nick said when Palamon walked in without knocking or asking if he wanted company so early.

'Life is a mean trick to spite us for we know not what,' Palamon grumbled, more or less ignoring Nick and finding more interest in the stones beneath his feet and the stones in the walls. He paced about, inspecting them cynically. 'How many?' he asked at last.

'I'm sorry?'

'How many flags to your floorspace, man? Can't you count, either?'

'I can count, sir, but haven't.'

'By my reckoning you have a dozen more than us. Why should you possess a grander chamber than two Theban knights, d'you suppose? No doubt it's Theseus's doing – you may be nobody, but you're an Athenian nobody, isn't that the run of it?'

Nick Bottom shrugged unhappily and waited for the intruder to go away again.

'Listen, fellow,' Palamon said after the tedious silence had given Nick the pleasant impression of drifting miles from human contact, 'you don't eat enough to keep a sparrow alive. You're pining for something, and if you don't stiffen your resolve you'll die. Unless there's an honourable reason, that's no good. D'you think Arcite and I aren't miserable and resentful? Of course we are! We'd rather be dead than stuck in here. We'd rather have died in battle – would have, too, if some nosy little shit hadn't poked about and found us breathing! But the point is, we don't give up like sissies! We keep ourselves fit, in readiness. Always be ready, hear me? This durance may end tomorrow. Everything

— 140 —

changes; you probably haven't studied the way of it, but this is a great truth. Everything changes. If it didn't our long perdition would indeed be beyond enduring, and even I should contemplate death with some fervour, for then there'd be no purpose to anything. Are you with me so far?'

'I'm in with you, sir. This is my room.'

'Never mind that. Grasp this: there has to be a principle for everything, and a principle is joined to a purpose. Now our purpose certainly isn't here now; therefore it's outside somewhere, in the future. There's your proof that everything changes, for otherwise the purpose wouldn't be discovered and there might as well not be a principle. You must attach yourself to this by faith, if you're anything near a man. Be fit, always ready – I don't say you'll ever understand the purpose, but at least then it will work itself out through you. I believe we all play a part, you see, however humble. Yours may well be to serve ours in some way.'

'I am abandoned, sir, and have no hope.'

'Is there no hope in that girl who loves you – Molly?'

'No one must love me. I am a wicked man.'

Palamon looked straight at this pathetic prisoner. He felt distinctions threatening to melt away, a sympathetic irritation swelling up in their place. 'I don't know what it is you've done.'

'It's too terrible to tell – I don't even know myself, but I've lost the company of my friends, so I must be terrible.'

'*I* can tell you are not a wicked man. At worst you've made a mistake. More likely you've been mistaken for someone bigger. Now I want you to do something. I want you to promise you won't give in so abjectly, that you'll eat what Molly gives, think less on past misfortunes and lost happiness, and direct your dreams to a better future.'

'That's a lot to ask.'

'You have time. Promise?'

'If it makes you happy, sir. All right, I promise.'

'Right. Now, a promise to a knight is a solemn promise and

— 141 —

means more than life. You have an obligation now, and that's more than you had five minutes ago.'

'Much obliged.'

'You may call me Palamon, while we live here.'

'Nick.'

'There's nothing wrong with that, either. Well, Nick, you'd like some occupation, I dare say? Molly once told me you were a weaver. Does that mean you undertake repairs?'

'If I had a needle I could stitch a rent or patch a patch.'

'Then we'll help each other. My friend and I have plenty of small work for you to rehearse your skills on.'

For the first time in an age Nick smiled – this was the arrangement he'd had with his fairy friends, who wanted no payment but employment. And Palamon's depression had lifted too. With a lighter step he circled the room. Wandered to the window. Glanced out, down into a pretty garden not visible from his own window. He looked. He stared. In the twinkling of an eye his life changed.

At that moment the rising sun broke over the garden wall and bathed the eager ranks of flowers in warm enhancing rays. The green grass glowed, the green stalks quivered towards this access of loving life, and all the flowers, white and pink, mauve, yellow, and bed upon bed of luscious red, were shot through at once in translucent delight, releasing their scents to attract the sleepy bees; and from the bushes slumbrous birds stirred and popped out to dance along the springy grass and greet the basking grub and wriggling worm. It was May, mild the air and fragrant with the promise of full blue skies and puffed white clouds like destinations for the exuberant traveller, whose lungs would fill with hope for the day. But Palamon didn't need to pin his dreams to the scintillating sky. There below in the garden walked his vision, his love at first sight, his perfect eternal beauty.

There, in short, walked Emily, sun-smitten hair in a braid a yard long, white dress peppered with tiny flowers, and flowers in her arms, for she was gathering the prettiest to fashion a garland for her head. To Palamon she was fresher than the very

— 142 —

season she was out to celebrate. Little wispy fragments of her gentle song came to him on mild currents of air like breezes from an angel's wings. Palamon was transfixed by melodious light. She passed from sight directly under the tower and he waited, breath held, heart pounding like an undisciplined child. What he couldn't see was the narrow gate in the garden wall.

The gate opened. On its far side waited a poorly disguised girl wearing a soft black leather jacket that had once belonged to Hermia, and a short white dress from the same source. The disguise consisted of a red shawl drawn over her hair. This was Gloria, who had not only benefited from Lysander's kindness but had also observed his acts of charity and determined to do likewise. Lysander's messengers and bearers were never searched and often embarked for the islands. Emily had befriended Gloria, and Gloria had agreed to this secretive postal service. In the shade of the great tower Emily passed over a new letter, perfumed with the flowers that had concealed it, and implored Gloria to see that it got safely to Scythia. The contents were as before, if better composed. The gate closed. Emily danced prettily back into the sunlight.

Palamon saw her emerge from under his nose and as she was going away his appreciation of her unattainable beauty felt even keener than before. He fell against the wall and beat it with his fists, and a cry of deep longing broke from his lips.

So piercing was his cry that Arcite awoke with a start and came racing to his aid. 'Cousin, what ails you?' he asked, glaring about wildly. 'Why are you so pale? What's getting you down? This place? Fortitude, my friend! We have no other choice.'

'No, you're way off course, Arcite,' Palamon answered grimly. 'I can take adversity and tear its balls off! No, this torture is exquisite – I've been stabbed through the eye, direct to my heart! Look out this window for me – I daren't, in case she's there, or lest she's gone. God, I don't know if it was a lady or a goddess! Must have been Venus, there in the garden as dew dried on the flowers – Venus!'

— 143 —

As Palamon fell on his knees and prayed, Arcite, with awakened curiosity, stepped past him. And at once he saw young Emily as well, and she struck his heart just the same. He too cried out and went weak. Yet when he spoke there was a firmer resolve, 'Such fresh beauty just wipes me out! Unless I can get to her I'm no better than a corpse – that girl has got to be mine!'

'Come off it! I'm not in the mood for jokes. I absolutely adore her. Don't mock my feelings!'

'Who's mocking! I tell you, I'm as devastated as you.'

Nick Bottom would have liked a look as well, but he didn't dare while these noble knights were getting so steamed up.

'This does you no credit,' Palamon said slowly, struggling to be reasonable when he wanted to kick Arcite's teeth out. 'We're cousins, sworn to assist each other, especially in love. Our solemn oath is binding until death. If you claim to love my lady you betray everything we stand for. I saw her first; it's your clear duty to help me, not break out in competition!'

'I was about to remind *you* of that! Your affection is for a spirit – Venus is who you saw. Go ahead, worship her! But I love a living creature, a pretty girl. You pray to your divinity, only make way for me to have that young girl's heart!'

'What specious garbage you talk – I've noticed before, but tactfully refrained from telling you what a jerk you can be. Now I'm warning you – lay off my girl, bub!'

'Hah!' Arcite exclaimed, but he knew he was on shaky ethical ground and decided to advance an alternative argument, more objective. 'You know what they say – you can't hang law on a lover! It's true – love's a greater law than any man can deal with. For love laws get broken every day by men of every rank. Isn't it true, fellow?'

'I want no part of this,' Nick said, 'for I follow my own inclinations in most matters and still get found guilty. I don't know what the law is, though if it's sensible I'm for it. I don't know what love is, for my one vision was a trick that was held against me. I only follow my nose, but it never brought me here.'

'What's he babbling for? Shut up, peasant! Keep out of this.

— 144 —

Listen, Palamon, let's face it – you're never going to stand in her grace and neither am I. We're damned here in perpetuity, like figures in some damned philosopher's anecdote. When you get right down to it, what's the good of our code? It's every man for himself – the code doesn't matter a shit. Look at our glorious leaders – what chivalry has there ever been between them? Dog eat dog. Go on, love if you want. *I* do, and always will, regardless of you. If ever I get a good break I'll take it without a thought of you, and I'd expect you to do likewise. We've both been suckers. Bugger off, plughead!'

They were no longer friends. Blood brothers they had been, sworn enemies they were from this day on. Nick Bottom thought it was simply further evidence of the madness of the civilised world. Although they hated each other they couldn't keep apart. Later the same day they returned to Nick's cell.

'I wonder,' Palamon said, 'if we could persuade you to vacate this chamber and move to ours?'

'Piss off, creep.' Arcite put it more bluntly before Palamon had finished. 'Gather your gubbins in a handkerchief and get lost. We need that window.'

'There's a decent view on our side too,' Palamon added.

Nick didn't think there was much to choose between either approach. He didn't say a word – knew he couldn't put up a fight against two trained killers – but meekly gathered his meagre rations and left them to their daily glimpses of heaven and their deepening hatred.

Molly was angry for him. She refused to feed them for a week. They didn't notice. Then she put too much salt in their potato. They didn't notice that either. She stopped doing her hair and wearing pretty dresses. They didn't care. After that she returned to her usual routines. She might as well have gone off in a cloud of pink smoke. Palamon and Arcite were obsessed. The sight of Emily was their food and drink, but the more they gazed the hungrier they grew. And thinner, sadder, more pathetic, until they were just a couple of stick insects rubbing each other up the wrong way.

Molly spent far more time with Nick now, pitying him, giving

— 145 —

him extra portions of apple pie, gradually coaxing him to talk about his past. He remained reluctant and only let out snippets in an embarrassed, halting manner which made it hard for her to reconstruct a coherent picture. Then, one day, he ventured so far as to ask Molly if she believed old stories about fairies. Her reply seemed to make him conscious of her for the first time. She said that when she was a child she would wander in the meadows and there see them at play near the river. She would watch them until the sun died, but was afraid of frightening them and never attempted to communicate. After that Nick was able to tell her about Oberon and Titania and his life in the forest, and Molly believed him and kept his secret. She knew as well as he that Theseus had declared fairies to be fanciful inventions without foundation or necessity.

Molly talked to her father, though not about fairies. Her father talked to Nick. The upshot was that the weaver, who knew about planting vegetables and fruit, was allowed to help in the old jailor's garden. No word of honour was given; the old man knew at once that Nick would be incapable of betraying his trust. Later, when he knew Nick better, he actively encouraged him to run off, assuring him no one need ever find out, but Nick said Theseus wouldn't have imposed his punishment unless he deserved it. He was also hurt that Oberon and the others had abandoned him, and that even Dewdrop had dropped out of his life. They were free, not he. Aside from which, Peter and Tom were banished. His old life was not waiting to welcome him. His initiation into manhood had been decisive, and he had cause to be unhappy.

Still, the jailor was a good friend who knew all about potatoes, aubergines and other edible exotica – stories to keep anyone entertained for twenty years. And Molly, though lacking the mercurial temperament of Hippolyta, and though probably no match for a young man born of Ariadne, was easy to grow very fond of. Indeed, Nick came to realise that his sudden access to elevated family vanities had done him no good. In an obscure way he almost knew that his troubles were rooted there.

Steadily, then, in the care of these humble and sufficient new friends, Nick adjusted, not resuming the naively optimistic nature he'd once had, but assessing his experiences and discovering that he could after all live with himself without being ashamed. Even better than that, he could live with Molly.

Sometimes, when he stood leaning on his spade in the tolling evening, gazing into the golden afterglow beyond the city walls to where the summons of the bells was unheard, he would think of his old cottage and his industrious hordes of friends, remember parts of conversations shared long ago with Oberon, and then he would grieve after the lost harmony of innocence amid natural images.

Molly would stand behind him in the shade of the tower and garden wall, watching him lovingly and knowing that the simple happiness she dreamt of would not come to pass, because on another such tranquil evening her lover must surely follow that softening golden light back into his own old solitary world.

Then he would turn and shoulder his spade and return to her in the cloaking dusk, and smile that faraway smile that made her yearning heart bleed with love's pain.

XXI

In due course Theseus visited Thebes, and his retinue numbered a hundred. So at last Helena addressed an anonymous letter to Perotheus.

Demetrius, beaming from ear to ear with excessive blind pride, brought out his three toddlers to be admired. One had black hair and brown eyes, one white hair and blue eyes, one red hair and hazel eyes; one was round as a berry, one thin as a sapling, one neither thin nor fat. All three were the same age and the third, named Arctos, the Bear, was his mother's particular favourite. Demetrius regarded all three as glowing proof of his vigour and range, and Theseus hadn't the heart to look askance. If it came to that, he allowed, even his own son Hippolytus, bore him little physical resemblance, yet the lad was such a fine blend of sturdiness and sensitivity that no one could possibly doubt *his* paternity.

On the seventh day Perotheus spoke privately to Theseus on behalf of Arcite, and Theseus agreed to free him immediately. Really he was taking advantage of the excuse to get home, for Perotheus ran Thebes like a barracks.

As soon as he was back in his own palace he sent for Arcite. 'Perotheus has spoken for you,' he said, 'and when a friend like Perotheus speaks, I listen. You're pardoned for your part in the defence of Thebes. Go home. But never re-enter Athens, on pain of death.'

At first Arcite couldn't believe his good fortune. Free again! Free to wander at will in the fields, free on the hills and under the sky, free to return to Thebes! Then a thunderbolt hit him; not free at all, but cast into exile! If it was purgatory before, now hell framed his vision. Bliss was in prison – Palamon was the victor. Day by day he had sight of Emily and paradise, and because fortune was changeable he might attain his desire in time. No such possibility existed for Arcite. He was severed from Athens and hope.

How unwise we passionate men are! he railed against himself. Not knowing the good we've got we engineer our own deeper despair. We go through life like some bum on a Saturday night, who knows he has a home but can't figure out how to reach it – and by God the way is slippery! Each time we distrust providence and try to make our own way we just stray further from happiness!

He carried on like that all the way to Thebes, lamenting that each step took him further from his goal, and made Palamon's way easier.

Perotheus feasted him and honoured him for his part in the great defeat of Thebes, and ensured that several eligible ladies were at hand, but Arcite couldn't build up much of an appetite.

'Theseus and me,' Perotheus said when Arcite confessed his problem, 'are men of a different stamp. We're takers because we're strong enough to take. No need for foppish melancholy, however fashionable you think it is. A girl's a girl – no need to make more of it. Put out the light and one's as good as the next. You kids today! No balls for the direct approach – no wonder our daughters grow insolent!'

Before long he was introduced to Demetrius, who soon invited him home to dinner. Helena was terrified and feared her voice would give her away. At one level she'd have loved him to identify her; at another she couldn't bear to contemplate Demetrius the cuckold. As long as he knew nothing her husband was really rather magnificent, confident, cocksure and commanding – just

— 149 —

the man she wanted. And he doted on little Arctos. A hint from Arcite would destroy the world.

He recognised her at once, but after a momentary embarrassment was able to control himself easily. She was pretty, but nowhere near as pretty as the dim prison had implied. Recollecting that exciting interlude was pleasant, but it had no connection with the lady at table opposite. She was no more than the charming wife of a new friend. The passionate creature he'd shared with Palamon had only existed in their imaginations, must have needed those precise conditions to come into that brief being. No erotic charge electrified this respectable dining room. Helena had no cause to worry.

True, when nurse brought in the three children to kiss their parents, when little Arctos noticed the lonely stranger and ran into his arms, Arcite's eyes filled with tears, but that aroused no suspicion. If he hadn't been in prison he might have been a father himself by now, Demetrius thought sympathetically. Arcite hugged his child, then set it down and watched it toddle along to clasp Demetrius's knees.

'I know who should bear my children,' Arcite said thickly, unaware of Helena's gasp. 'I love her hopelessly. Now my rival will have her and I can do nothing!'

'Tell us,' Demetrius said, unaware of Helena's head-shaking. 'We have some weight in Athens; perhaps we can help.' And as soon as Arcite described his love, unaware of Helena collapsing from relief and jealousy, Demetrius interrupted. 'Why, that's Emily, Hippolyta's kid sister!'

'You know her? May I hope, then?'

'She's . . . well, she's . . .' But Demetrius didn't know how to account for what he found so forbidding in the virtuous girl. 'She *is* jolly pretty. We said so, didn't we, darling, when she was here the other day?'

'Pretty, perhaps,' Helena said haughtily. 'I don't believe either of us could have said she was jolly.' Her son left Demetrius and came into her arms. She kissed his head, patted his bottom and sent him to his brothers, smiling fondly. 'Frankly,' she added,

— 150 —

daring to look directly at her lover, 'I don't believe she'd make you happy. She's terribly . . . sublimated: is that the word?'

'No matter the word,' Demetrius said. 'The deed is all that counts. Love's a chaos that makes mismatches every day. Let Arcite love whom he wants. Forces greater than us will determine the thing. What looks impossible one day may be achieved the next – my children are living proof of that! I hope Emily will be yours one day, and then you may know as I do the pleasures a good wife can give.'

And that was that. The unsatisfying hints increased the mystery of Arcite's passion and doubled his desire till he couldn't eat or sleep. Palamon was experiencing the same difficulties:

'Oh, Arcite!' he wailed in his cell, 'I bet you don't give a shit about me now, do you? I bet you're strutting about Thebes as if you own the place! You're free to gather our friends and come and wage war on Athens, and you'll be able to get my love and wed her, you rotten sod! You've got all the advantages, while I have nothing but the pain of being stuck in here, compounded by the pain of adoring a girl who doesn't even know I exist!'

He hit his head against the cold wall until blood ran in his mouth, then turned on the gods for taking so little care, cursed them, cursed the wretchedness of existence, the needless malice of life from beginning to end.

It's hard to say which of them had the worst of it. Palamon could see his beloved every day, but she had no idea and he had no hope of release. Arcite could walk or ride anywhere he wanted, except to the one place that held meaning.

And Emily, whenever the coast was clear, wrote another distressed letter and waited indignantly for the women to come and save her from her luxurious but loathsome imprisonment.

Arcite was robust and his decline was so slow that at first no one saw how love-sickness was eating away at him. But it was inexorable. He took to avoiding company almost as he avoided sustenance, and grew so bowed down and hollow-eyed that he looked like a stranger to himself.

— 151 —

One night, in a dream, winged Mercury visited and commanded him back to Athens. He decided to go, reconciling himself to the prospect of death with the hope that he might get one last glimpse of Emily before Theseus swiped off his head. Then, by chance, he saw himself in a mirror and hit upon a plan. No one in Athens would know him now. He disguised himself as a poor labourer, left instructions for friends to send money periodically, and taking only a squire who knew his right identity set forth on his desperate quest.

Barely a month had passed since the Great Eleusinia, when initiates of the secret cult – most men of substance, including Theseus – had proceeded along the Secret Road and undertaken rituals of purification which freed them from their clotted sins and put them close to deities who could guarantee immortality. These men were easily spotted: they walked about gracefully, holding themselves erect and wearing an expression of almost asinine beatification. As long as that state lasted they were unlikely to scrutinise or challenge anybody. So it was a propitious time for Arcite to reach Athens. Cleverly calling himself Philostrate, because his real name was a bit of a give-away, Arcite slipped into the city and found work rolling out the casks of ale at the Bull.

He was on hand to observe one of the six main festivals in the Athenian calendar, the Thesmophoria, and thus it was that he caught his next glimpse of Emily.

The Thesmophoria was a sort of Ladies' Day, whose chief event appeared to consist in the sacrifice of pigs. A number of squealing porkers were rutting about the square all afternoon. Then the ritualised but gruesome slaughter began. Hippolyta and Emily sat on thrones at the top of the steps and the stubborn pigs were dragged in below them, some magic words were spoken, the knife blessed, the neck widely opened, and then blood overflowed the buckets and poured down the steps and everywhere, till women were splashing about chanting 'Pig! Pig!' over and over.

—— 152 ——

Emily didn't chant, not that Arcite could hear, but she did look transported with uncharacteristic lust, as if she regarded every pink barrel of a pig as a beastly man. Arcite adored her.

As for Athens, he found it a topsy-turvy world much as Demetrius had glumly predicted, with the women blood-happy and fighting fit, and the best of the men floating about like vestal virgins. Nevertheless, disguised as Philostrate the honest if ignominious labourer, Arcite whistled through his work, and because he remained a well-built knight despite weak appearances his strength and willingness soon earned him promotion. He worked his way up assiduously until he became a page in Emily's household. Breeding showed. Soon he came to the attention of Theseus who, gratified that one of humble origins could show such gentility, made Philostrate an example; made him, in short, his personal squire. For all this he was no closer to winning Emily's hand, for even the democratic softy Theseus wouldn't give his sister-in-law to a mere enhanced working fellow.

The years were drifting along as innocuously as clouds. Palamon had now endured his martyrdom seven years, and he'd come to the end of patience. Lysander had been visiting him for some time and the two men had become friends. It was Lysander who finally agreed to help, providing food and drink, a long rope, and directions to the great forest where he had once fled with his poor beloved Hermia. Palamon's plan was to get back to Thebes, raise an army, return and either die nobly or win the elusive hand of Emily.

It was May again, the night he fled and holed up near the edge of the forest, and he had no idea that Arcite was in the habit of riding out in the early morning to celebrate the season and pray for better luck to conquer Emily.

The busy lark was high on salutations to a grey dawn, the sun just breaking over the far seas, when Arcite on a fiery charger galloped across the damp fields, reaching the forest before the warming air had dried the silver drops that hung from every leaf. He dismounted and started collecting leaves for a garland, singing the praises of May as he wandered from tree to tree. He stopped

— 153 —

before one particularly dense thicket and fell suddenly into deep gloom. It's like that for young lovers, just as it is for people trying to hurry along the sale of an old house, the purchase of a new – up one minute, down the next. Up, down, day after day, week after week, in debilitating helplessness, fulfilment endlessly and gratuitously deferred – how much disappointment can a man endure?

Arcite lamented the entire history of Thebes and the lines of descent that had led to his birth and abject condition. But basically he blamed Emily for the entire mess. He knew that if she'd only weaken for him his history would come bright again and he'd be the saviour of his race.

Hiding on the other side of the thicket Palamon heard every infuriating word. This was handy, since Arcite was nothing if not thorough, and soon Palamon knew about the pseudonym and the deceit that had enabled his cell-mate to wangle a job with Theseus. All thoughts of completing his escape left Palamon. He sprang out and accused his treacherous friend of leaving him to rot, breaking his word to Theseus, seeking Emily's favour, and being an absolute shit. 'Choose your weapon,' he concluded. 'I don't care how it goes, but you're not getting out of this forest alive!'

'That suits me, you little prick. You've been a thorn in my bollocks as long as I can remember, but I won't finish you off right now. You look like a bum, but I'll give you the benefit of the doubt and treat you like the knight you once were. Stay right here. I'll go back and return before dawn tomorrow fully armed, with enough gear for you. We'll settle this honourably or not at all!'

'Fine, just make sure you do come back – you've a habit of leaving!'

'I'll be here again tonight, with blankets for you. I wouldn't want anyone to say you lost because you took a chill.'

It didn't occur to either of them that even if she knew of their ordeal and their stylish battle Emily might simply not be interested. She was the chosen lady, whose role in all this was clear. Anyone of their class would have found their assumptions perfectly rational.

When Theseus called for his squire that evening he was informed that Philostrate had been seen riding out with a sleeping bag and a sack of food. He nodded, as if that was in order, and went to his study. He waited, noted the time of his squire's return, and then slept lightly.

Now Dewdrop still lived in the forest, yet although he was capable of foraging the sad fact is that since Nick's absence he'd gone into decline. He missed his only friend badly. His coat had never shone but at least it used to be soft and attractive. Now it was unkempt, stuck with burs, and in patches the hair had dropped out altogether, revealing sores and a sorry black hide. His bones were practically visible through his stiff sides and he looked twice his age, like a worn-out working donkey from a treadmill.

As soon as word came that a man was in the forest, near where Nick had lived, Dewdrop made his slow way to that spot, hoping he might hear news of his master. He arrived shortly after Arcite and waited prudently behind the very bush where Palamon had been concealed the previous day. What he saw was strange.

Like brothers these two fine young knights assisted each other in buckling on their armour, but neither uttered a single word and as soon as both were fully protected and armed they commenced battle. Their ferocity exceeded anything Dewdrop had witnessed at Thebes. Lions and tigers didn't use claws and teeth as unremittingly as these two laid into each other with their great swords. Dewdrop was frightened, yet he knew there'd be no further chance to learn of Nick's whereabouts, and since he also knew by their smell that these were the men Nick had saved from the battlefield he assumed they would know something and be pleased to tell.

So, although they were up to their ankles in blood he coughed politely and spoke up. 'Excuse me for butting in, but have either of you gentlemen lately seen our old friend . . .'

He got no further. At the sound of a cultured voice, Palamon

— 155 —

and Arcite ceased hacking, thinking they'd been caught out in what was, after all, an unsanctioned battle – an offence punishable by death. They peered anxiously into the bush and, as no one came out to clap them in irons, quickly realised that their best bet was to kill the intruder. Still without a word they plunged ahead, flailing indiscriminately. One swipe opened Dewdrop's flank before he could kick out. Another lopped a chunk from his hindquarters. Then he was away, weaving and sliding between the trees, easily outrunning his heavily armoured assailants, who stopped perplexed when they couldn't find the rider anywhere.

Miffed, but with the main account unsettled, they resumed first positions, took deep breaths and raised their weighty swords. They hadn't been going more than a few minutes, however, when a much more terrible party discovered them.

Theseus had observed the curious departure of Philostrate, laden with armour. As it was May he had reason enough to satisfy his curiosity without drawing attention to it. Not alone, then, but in a jocund company of knights and ladies, Theseus rode out not long after Philostrate, hounds racing ahead, hawks soaring above. At worst he expected to find his squire with a friend engaged in illicit hunting. What he saw astounded him: two knights attacking each other as furiously as wild boars, each stroke of their bright bloodied swords enough to fell an oak. At once he spurred his massive horse and was in between them, his club raised mightily.

'Hold!' he cried with dreadful authority. 'Or you'll feel your skull bite into your brains! He that strikes next is dead, by mighty Mars! What kind of men are you, that dare this fight with no officer standing by? Who sanctions this outrage?'

'No one, sir,' Palamon answered. 'We both deserve death. We seek no mercy. This is Arcite, your enemy, latterly your squire.'

'What!' Theseus roared. 'What treachery is here? Wheedled into my good grace and thought to poison me, eh?'

'No, sir!' said Arcite. 'This is Palamon, who escaped prison for the very reason that I returned to Athens; love of the lady astride that lucky colt yonder! Let me die in her sight! Him too!'

— 156 —

'I grant your wishes, by mighty Mars the red!' He didn't even mean to dismount, thinking to club them as they knelt on either side awaiting justice. He raised his arm, but the blow didn't fall.

Hippolyta had cried out. All the gentle ladies cried. They thought it a great pity that two gorgeous young men of great estate should be in this extremity because of love. They saw the bloody wounds and cried with Hippolyta, 'Have mercy, lord, on us women!' Except for Emily, who didn't give a toss. She thought it inexcusable that such ruffians had the nerve to squabble in her name, and summary execution for that and for spoiling a morning's hunting seemed quite appropriate.

Theseus slowly lowered his club and ruminated. He was angry enough to kill them, and they were contrite enough to be killed, but it was true that any man would help himself in love, even break out of jail; he didn't approve of such licence, but he comprehended it. Beyond that he found it hard to ignore the piteous weeping of the ladies.

Oh, hell! he murmured to himself, fie upon a lord who'll have no mercy, but must always be a lion in word and deed. It shows little discretion to make no distinction between cases, and to regard pride and humility as identical before the law. Men have their reasons, and justice must bend a little towards mercy!

As he thought this through he began to lift up his eyes, and the darkness of his wrath faded with the rising morning sun, and he addressed the malefactors and the tense assembled company.

'How mighty and how great is the god of love!' he declared in tones of awed resignation, as if finally conceding defeat to something beyond his ken. 'How puny are all our defences of law and custom, our art and statecraft, philosophy – nothing holds hard against this mighty force. Look at these knights, who could have lived royally in Thebes! Emily knows as little of them as a cuckoo or a hare – pathetic! Yet anyone may be struck down the same, young or old. Right, then – at the urging of my gentle Queen who kneels here now, I forgive you boys. But you'll swear never to make war on me or my lands; rather, you'll be my friends in every way available to you. Do you accept my terms?'

—— 157 ——

It was a moving occasion, Palamon and Arcite kissing the club and swearing allegiance, everyone watching in pious exaltation. But there was still something outstanding, which needed considerable diplomacy to resolve.

Theseus spoke again. 'Boys, you're both eligible, but the plain fact is Emily can't wed both of you. I speak for her in this matter, and can't decide which of you is fitter to become my relative. Attend carefully, then, to this proposal. Both of you depart now, and in exactly a year come back with a hundred knights apiece, armed in readiness for a tournament, which will be held on this very spot. Meanwhile I'll have the ground cleared and prepared for the spectacle. Whoever then slays his brother shall win Emily. We'll let fortune determine the outcome, and there'll be no two ways about it – one of you'll be dead or captured, the other will have fairly won fair Emily.'

'We thank you, lord!' they said in unison, and sprang up jubilantly. Everyone rejoiced to have so wise and compassionate a ruler as Theseus. Two hundred knights to do battle for a wife! What chivalry, what spectacle, what evidence of control over the savage passions! Really, what a triumph for reason!

'But I don't *want* to be married!' Emily whined to her sister.

'Ungrateful minx!' Hippolyta snarled. 'But for me Theseus himself would have had you by now, more ways than a compass has points. But he loves me and my son. You just don't know when you're well off!'

Emily pouted, and the tears rolled down her pretty cheeks as she thought she hadn't a friend in all the world. In another part of the forest, Dewdrop felt much the same, though he had no one to tell it to.

— 158 —

XXII

LYSANDER HADN'T RIDDEN out with the hunting party because his conscience troubled him. He heard their noisy return and met them, as soon as possible asking to see Theseus alone.

'I can't advance any more for your charities,' Theseus said affably. 'I've found a new project that'll strain the purse of every citizen. Want to hear of it?'

'Um . . .' Lysander dithered until he had closed the door on the boisterous party. 'I'm afraid you won't think me your friend when I've said my piece, sir. I have transgressed.'

'What? Even you? I can't believe you've been skimming the funds – even if you were bankrupt you wouldn't do that!'

'Of course not – no, but worse, I think. My lord, I helped a prisoner to escape two nights ago.'

'That *is* serious. I have great respect for my jailor's peace of mind. He grows the best greens in Attica. Have you shamed him?'

'I hope not. I waited overnight in the prisoner's cell, until Molly brought his breakfast; then I went down with her and informed the old fellow of what I'd done, assuring him the liability was mine and that I'd confess to you. The jailor is a blameless man.'

'Kindly spoken and courteously done – think no more about it, Lysander. You clearly acted charitably, as is your nature.'

— 159 —

'I clearly broke our law.'

'To serve a young knight imprisoned by love – I came upon him this morning, with his antagonist. Worry not, my friend, for your charity served a greater purpose than you knew; none of us can predict the fuller purposes that guide our deeds. My new great scheme is born because you gave Palamon a rope and enabled him to encounter Arcite, and me to meet them both. I'm going to want your suggestions. And remember that carpenter I banished a few years ago? Quince? By now he'll be an expert in every byway of his craft, so we'll need him here for this. Rescind the order and have him placed in charge of a team of carpenters. I'll need the best stonemasons, good chisellers, sculptors, painters – ah, but first the best draughtsmen, best architects . . . I'm revolving the ideas, but I must have men of vision to implement them.'

His enthusiasm was irresistible. Soon the city thrilled to new activities, urgent comings and goings of men with plans and optimistic competitive costings; soon a prize was given, a contract signed and preparatory work commenced; soon a large tract of the forest was cleared, trees turned into scaffolding, the space dug over and seeded to become one corner of the vast stadium; employment was found for many, and strangers flocked to Athens to find work; thirty men had the daily task of removing small stones from the ground; others, ropemakers, water-carriers, wagon-drivers, cutters, carvers, heavers, plasterers, kept up their noisy labours from dawn to dusk, ploughing deep tracks into the old green meadows, terrifying the innocent life of the forest and inadvertently slaughtering thousands of plants and fairies so bemused by so much life they forgot to leap aside when a cartwheel squelched them into the mud, or when a tree shattered down and pinned hundreds. It was a nightmare time for the forest dwellers, and those that survived soon learned to retreat first and preserve curiosity for a better day. The city had eaten a third of the forest, and gradually the great building emerged from the half-digested mulch and rose higher and ever higher into the sky.

Nothing like it had been seen on earth before. The faced stone wall was longer than the city wall surrounding Athens, and sixty feet in height, forming a perfect circle. Peter Quince, who had supervised the marking out of the ground and the erection of the scaffolding, was properly credited with the success of this engineering miracle, and he drew admiring whispers wherever he went, and parents named their sons after him. He had a special hat designed to mark him out as Quince the Master. It was a hat so high he had to tie it under his chin to keep it in place.

One evening when the work was well advanced Theseus rode out with Hippolyta to show her around. He told her how many oaks had gone to make the gates at the southern entrance and she expressed appropriate incredulity. Inside the perfect circle was a bare extensive grassed plain. The walls were distant and ridged in the lowering light. Seating was provided in several ranks all the way around. Three structures interrupted the seating, north, west and east. Theseus smacked the rump of Hippolyta's horse and rode with her to each compass point in turn. He said he had considered over two hundred deities before making the final choices. The temple in the north wall served Artemis, or Diana, and was full of images of chastity and the hunt; in the west wall was Mars the terrible war god's image, and in the east stood Venus, goddess of love. The perfect life circle, with men entering at the southern gate and seeing their essential pursuits represented.

'It's so simple,' Hippolyta said, 'and yet profound. It's unforgettable, Theseus, the essence of things!'

He smiled modestly. This was the response he'd hoped for. Now was the time to spring the surprise he'd been planning longer than the circle. 'I think we've had a good marriage. We've produced a magnificent son, despite the injuries men did you in the past. Anyway, I've had no regrets, and throughout our marriage I've tried to give you whatever you wanted. One thing has troubled me, though: you haven't been free to choose the life I've given. At first, I'll admit, I didn't grasp the need, but

— 161 —

you've shown me a woman can feel, even think, as well as a man. Hippolyta, I now release you, absolutely.'

'Ah, yes, but . . .'

'You'll say this is another extension of my control, releasing you at my discretion again, not at your request, so let me express it this way: I love you as a husband loves a faithful wife, and hope you choose to stay with me. I will grieve if you go, not rejoice. But the choice is yours and unlimited. You are at liberty to stay or go, go and come again, take ship anywhere you wish – I shan't restrain you at any time. All I will not do is abrogate my own position, for I am and will remain Theseus, fully accepting my own duties. My rights do not include commanding you, however, unless you consent. And as you are free so may you keep your own counsel in this and every other matter. You do not have to discuss with me. I free you, and I take no pride in saying so, for you should not require to be freed. You are free, though. I have said.'

'Theseus,' Hippolyta answered gravely after she'd ridden in thoughtful silence awhile, 'don't tell my sister. With these unconditional conditions I am yours. I stay, and willingly, but Emily would go. Keep her freedom until she is mature enough to be impartial.'

If I hadn't interceded, Hippolyta reflected, he'd have clubbed those two knights to death and none of this would have arisen. I saw him come up with the idea on the spot, but from that chance notion of a deferred tournament he's woven a concept of the nobility of life and the possibility of governing it, of embracing men's natural propensity for chaotic destruction, moulding these forces, containing them, confining them, controlling and transforming them within a structure whose intellectual elegance is matched by its physical harmony. Within this stone circle triumph and despair will exist together, and nothing need spill over, all held within this perfect O. A man whose shaping power can make a pattern of human emotions is almost godlike.

'You should be proud of what you've achieved here,' Hippolyta said. 'People are coming from all over the Aegean to marvel, and those with the capacity for thought will apply your logic to the messiness of existence hundreds of years from now.'

'Ah,' Theseus exclaimed nostalgically, 'the Aegean!' He reined in his horse. They were now directly below Athens and the city threw back the last embers of the sun, black land below it, black hills around, black sky above. The two horses grazed the night grass. 'You know why I called it the Aegean, of course?'

'For your father, Egeus.'

'Not everyone knows how his death altered me, yet it bears on this, and every decision I have come to. He made me promise to hoist white sails on my return from Crete, if I had slain the Minotaur. But such a lot happened on those voyages, and between setting out and sailing home I'd loved and left Ariadne. Anyway, when it came to it I simply forgot about the message in the sails. Egeus saw the black sails and read them as a sign the Minotaur had beaten and eaten me. At once he threw himself off the cliff to perish in the rocky sea that remembers him. Is it a sad story, or a pointless, laughable error? Doesn't fate treat us to such absurdities throughout our lives, no matter how careful our rules of conduct? I remember my landing and my ride to Athens, jubilant celebration and condolence for my loss colliding with equal force. Why do the gods play these games? To tell us we're nothing, or make us reflect further on our farcical transience, our inept laws? Hippolyta, I *am* authority, yet I am as confused as a child.'

By this time darkness had fallen, and they rode home in sombre mood.

A few days later Lysander came to Theseus on another delicate matter. 'Palamon has asked me to be one of his hundred. Given the illustrious names he's assembled so far, that's an unlooked-for honour. Demetrius will join Arcite, apparently.'

'But there's no compulsion, Lysander, and you're a man of peace. Do you want me to explain to him? That's easy enough.'

'No, I want to accept.'

'But what of your children, should you be mortally wounded?'

'It's for them I accept. They're too young to be proud of my pacific temper, and although they know there's strength in virtue they admire those knights who hack out the freedoms we enjoy. And I'm afraid their friends taunt them with having me for a father; I tax their parents, who naturally resent the demands of human kindness. So I want to redeem myself in my children's eyes. As for myself, since Hermia's death it's never bothered me that I must die some day, only that that day has seemed so far off. So I'll fight, though I'll not kill anyone.'

'Not . . .' Theseus paused, then his eyes widened. 'Yes, Lysander, that's it! That's what was still wrong in all this – surely we can control the event to such a fine conclusion! I will put it out that *no one* is to be killed in the combat – oh, the beauty of it now! In Athens even death can be contained within the bounds of law – and thus do we learn to shape our destiny as men and rise above brute creation! Leave me, my friend, for I must pray for guidance. Thank you.'

Let the simple clarity of the contest, he prayed devoutly, stand as proof that a purpose exists, showing that what is brutal in us can be channelled to serve what is best, and that what is best has your approval.

Night fell. Thunder rolled and cracked above the field.

In the darkness of the tower Nick Bottom listened. He was content in his way, and grateful for Molly's love, and yet he felt deceived somehow, diverted from his true path in life. He remembered the promise Palamon had extracted from him years before, to keep him alive. It had seemed reasonable enough that he should serve the young knight, that would have had meaning. But he hadn't helped Palamon to escape, and he longed for the life of his cottage in the forest. Athens revolved around the tower and he knew that exciting events were occurring, but he had no connection with them, so what was it all for, and where did he fit into the scheme of things? If there *was* a scheme, which Nick profoundly doubted.

— 164 —

XXIII

CITY OF COLOURED cloth, canvas and linen grew up at the edge of the forest as the notorious knights arrived and set up temporary residence. Some tents were grand and beautifully furnished, others humble, even dirty; all produced quantities of refuse which were slung in amongst the trees. Sanitary arrangements were rudimentary. Everything ended in the forest, with the result that spring brought a less attractive range of fragrances from the green wood that year. Knights and squires, horses and donkeys, yapping curs, corralled cattle, pigs; from a distance the tented city was quite beautiful, but the denizens of the forest experienced the full foul stench of human settlement and wondered if Theseus had instigated a deliberate policy of genocide. Fairies survived the poisonous vapours, but innumerable small plants perished and trees died, copses dried out, new and nasty sub-species proliferated, that fed on filth and spread it further into hitherto unspoiled reaches of virgin cover.

It was Puck who ventured out and discovered the temples in the arena. Puck hadn't been in Athens since he heard Nick Bottom denounced as a traitor and condemned to death, but he'd seen Theseus break up the fight between Palamon and Arcite and knew what the fight was about. This he'd reported to Oberon, but he'd been unable to warn of the destructive scale of the event, and so for several months he'd been in disgrace. By flitting from temple to temple he hoped to redeem himself, for it's well known

— 165 —

to anyone who haunts temples or betting shops that men at their most pious ask for far more than life or health, and Puck was a subtle eavesdropper.

Most men chose Mars, and asked for victory; some sought Diana's protection; very few bothered Venus. What struck Puck was the similarity of men's minds. Having accepted Theseus's ruling that no one was to be killed, most of these fierce veteran fighters would round off their flowery lists of requests with a loaded allusion to Chance. 'If there is to be an accident, for accidents do trample on our noblest intentions, let the sufferer not be me; rather, with my blessing, let the sad blow fall if it must on my noble brother and sworn enemy . . .' and here they would name the rival in prestige or love, who was ardently naming them elsewhere.

Puck had great fun impersonating Mars or Diana and gravely granting these sincere, appalling requests, and all the knights came away from the temples standing tall and smiling with knowing condescension at the hapless friends they had consigned through Chance to Fate. Puck was a pernicious booster of confidence.

To Mars Demetrius made the unsporting suggestion that as Lysander had so much less to live for he was more disposable. To Venus Lysander himself actually confirmed this. Puck thought he must be the idiot of the mortal tribe, though none made a very favourable impression. However, it was the night before the tournament that afforded him his best amusements, for then he pronounced on Arcite, Palamon and Emily in the space of an hour.

Arcite's demands were simple. He prostrated himself before Mars with an ease that bespoke long familiarity and confident service. 'You know me, Boss,' he began. 'I thought you'd deserted me at Thebes, but now I realise you had to do that to bring me to Emily. You know how I've suffered since – that's all right, I'm not complaining because I know you arranged this climax. So I just ask what you're expecting me to ask: Give me my victory tomorrow. I seek no more.'

Puck stopped himself laughing at the youthful arrogance, which outdid the vanities of the other knights. He made the big rings on the temple doors, and the doors themselves, clatter furiously enough to startle Arcite. Then he made the altar fires flare until the walls glowed red. A sweet smell rose up through the stone floor and permeated the temple with scents reminiscent of Emily, but Arcite didn't amend his plea. At last Puck summoned a terrifyingly deep and resonant note which, as it made the temple tremble, shaped into the single word: Victory!

Arcite leapt to his feet, threw bunches of incense on the fires, and hurried into the cool night air full of joy and plans for his future.

In the temple of Venus Palamon knelt and composed his thoughts. 'The outcome of this tournament wouldn't interest me in the slightest for itself – win or lose is equally irrelevant. I love Emily. If I can't win her then put me out of my misery tomorrow. If I'm dead I won't mind if Arcite has her. But give me my love, great lady, and I shall die in your service.'

'Downbeat,' Puck said in a low feminine voice, 'but sincere. OK – granted!'

And with that Palamon left the temple, glad of heart if unclear whether he'd been granted Emily or death.

Emily herself, last and in a way least, put her complaint against the chaste Diana. 'Frankly,' she said, forgetting to abase herself, 'I'm disappointed with the way things are going. None of my letters has been answered. Tomorrow's going to be the worst day of my life, and all my sister can do is insist Theseus knows what's best. Chaste goddess, I want to stay a maiden; I'll never love a man, I am of your company. I love freedom and the wild wood – don't coop me up as some vain bully's nurse and whore! Mothering his noxious brats! Yuck! All you have to do is send amity to Palamon and Arcite, quell their horrid lusts, turn them from me. If you can't manage that, then at least let me have the one who will bother me least – but even the thought makes my tears flow! So far you've helped protect me from the drunken fumblings of that old hypocrite – *please* let me serve you for ever as a maid pure and true!'

For a while nothing happened, then one fire died and immediately sprang to life; the same thing happened to the others, and bloody red drops ran from the brands.

Diana's impatient voice came through. 'You'll marry one, but I can't say which. You'll just have to make the best of it, like everyone else. You're not fit to bear children, so take comfort in that. I've better things to do than listen to you, so I'm off.'

'Wait!' Emily cried in vain. 'What do all my prayers amount to, then? How can you slight me so?' But she got nothing for her pains and rode home deeply dissatisfied.

Puck didn't gather anything useful for Oberon, either, but he'd had a good laugh. It was a pity he didn't follow Emily, for when she reached the palace she heard the tail-end of one of Theseus's grand public orations. He was offering a general amnesty to his prisoners.

—— 168 ——

XXIV

MOLLY USED HER largest frying pan, filling it with as many eggs and rashers of bacon and mushrooms as could be burnt at one time, because she wanted to give Nick Bottom a breakfast he would remember. The news reached her less than an hour after Theseus had spoken, and she informed every one of her prisoners that they'd be released in the morning. Nick was the only one she cooked this treat for, though, and while she took it to him her father had the joyful task of freeing the others, giving each man a handshake and a coin to see him fed for a week. They were only guilty of crimes such as using bad language in front of ladies, which hadn't even been punishable until recently.

Molly placed the tray on the carpet Nick had woven and got back into bed beside him. He groaned lazily and affectionately rubbed warmth into her arms. 'What do I smell? Is this bacon?' He turned aside and lifted the tray, his eyes showing how pleased he was.

'Get stuck in, Nick, you'll need a good breakfast today, there'll be plenty to do.'

'Aren't you eating with me?'

'When you're gone I'll try something.'

Nick had bacon dripping with egg halfway to his mouth. He slowly replaced the fork on his plate, chewing and swallowing before attempting a reply. 'I said last night and repeat this

— 169 —

morning, my love, I don't mean to go anywhere without you.'

'I know, but I'm not happy about holding you to what may only be the consolation of poverty. You must find your freedom in the world and only then, if you freely desire it, come back.'

'I'm old enough to know what I want, Molly.'

'But you wouldn't marry me.'

'Apart from the public showing of the thing we *are* man and wife, have been since we consummated our devotion. But I'd be a poor husband with no end on my sentence and no prospect of continuing my trade. But I don't want to part from you – I expected you to come too, at least to help me taste the city air today.'

'No. You may well meet old friends, and then you'll have much gossip to swap. Anyway, you'll be gathering new impressions of the city, and today is the great tournament they've talked of all year. I'd be in the way, Nick, for you'd be looking out for me and so forget to savour it to the full.'

'What rot! The people of Athens don't attract me! Gathered together men only turn to destruction. I love loneliness and you, and need no test to know that. Do you love me?'

'I cried all night after you went to sleep. These last months have been my happiest since I was a child. But I want to know you're with me of your own real free will, having tasted freedom again, and not because you've only tasted me.'

'Molly, my girl, I neither have nor ever want free will. Don't offer what I've no use for. I'm bound to you, as I trust you are to me; freedom only finds a meaning with that constraint. I've had more than enough time to think *that* through!'

Well, the breakfast went greasy cold and the loving squabble continued upwards of an hour, but in the end Nick conceded just to content Molly, and he left laughing, assuring her that he'd return well before nightfall and never part from her again.

She'd laundered his clothes and he'd kept them in good repair, so nothing about him made anyone look twice. Because he'd regularly worked in the garden he didn't even have a prisoner's complexion.

At first he simply wandered about the streets remembering and enjoying them, then he revisited old haunts hoping to bump into Francis, Robin, or even Margery, who'd know what had befallen his friends. But the new girl at the Bull didn't recognise his descriptions. A little downcast, Nick was tempted to go to Molly right away, but discerning the general traffic of the crowds out of the city he thought he might as well follow and perhaps watch enough of the spectacle to gather colourful accounts to render to his loved one later.

The morning was already hot and the way was busy; it seemed the entire city had turned out, some rudely prancing past on horseback, some in bulky carts and fine fashionable carriages, most, like Nick, afoot and wending slower as the crush increased. Everyone was jabbering excitedly, as there'd been plenty of time to learn the names and qualities of the participants; never had so many commanders and tyrants of distant lands been gathered together in one place to test their strength and skill. Bets were laid on every side; even Nick had a struggle to keep from placing his money on the names that were shouted most convincingly.

I was with Palamon and Arcite when this blew up, he reminded himself incredulously. I too saw Emily in the garden – a pretty little kid, though she'll never hold a candle to Molly. So many people, and most are jerks who don't even know they're caught up in an idea. Frightening.

Yet, ridiculous as it was, he found himself churned into the spirit of it, and not unwillingly. So much noise, such clashing bright colours, such leaden heat, such lemon light! It was exhilarating, and very soon it was too much to take after his long tranquillity, and even as he queued for the arena Nick started feeling nauseous, had to push out from the sweaty throng, move over to sit against the great wall, whose shade just took the beating sun off his whirling head. For some reason he recalled Thebes, the parched heap of bones, the chopping swords and gaping wounds, the lust of blood. He opened his eyes and saw bickering, shoving Athenians, and the scenes so nearly matched

— 171 —

he thought he was mad and waited on only until he felt stable enough to rush back to jail and Molly.

Then a strange thing happened.

A captain, bearing the Minotaur pennant of Theseus's élite private guard, approached and stood over the sick weaver. 'Arise,' he said. 'Follow me. Orders of Theseus.'

Nick knew better than to argue. He pressed his back and hands against the wall to get to his feet and the captain waited patiently, even courteously. It made no sense. Unless the amnesty hadn't extended to him. He was too unsettled to object, though, and when the captain ushered him through the intimidating gate and then directed him up a flight of stairs that no one else was pushing towards, he accepted his fate with blank indifference.

Instead of coming out into fierce sun he entered a lovely cool blue light and his indifference melted into gratitude and a stirring of his old curiosity. Nick was quick-witted enough to realise that he'd been shown into the royal enclosure, where Theseus and Hippolyta and a select few could observe the débâcle. In the row to which he was directed Nick saw the back of a stiff man in a funny towering hat. Above, though he didn't risk more than the odd sidelong glance, the mighty Theseus was enthroned, Hippolyta and Emily at either side, little Hippolytus playing with toy bulls at his father's feet. Theseus made no acknowledgement of Nick, but why should he? Nick meekly sat and fretted. At least he was still under that blue awning, and off to his left side white gauzes soaked in water had been hung, so that the warm breeze cooled a little in passing through and made the enclosure as comfortable as a marbled inner room of the palace, or Nick's secluded cottage.

Gradually he adjusted to his privileged situation, and watched the long ranks of seats filling, and the solemn knights marching in and taking up position in two aggressive lines. Their squires scurried to horses and donkeys, carrying various weapons out to their masters, who enjoyed the attentions of the crowd. The great knights with chariots urged their horses forward and brought them back again just to display their prowess and expensive livery. One even made an inspired race the length of his lines, returning nearer the cheering crowd and sweeping neatly back into his first position. He turned and made an exaggerated bow to his fans, who increased their bets with absolute convictions that by the end of the day they'd stagger home rich as well as tipsy.

Nick turned to his neighbour to learn the identity of the conceited charioteer. 'Excuse me, sir, but would that be Lycurgus the lionheart?' he asked, and forgot his question instantly. 'By all the gods! Is it *you*, Peter Quince?'

The master carpenter's jaw dropped, his eyes nearly popped out. 'Bully Bottom! You can't be! You've been dead since I went to renovate Thebes!'

'I've long been the guest of tall Don Jon,' Nick laughed. 'Is that why none of my pals ever came to swap tales with me? Was I dead to all the world?'

The two men embraced there and then, and tears mingled on their cheeks, old differences forgotten in their joy or, if remembered, welcomed as necessaries in the dense fabric of friendship, which in time values its full store of shared memory, good and bad, sad and glad together. However, before Nick could compliment Peter on his prosperous appearance, before he could ask about the old crew, a palpable silence swelled the stifling air of the arena. For a panicky second thousands of expectant Athenians stared hard at Nick Bottom, then a magisterial voice filled the enclosure and reached out evenly to every ear in that vast and suddenly concentrated space.

'In his high discretion,' Theseus began, 'your lord has considered it destructive to the blood of chivalry for mortal battle to be waged in this noble contest. He has, therefore, modified the original plan, and now dictates the manner. No one may bring into action the poleaxe, the short knife, or short sword with its biting point; there'll be no bows; the sharp spear only in the first charge, or for a man to defend himself on foot. He that is caught out will be taken, but not slain, and brought to one of the stakes you see at either end. He can be taken by force

— 173 —

and must stay once placed there. As soon as the chief of either
side is brought to the stake the tournament ends. Right, men,
with your long swords and maces go out and lay on hard! God
speed! Fight bravely! This is the lord's will!'

As he concluded the voice of the people blew at the skirts of
heaven, so loud and unanimous was their enthusiastic chorus.
'God save such a lord, who is so good he wills no destruction of
the noble blood!'

Then the trumpets sounded and at their sound Arcite rode out
from the temple in the west, bearing the great red banner of
Mars, and Palamon rode from the east, bearing the great white
banner of Venus. They took their positions and waited until the
cheering subsided in a wave that wanted to come again, and in
that swollen near-silence Theseus spoke once more.

'Now, my proud young knights – do your duty!'

Trumpets sounded for the charge, upraised spears shone as
they were lowered, and the thunder of a thousand hooves exploded the charged stillness. Horses whinnied and neighed as
spurs and lashes pricked them to fury, riders bellowed commands, challenges, the crowd roared encouragement on one
side, disparagement on the other. In the first clash the noise of
breakage was as if the earth had split apart; shields shattered
under showering mace blows, spears snapped like kindling,
harness gave way so that horses and riders swirled giddily out of
control; out came the long swords to hew away helmets, shred
them and open the brave kernels within; gruesome streams of
bright new blood burst forth; maces mashed arms, ribs, horses'
noses and unprotected eyes; in one wheeling mass of riders the
whole turning, fighting pack collapsed in a sickening awkward
heap; horses were going down everywhere now, hurling off
knights under the bumping wheels of chariots. One was captured
and dragged back to the stake, one was forced to the stake on
the other side. Demetrius, laying about him with mace and long
sword, fought towards Lysander, who defended himself but
feared hitting one of his own side, assuming he was the only one
who didn't know the disposition of allies or the colours of

—— 174 ——

enemies. In truth most knights only knew a handful of their own, and had earmarked only a few specific enemies to aim for. Niceties gave way to practicalities and all save Lysander simply whacked away at whatever came within range. It was a wonder none was killed. A miracle, the crowd was beginning to believe – and Theseus had ordained it. What a lord! What majesty!

The battle raged on till scarcely a man or beast stood that was not blood-stamped. Nick Bottom had no stomach for it and he had occupied himself by studying the corner of the field where grooms had led the donkeys to give them water and a few oats.

Lysander was fighting off two growling knights when Demetrius dealt him a mighty blow across the back. The three then dragged the unconscious body roughly over broken wheels and spears, all the way to the stake. Fortunately Lysander's twins had been in a position to see how courageously their father fought, and the cheating blow that laid him low. What they couldn't see was his condition now. He spat blood and tried but failed to stand unaided. His captured comrades, all wounded, gathered close and forgot the continuing battle in their gentle concern for this good and modest knight.

Now the field was wearying, but still men bludgeoned on with slow heavy blows that made them wheeze and stagger. Odd loose horses cantered or stamped nervously. There was a danger of the mood shifting from what was engendered by clean shows of courage to something perverse, shaming to watch or be in. Five more of Palamon's men were brought to the stake within a couple of minutes, three of Arcite's. Then Arcite was face to face with Palamon at last, and all the loathing and self-righteousness of a twelve-month past came foaming to the surface, all the old irrational ferocity.

'To the death?' Arcite demanded.

'Yours, certainly,' Palamon replied with aristocratic disdain, and charged into his old sworn brother with a yell like a great beast tormented in some steel-toothed trap. This chilling cry was heard by Lycurgus, King of Thrace, and Emetreus, King of

— 175 —

India. Emetreus strode over and before anyone had a chance to gasp warning he plunged his sword into Palamon's hip, and immediately the remaining knights clustered here where the fight was most urgent. Twenty of Arcite's men surrounded the stricken but undefeated Palamon and began hacking a path towards the stake. Lycurgus, with at least twenty of Palamon's knights, flailed mercilessly to the rescue, but just as he was about to free him, Arcite's long sword slashed the backs of his legs and Lycurgus fell in agony. At that moment Palamon swung up and back with his great sword and caught Emetreus so powerful a blow in the chest that he was flung backwards off his horse. Even so, Palamon was soon outnumbered. His men could neither reach him nor fight close enough to capture Arcite.

Theseus stood in his enclosure and saw Palamon at the stake. He signalled for a trumpet sound to stay the tired swords.

'Hold!' he said in a commanding voice that wasn't raised yet carried firmly. 'No more, for it is done. I will judge impartially, as I promised. The man who by his fortune has fairly won the game shall win Emily. That man is Arcite.'

The people, who should have been hoarse by now, cheered loud enough to make the sixty-foot-high walls tremble.

'Sounds like that's it, then,' Nick Bottom said, opening his eyes to survey the carnage below. 'The more inconsiderate of the pair has won a girl he's never spoken to. She may have a voice like a duck for all he knows. Did you enjoy it, Peter?'

'All my year of fine labour,' Peter groaned, shaking his head dolorously, 'gone for this bestial display! I thought it would be a romance, like one of our plays we used to rehearse so feelingly, only on a grander scale. Is war like this, bereft of spirit so? All I can think of is poor Snug the night I saw him done for – I thought that deed was an aberration, and I asked for justice. You were there with me. What fools they must have thought us!' He sighed in his disillusion. 'I suppose we may go home now. Will you come and get drunk with me?'

'That makes sense. And Peter, I'd be proud to have you meet Molly, she who'll be my wife once I'm back in work.'

'Where will you find work, Nick? Let me help to set you up.'

'Oh, no need for that – I'll return to my cottage and tidy things up for a few days, make it fitting for a wife to live in. You'll see, we'll be right as rain soon.'

Peter Quince looked dubious, as he always did, but their conversation was cut short by new events. Arcite, having removed his helmet and mounted his charger, made a circuit of the arena and came tripping confidently towards the blue enclosure, eager eyes seeking out his prize. Undeniably glamour attached to him now and even Emily, though the thought of this streaked bloody man breathing on her was loathsome, had to respond to the occasion: she managed a nod and a wan smile with less effort than she would have supposed possible.

I'd rather bathe in cow dung than have him near, she thought, as her winsome smile sent doves into the air. The moment he lays a finger on me I'll cry rape and have his head off.

'I see the fate decreed for you is no longer so oppressive,' Hippolyta observed, touching her sister's hand in friendly gesture.

'He's a man,' Emily answered non-committally.

'You can say that again! Wow, if I was you and had all this put on for my benefit, I'd be getting the bed warm by now!'

'Well, I'm something short of your imagination, sister,' Emily said softly, and she leaned forward to take a closer look at the stranger who dared behave as if he'd won her heart.

As she shifted and the people sighed with her gracious beauty, Nick Bottom also moved, suddenly alert, for he'd seen something unbelievable. There, in amongst the pack-horses, stood a scarred and skinny and rather pathetic animal that he recognised and pitied and felt responsible for all at once.

'Dewdrop,' he murmured. And it was no more than a murmur, not a great cry anyone could hear. Even so the murmur travelled directly and the sad donkey, taken by surprise, looked up sharply to see his long-lost master.

'Nick!' he answered, all in the moment of Emily's leaning forward.

— 177 —

Like all aristocrats, Arcite's charger was highly strung. It had been schooled in battle where no noise would distract it, but it saw Nick Bottom from the edge of one eye, and it saw Dewdrop from the other. And it distinctly heard the donkey speak, and on that instant danced aside, rearing as though a serpent coiled in its path. All this directly below Theseus. Who watched aghast and helpless as Arcite tumbled off the staggering horse and fell on his unprotected head, his body twisting so awkwardly into the rearing, falling beast that his ribs were smashed by the hard pommel of his own saddle. It was a grotesquely elaborate and ludicrous treatment of a simple fall. The horse snorted and got up, dragging Arcite and raking him over a splintered spear. Then Arcite lay as if dead, blood running over his face. Men hurried forward to bear him quickly back to the palace. Shock was everywhere. Everyone seemed to understand what this accident signified; the world of order that Theseus had imposed had just fallen apart, and all was inscrutably cruel once again.

'Oh, shit!' Nick Bottom exclaimed. 'Now I'm for it! But I won't submit this time. Peter, do me a favour – see Molly and tell her I've fled – I have no choice!'

He spun from his seat before his friend could turn from the accident and ask what he was saying. No one noticed him go or suspected him of anything, unless perhaps Theseus, who knew everything.

He was out of the gate in one breath, astonished that a dozen spears hadn't found his back. As soon as he hit open ground he ran for the familiar safety of his forest. And as he ran noticed that the meadow wasn't where it had been. Then the forest wasn't as close as before, either. Prison had tricked his memories. Nick kept running.

Eventually there were trees, but not the old entrance, no sign of the abandoned dwellings. Eventually there were parts of the forest he recalled, though they seemed back to front, as if he'd reached the far end instead of the properly familiar beginning. He was dizzy and breathless now, quite disorientated. So he stopped. Waited. Listened for pursuers. Where was all the forest

— 178 —

life? He heard none of the creatures, saw none. Where was his cottage? How, no matter what the deprivations, could he have forgotten the way to his own safe home?

Nick ran this way and that, remaking landmarks in his mind and calculating feverishly to point himself in the right direction. Dozens of times he must have worked out logically where his cottage had to be and set off doggedly to find it, but every time with the same dire result. His cottage had vanished and with it the greater part of the forest, and with that his cherished memories, his long childhood.

That which remained, he now began to perceive, was callously despoiled. He called his old friends, careless whether or not the soldiers heard. Cobweb, no answer. Peaseblossom, Mustardseed, no answer. Puck. Titania. Oberon! Oberon! No answer. No answer. No home, no friends, no return for trust and happy love.

Night fell and Nick lay shivering and alone in the world. Or not even in the world any longer. He could not go back to Athens without losing his life, and so had to accept that he'd lost Molly. He could not reclaim the forest either, for that lay destroyed about him. No, he just lay shivering and alone, and without a world to be alone in, a negligible part of nothing.

XXV

IN THE FOLLOWING days Athens was like a city besieged, and whereas before mothers had carried babes into the streets to marvel at the passing parades of fine knights from far beyond the seas, now these same mothers trembled in their homes in dread of those same killers. The cause of tension was Arcite's fall. Many comrades were spoiling for a fight to avenge his disastrous accident, which they preferred to see as a cunning trick that had robbed them of their due glory. At last Theseus called the best of them together to visit Arcite and see for themselves how every known prayer had been brought unavailingly to his aid. Weak and feverish as he was, Arcite assured them he bore Palamon no grudge. He'd asked Mars for no more than victory, he admitted, and Mars had given him that. He should have remembered a long happy life as well – the gods were renowned for pedantic quibbles.

Diplomacy worked and the knights, agreeing that no clear blame could be laid anywhere, grudgingly dispersed. By nightfall the tented city was gone and the people of Athens could breathe relief. Only now they had a new concern: if Arcite died, the miraculous powers of Theseus really were faulty, so some of the old resentments were heard again; gratitude has a briefer life than ingratitude. The people had never liked Egeus, and Theseus was something of a usurper. Others had better claims to the

— 180 —

throne until he killed them. And then, many of his reforms were more restrictive than liberating . . .

While seeds of disaffection germinated in the fertile common ground of ordinary envy and resentment, Arcite's hold on life slipped. Palamon and Emily were summoned to his bedside.

'What is this life?' he asked with enfeebled bitterness. 'What is it men seek? In love I was alone. In my grave I'll be alone. Emily, my love, my death, my enemy, since my life can no longer endure, my ghost will continue in your service.' Then he winced and cried awhile, then rambled about a bear-like son who could have loved him and a long-legged woman who stalked through his dreams.

Theseus and Perotheus were called. Just before the end Arcite redeemed himself by attesting to the virtues of Palamon and imploring Emily to consider this courteous gentleman if she ever again thought of marrying. Then cold death, that had been creeping from his feet along the length of his impassive frame, overcame him. His last words were despairing. 'Mercy, Emily!'

The sad news was put out and general mourning ensued. What hope was there for less privileged folk to delay death's embrace? Unwilling to carry the burden of such hopelessness the people shifted the weight to Theseus. They wanted him to take the bitter edge off mortality, give joy and purpose back to their lives. Theseus shook his head worriedly.

'Look,' Perotheus consoled him pragmatically, 'no man ever died who didn't live a bit first, and no man ever lived who didn't die. There's no escaping it. This world is just a thoroughfare of woe, and we are only pilgrims passing to and fro.'

'That's a great help!' Theseus said drily. The best he could come up with was to make a grand public statement of the Theban's idiotic end. Formal solemnity with fireworks would put some spirit into life. So he instructed that a great funeral pyre should be built out in the forest, where Arcite had first fought Palamon. He wanted a fire which wouldn't burn out until well after dark; everyone would be moved by that. There was

— 181 —

something philosophical about seeing fire consume a mountain of wood.

Then Theseus prepared himself to meet a sadder situation. Unaccompanied, he visited Lysander. Gloria, who met him, didn't know whether to prostrate herself or hide behind a towel. Kindly, Theseus paused long enough to smile. 'Don't fear me,' he said gently. 'I know you've been a good and faithful servant, first to your mistress, and ever since to your sad, saintly master. I wish to speak privately with him.'

'I haven't left the house since he was brought in bleeding so bad,' Gloria said. 'I don't know what we shall do, sir!'

'You will be provided, and if Lysander wishes you shall be the mother his sons lack, given all the recognition due to a lady of noble birth – and a housewife of any sort.'

'I wonder, sir, if I may slip out while you're with my master – I have a message that must be delivered by my hand personally, and this is likely to be my only opportunity.'

'Of course. I won't leave him until your return.'

With her heart in her mouth Gloria hurried away to the palace, to find Emily and hand her the reply she had so long awaited.

Theseus ducked and entered the sick room. Lysander's twins sprang up and stood at attention. Lysander himself struggled to raise himself on his pillow, until Theseus motioned him not to stir and begged the boys to take their ease. He drew up a chair and sat near. 'How is it?' he asked tenderly.

'Near the close,' Lysander replied without a trace of regret. He was as serene as his wife had been, and Theseus wondered at his serenity, which appeared so much better than the bitter whining of Arcite's and most men's leavetaking. 'Permit my boys to speak for me,' Lysander said faintly, 'for I am short in breath.'

The boys stood up side by side, and, with frequent glances to each other, then to their father, they recited his instructions. 'Father says hatred attacks the man who hates. We are not to nurse hatred for Demetrius, though we saw his mean blow.

'Father says Demetrius acted from petty spite and never meant to kill him, so he must grieve or not as he thinks fit; we should

—— 182 ——

not waste our lives in anger – there are better ways to waste life.

'Father says we must not plot to hurt Demetrius or his varied progeny, but live our own lives as the future brings them to us, not as the past would deform them before they reach us.'

'Your father is a good man,' Theseus interjected. 'None is better.'

'Father says he dies not to abandon us but to go ahead and scout the unknown territory; he will find Mother there.

'Father and Mother will make ready the house so we needn't dread our own deaths. We shall be reunited at last.

'Father says no one knows what lives behind death, but if it is bad he will do battle against it. We shouldn't seek to join him before the allotted time, lest he be still fighting the bad. But when the time is right, Father says, he will gather us to him and we shall be happy eternally.'

'Your father is wise as well as good,' Theseus said.

'Father says life is brief, though it may appear protracted. He advises us to follow love and truth while we abide here, so we may hope to know a little peace.'

'I have no words to add to those of your father,' Theseus said with tears in his noble eyes. 'But, boys, I do have a few words to share with him in private – may I ask you to withdraw for a few short minutes?'

They looked at their father, who nodded assent, and then silently they left the room.

'I have only this to say, Lysander: when you first arrived at Court I misjudged you. Your letters of introduction aroused suspicion and I made secret enquiries. Ariadne's sister, Phaedra, is my friend, and it was she who revealed the truth. I have known for years that you were my son by Ariadne. Your reasons for not declaring yourself are your own, but, my boy, do you wish your sons to have the benefit of your true heritage? If so I'll treat them as the equals of my own son Hippolytus – but if you would prefer they should never know their descent from Theseus, I will respect that wish.'

'Father, I want them to live a full span. Power and position

—— 183 ——

cannot ensure that, and may well work against it. They would have your protection until your death, but then they'd have more enemies than a cat has fleas. That's the way of it.'

'Very well. I shall oversee their welfare secretly, if you will permit it, just as I've tried to do for you.'

Lysander nodded and closed his eyes. He was too near death for the conversation to continue. Theseus invited the boys back inside and eulogised their father movingly. When Gloria returned he spoke further to her and then, surprisingly less despondent than he'd been earlier, he walked back to the palace and looked for his best companion, Hippolyta, to whom he could unburden his mind of all its ponderous matter.

Lysander's burial was a small affair attended only by close friends and servants, with Demetrius, Palamon and Theseus among the pallbearers. By contrast the funeral of Arcite was a State occasion, a public holiday on almost the same scale as the tournament. Another sizeable part of the forest went into the conflagration and in the evening, as the flames calmed down and people stood together arm in arm romantically and dreamily inclined, Theseus made what he hoped would be his definitive speech on the conduct of life.

'Friends, I have had the temerity to shape the law, even though I am only a man. Like you I look to the gods for understanding, and I know they also look higher, even to the Prime Mover himself, Jupiter. Now when Jupiter first made the holy chain of love that links us all to one another, and all to heaven, the effect was as noble as the intention. Jupiter knew what he was about when he bound fire, air, water and earth and fixed their boundaries, and when he established the firm bounds of time and space on our wretched earth, and gave a certain number of days to every living thing. It was chaos and darkest night he cleared away so we might see the true path where it leads, and how to stay well in the middle of it. By observing his creation and its perfect harmony we can all see that our First Mover is absolutely stable, absolutely eternal, and that every part and particle of life derives from his wholeness. Thus we should understand why

— 184 —

nothing in *this* world is eternal, because everything is only a part, and every part is so designed that it can find its way back to the whole at last. The whole is the eternal, and Jupiter alone is whole. All else perishes in time. See how the stones of our palace steps wear down generation by generation, how the river sometimes dries to a trickle, how towns wax and wane like the moon above us now. Every thing has its appointed end, and so it must be with us. A king must die as must his page. Some in bed, some at sea, in battle, piously, long before we can bear to part company – all this is done by Jupiter, so we shouldn't rail against it, for we serve his purpose knowingly or not. It's wisdom then, it seems to me, to make virtue of necessity and take in good part what we can't avoid anyway; to do otherwise is to make a rod for our own poor backs. And again, surely there's something to be said for a man's dying at his finest hour, before he falls apart in age and wretched misfortune. Surely it's best to die while you have a good name? Now Arcite, dutiful and highly honoured, is departed from this foul prison of life – isn't he more fortunate than us? Friends, we should go from here with hope, not heaviness. Here is Emily, who would have been Arcite's wife. Here is Palamon. Let mourning cease. Let these two, who never thought to win such happiness, be made man and wife, with my blessing and the blessing of Arcite who smiles on them from heaven. Come, friends, let us wend slowly homewards and take our rest. The best of knights has won the best of wives, and our sorrows are required to end, for the pattern is thus restored. Thoughtful pleasure is warranted after the ceremonies of parting from a young hero.'

Although his words weren't heard or understood by everyone the general sentiments wove naturally into the warmth of the night and the communality of a long vigil at the blazing pyre. Palamon wept unashamedly for his childhood friendship, and for this marvellous revival of his good fortune. Venus had answered him perfectly.

Emily neither wept nor sulked. She accepted this revised alliance as an irrelevant gift, of consequence only to the misled

— 185 —

giver. Her mind was filled with three words that outshone all the speeches the tedious Theseus had ever made. These three words comprised the message Gloria had brought her in secret the day Lysander died – thrilling to imagine the dangers its various carriers must have risked as it was passed from hand to hand, from boat to ship, through stormy seas, to land to rider, to Gloria, to its desired destination in the pretty little hands of the fair Emily. She saw the words circling the moon, she saw them in the glowing timbers, she saw them writ large behind her eyelids, and she heard them in her blood like a distant promise of terrible thunder:

PATIENCE: WE COME

XXVI

AWN IN THE forest, light as drab as sodden newsprint; stodgy grey bark, grey bushes, grey scrubby patches of grass on a grey ground, all informed by the continual dreary dripping of drops of dew from the tired grey leaves overhead; shapeless gobs of charred black wafted in from the previous night's fire gave the only variation to the generally flat tone. Even Nick Bottom, huddled under a makeshift shelter of dead broken branches and a busted cartwheel, was as greyly indeterminate as his surroundings. Where had the deep dark greens and browns gone, the depths where the day-long sun never penetrated? All was thinned out and open now, lacking the fascination and the mystery of receding shapes and bends. Where were the pastel-blue shades at the lips of bonny bright clearings, where the colours that had been yellow and lime-green and scarlet with exuberant, unchallenged life? No life revived to meet the dawn, until one of the charred fragments burst, not into flame, but a sharp trilled song, and proved itself a blackbird.

Nick opened his eyes and stared disbelieving at the bird. It carried on singing and dipped its head, fanned its tail a little, but no mate answered. And the drip, drip as the damp night shrank away was unabated.

Reluctantly, Nick persuaded himself to get up and shake about, thrashing his arms and stamping numbed feet. The blackbird shrieked and fled. Nick made his way to the nearest

— 187 —

dribbling stream and cupped his hand to drink. Fortunately he breathed before drinking and then examined the water more fastidiously. There was a place below the city wall which released a stream like that. Nick turned away and endured the longer walk to the river. That, being well away from the site of the camp, ran pure as ever, and after he'd quenched his thirst and splashed his face Nick felt more like a human being, one who could at least recall what being alive had been like.

Well, Nick, he said to himself, you thought you knew loneliness, but here are none of the comforts you had then. Yesterday you awoke with tender Molly, and a hot meal and a fairly likely future. Today your guts grumble and your skin complains and you've no future but more of the same or worse. It's a bad job, Nick, and you'd better pull yourself up before you get as maudlin as those pitiful knights.

He clapped his hands as if about to get down to heavy work, looked around hopefully, clapped his hands again and, seeing nothing of promise, took the initiative and started walking to where his cottage used to stand, humming a frivolous tune for companionship. Nick had no receptacle for his faith but his own volition and common sense. A man moving is a man alive, was his practical belief. You could be reflective on the move, but your reflections couldn't turn stagnant because movement itself was too affirmative to allow the backward slide. So he walked and hummed and talked to himself, and observed that the monotonous grey was fading as the rising sun drenched the land in its fresh new dyes. Soon there were colours enough to warm his creative heart; he admired the textures of the fields, the sparkling highlights fairy-dancing on the endless weave of the river, the flowers, rabbits by the bank, larks ascending . . . Nick breathed deep and forgot hunger: here was beauty enough to sustain him for several days, and whoever needed to plan confidently further than that?

The gigantic wall of the arena loomed dimly in the distance, but there were no soldiers and he was safe to wander past the remains of the fire, down to the rubbish-strewn bank where trees

— 188 —

and a cottage had once sheltered from careless intruders. Soon he located broken pieces of furniture which he recognised as fragments from his former life: a chair back, two table legs, a twisted loom. He sifted through, not too closely, not allowing himself to bother too much, simply on the off-chance of retrieving something for use. Hard to say, then, whether it was mere chance or some better organised providence that arranged his movements to take him to the brink of the river, persuaded him to tarry on the edge, directed his eyes to gaze at one not very interesting object until he reached out and tugged the shaft of burnt stick out of the wet earth and unwrapped the dirty linen which had been impaled with it. Chance or providence it was certainly astonishing to Nick when a bedraggled but otherwise unharmed Oberon turned to blink at his deliverer. And not only Oberon, for beneath him, protected by him, crouched Titania. They leapt free and immediately tested their wings in two dizzying little blurs of colour. They flew spirals up and down and darted amongst the leaves of grass, under buttercups, over daisies, in and out of cowslips, delighting in the glorious day as if it was the first of its kind.

Nick, meanwhile, set to work turning over every stone and bit of wood, moving and unlocking every possible trap he could find until the air around was dense with whirling laughing fairies – hundreds, where there had been tens of thousands, but hundreds were better than none at all, filling the air like flurries of dandelion seeds and dragonflies.

'Mortals are wicked fools,' Puck declared angrily, trying out his wings and finding they would still carry him, if at considerably reduced speeds. 'I'll make it my business to do 'em mischief henceforth!'

'But you always have done!'

'Playfully, not in earnest malice.'

'It was a mortal who saved you,' Oberon warned him.

'No, it was Nick, and he's different.'

'That's true,' Titania said softly. 'In all our travels there are very few like Nick, and none so truly innocent as he used to be.'

'I am not as I was,' Nick admitted soberly. 'Those halcyon days are wiped out now, and there's no return from knowledge to nature. I'm a changed man, and I've all but lost you, but I'll do what I can to help you here.'

'There's nothing to be done,' Oberon said gravely. 'This has happened. Ignorant men have destroyed what they disbelieved. We cannot make a forest, Nick. We must move on to find the virgin places far from men. The forest has ended and we must begin our wandering, though we may never find a homeland sweet as this.'

'With all your travels, friends, couldn't you have foreseen this?'

'We can only be in one place at a time. I knew an end was made here, as there is no future to be returned to in this place, but that didn't provide a means of avoiding our disaster. But be of good cheer when you think of us, because we know there are new places – we have visited ourselves there, and even though we separate, we survive.'

'And,' Nick hesitated to ask, 'what of me?'

'I'm afraid we shall not meet again in your mortal life. You too must go from here, and though I search the world I never find you.'

Just then Nick heard a heavy sort of noise some way behind, but the fairies didn't vanish so he knew it wasn't soldiers creeping up to arrest him. It was no threat at all. There, chewing through the rubbish, was his poor old friend Dewdrop. It was evident that Dewdrop had come to be near Nick Bottom, but he didn't come closer, preferring to chew nonchalantly, as if he hadn't taken in any of the riverside commotion.

Nick tried to be equally relaxed as he strolled over, but the closer he came the clearer was it that Dewdrop had suffered terribly. The old long cuts had healed but left ugly welts; his coat was dreadfully shabby, his back drooped, his legs and flanks shivered as nervously as paper in a breeze; worse, there were recent cuts about which greedy flies buzzed. Teeth had torn at him. The noble horses, Nick guessed, taking it out on Dewdrop

— 190 —

for unseating Arcite. When he extended his arm his donkey flinched away.

'There, there, old pal,' Nick said sorrowfully, and touched his friend's sinewy neck. 'Don't fear me, I shan't do you harm. There, there, now, you know me, don't you? How you've been in the wars since we parted! Forgive me, for not looking after you as a friend should – or anyway, if you can't forgive, just let me bathe your wounds. I'll look after you, Dewdrop. To tell the simple truth, I think I need you more than you need me, though my wounds are beneath my skin where the eye needn't grieve.'

He led his limping donkey to the river, found a cloth and rinsed it through and through, then cleaned the wounds and spoke lovingly all the while. Dewdrop didn't speak – he'd suffered too long at the hands of men to use their tongue with pleasure – but in his balance and attitude he made it plain that he too was relieved to have found the weaver and a touch of kindness at last.

So engrossing was this glad and sad reunion that Nick failed to see for some time that all his friends had silently taken their leave. What he then saw was meat, bread and wine, and he knew they'd used their powers to scavenge about the city, and had brought him a feast as their token of parting in friendship.

Nick sat and ate his fill.

'Well,' he said, as robustly as he could, 'Oberon has shown his tribe the way, and we must use his sense. Today is a beginning, Dewdrop. What once was is gone, and it serves no purpose to wait here moping with memories and planning on might-have-beens. Even in my innocence you couldn't have said I was that sort of dreamer!' He paused, waiting for the sarcastic retort Dewdrop would have furnished in happier times, but none came. 'Well, let's study the situation, old pal. We can't tarry here with the best of the forest robbed from us. We can't return to Athens – those noble nags have got it in for you, and their masters would pretty soon have it in for me. We don't fit too nicely into civilised society, though I've never been against a bit of good company. I reckon we sustain ourselves best outside city

— 191 —

bounds, living by natural laws which don't have to tally with Theseus's. I've great respect for the man, and should tell him so to his face, but I don't suit the pattern, so I'd best be on my way. We'll find the sea, then take passage to another country.'

He wanted to say more, build a momentum as Theseus could, but it was beyond him. So, feeling plenty had been left unsaid, feeling less optimistic than he wanted to, Nick Bottom wrapped his remaining food in a cloth, put the cloth on a stick, the stick over his shoulder, and set off at a pace Dewdrop could easily follow.

They walked all day, keeping well away from main roads, and although he chatted to his donkey most of the time Nick couldn't stop his thoughts returning to Molly. Their love had evolved so quietly that he had taken it for granted, as he took every turn in fortune for granted. He was coming to understand that that didn't mean his love was superficial. Now he remembered her unprompted kindness, her prettiness, her ready understanding of his temperament, her straightforward honesty, even her affection for her father, and it dawned on him that the loss of Molly was just as momentous as the loss of his precious innocence.

'There are stages in a life,' he observed as he walked. 'But you don't know until you pass out of one and lose it. We must be commencing a new stage now, and who knows but it will be as rich as those we've lived through hitherto? I do wish Molly could share it, though, for it doesn't seem to me she was a stage I could finish with ever. I shall have to be a sadder and a wiser man, shan't I? But I'd rather not. I love Molly and need her love, and the right thing would be to watch our children grow and have bacon sandwiches together, and make new dyes to delight her with, and learn her kindness and its source.' He fell silent and trudged unhappily for several miles. Dewdrop followed. Both had downcast heads. 'Fair enough,' Nick Bottom declared at last, 'I'll try and think no more of that. It's painfully obvious we generally don't get what we want in life. I'll tell myself she isn't pining, and that my pining is one-sided and childish. We'll find a cove with a path down to the sea, and there we'll pass the night.

— 192 —

Tomorrow we'll find a ship and then there'll be no looking back. Cheer up, old chum, misery has its duration, as all things.'

They rested in a little grove near enough their destination for the smell of the sea to be distinct and appealing. The sun was sliding away but the air was mild and that tangy smell was making Nick impatient to be setting off from land. Currents of memory travelled through the earth wherever he put his feet, and only the sea would free him. But when he readied himself to continue Dewdrop pointedly ignored him.

'You think this is a good spot to camp tonight, do you?' he conceded. 'Fair enough – it's an improvement on last night and that's the truth! So at least we are advancing, eh? Tell you what, I'll just stroll on to get a look at the sea. You rest up and I'll rejoin you later. If you're awake I'll tell you stories. Even if you're asleep.' He grinned and stroked Dewdrop's shabby coat, sincerely grateful for the comfort he could give and get.

The cliff was much nearer than he'd supposed, at the top of the first slow incline, and a little way along he saw there was a broad sloping track that zig-zagged roughly but usably down into a long silver sandy bay.

Nick dropped on to his stomach in fear.

Below were anchored five of the biggest ships he'd ever seen. Longboats were working between them and the beach. The light was poor down there but he could make out horses strung on lines being led ashore, and many more horses already crowding a long stretch of beach. Fires had been lit at intervals, and around the fires were soldiers, just as he'd seen in Theseus's camp the night before the attack on Thebes. But Nick knew Theseus had no army out because there was peace in Athens, bought with the death of his forest. These soldiers were arriving, and there must have been hundreds exercising on the sands.

I'll get no passage out from *this* bay! was his first thought, and he nearly scrambled back to Dewdrop there and then. But he had to learn more.

Why should I care? he asked himself as he descended stealthily

— 193 —

from rock to shrub to rock, realising that the path was good enough for that entire army to march up.

Athens ain't my business, he told himself, and he believed it, too. Yet still he crawled closer. And then at last he saw the soldiers by firelight, their golden bodies and braided hair, their muscular thighs and arms, their great bronzed breasts – this was the terrible Amazon tribe, which outfought men and ate them and drank their blood and followed unnatural practices!

Nick shook with fear and awkward arousal, and clung behind a rock unable to retreat. He remembered another night, standing with Tom Snout and Peter Quince, remembered taking a sheet from his jerkin and hearing his own voice read out 'Cum quik', and the accusation that sang from the angelic child, and the sight of Hippolyta, who had wrapped her powerful legs around him and laughed in his arms and told him Titania had sent her to make a man of him; he remembered his ecstatic awakening as a man, then seeing his vision transformed into the warrior queen, wife of Theseus – 'Cum quik', and the charge of treachery and the sentence that wrote off his friends and most of his life.

Not knowing how he had moved at all the weaver found himself huddling in the grove next to Dewdrop.

'I wasn't set free at all,' he babbled. 'It was another cruel trap. I have led us to a terrible vengeance. Yet how could Theseus know I'd choose this bay when I didn't know it myself? And why am I pursued? Where is my offence? I lay with Hippolyta. I let Palamon see Emily through my window. I called to you and caused the death of Arcite. Am I Jupiter?'

He talked on, sometimes silently, sometimes aloud, sometimes almost making sense of the tapestry of events, but as long as he saw himself as their central feature the presence of the Amazon army threw him off balance. Time and again his fractured brain replayed the scene with Tom and Peter and his reading of the letter, until he believed he had driven himself mad and might as well go throw himself in the sea like Egeus for all the peace he'd ever find.

But then, though he hadn't been working consciously at this

side of the pattern, understanding came upon him. 'Snug the joiner was no spy! And if he was no spy, no more was I a traitor. I can't say I blame the women, but I never threatened the rule of Theseus and I deserved no punishment whatever. By gum, Dewdrop, I don't believe this army is here to capture me at all! It's Athens they're after, and I bet Theseus knows no more of this than me – none of us knows anything, we just blunder about and get entangled and *look* connected!'

Dewdrop turned his head slowly and by the moon's little light Nick still saw that the expression was as condescending as he deserved. Still the same old Dewdrop, cynical, derisive and utterly loyal! Without waiting for his master to stumble towards the necessary decision, Dewdrop shook himself and struggled to his feet and quietly commenced walking back in the direction they had fled from.

'Don't worry,' Nick assured him, 'you needn't come the whole way. I know you want to avoid the company of my callous fellow men. When we near the city you wait beneath its walls. All I intend is to warn Molly and her father. If I were a man who'd be listened to I'd warn Theseus, but I reckon he'd arrest me before I got a word out. At all events, I must save Molly, and if I have to die thereafter, well, what's the odds!'

And so curious is the texture of a man's desires that the journey back to Athens, no matter the fears that prompted it, was light with happy yearnings. Even Dewdrop's step was jauntier now, and they kept to the main roads and made good time by starlight and moon.

—— 195 ——

XXVII

THE MOST NOTABLE feature of Palamon's apartment was an enormous bed draped in creamy satin. Its austere beauty would have chilled the balls off a bull; if Diana had demanded a new altar this cold centre-piece would have served the purpose well. When it was installed Palamon thought it the perfect shrine for Emily. As the nuptial hour approached, however, he realised he'd left something important out – he just hadn't connected sex with his feelings for Emily. To adapt his apartment at short notice the best he could do was bring in a lurid red arras, a few scatter cushions, and a small but shockingly explicit fresco depicting an amorous forest interlude. This was still drying when the wedding ceremony took place.

It was the first thing poor Emily saw when she entered, for she refused to acknowledge the giant bed and came into the room with her eyes averted. She saw a sketchy forest, glanced lower for the classical subject, and saw a leaden-winged Titania going down on a hairy Oberon, who had a grotesquely obscene leer on his mug. Before even seeing what Puck was up to Emily fainted.

The arras had been pulled tactfully in front of the fresco by the time she awoke. She was lying out perfectly straight, like a corpse, covered from neck to ankle in a white nightgown. Quickly ascertaining that she hadn't got to heaven, Emily sat bolt upright and glared at her husband, whose cheerful red nightshirt added fuel to her fury.

— 196 —

'Have you done it?' she demanded coldly.

'I called your maidservants as soon as you fainted. I returned a few minutes ago and dismissed them.'

'But have you done it?'

'I flatter myself that you'd know, beloved.'

'Are you going to do it?'

'Emily, you are understandably hesitant, but rest assured that what we'll do is done by men and women everywhere. Far from unnatural, within marriage it is a sacred duty.'

'When you've done it I'll denounce you and Theseus will have you castrated and killed.'

'I know the law, but, you see, we're the envy and dream of Athens tonight, and whatever we do will be what is expected. I don't mean to hurt you, and there's no reason for you to hurt me as you're doing now.'

'Other women find you attractive, I suppose?'

'Well, frankly, everyone finds me attractive, yes. We are made for each other.'

'I am maid for no one. My only desire is to keep my vows of chastity. Soon I shall be delivered. Palamon, can't you understand that I have no interest in you? Why must I be tormented?'

'You are my wife. I don't mean that's why you must be tormented – you're very frustrating, Emily. I've loved you constantly since first I saw you in the garden. I am alive only for this moment.'

'Why not die now, then, and take it with you?'

'This *coming* moment.'

'You conform to type – beneath the show of courtesy the beast slavers and I must be sacrificed. No one hears a virtuous maid!'

'Emily, my dear, you've long known that either Arcite or I should have you. I am no more a beast than any other fellow. You'll find no impropriety here.'

'Save that no one consulted me! I didn't ask to marry. Quite the reverse. I'd rather die!'

'But it isn't a matter for choice. Marriages would be impossibly complicated if *women* had a say! You get the honour reflected by me – I give that willingly. I don't understand your attitude. You seem to want a man's authority without the burdens and challenges that validate it. I wonder if you've ever seen a man – do you know that we are different?' In a hot-tempered impulse he suddenly wrenched his nightshirt over his head and flung it at her. 'Look at me! Can you hate what you see?'

Emily obeyed. What she saw was neither horrifying nor appealing. 'Hah!' she cried. 'Walnuts and an almond!' And she laughed cruelly at his far from straining equipment. 'Here, then,' she countered his unfortunate attempt to placate her. 'If I can't plead with you and can't beat you off, here, if this is what you demand – ruin me!' And so saying she sprang to her feet and flung away her nightgown, and there she stood in the middle of the gigantic bed, rigidly at attention, beautiful and as inviolable as a statue. 'Hurry up,' she said grimly. 'Get it done!'

'No,' Palamon protested, suffering worse agonies than he'd endured in prison. 'This isn't the way it's supposed to be. You are more wonderful naked than clothed, Emily, but you face me with such defiant ignorance that you disappoint me in yourself. You're wilful and strange, and only have tenderness for yourself. You may have the bed. I shall retire to my room and have one of your maidservants. Good night, selfish!'

Emily was taken aback by his prompt departure, but took it as a victory, donned his red nightshirt and paraded up and down while Palamon vainly awaited her contrite knock at his door.

They weren't fated to be famous lovers, but to fade from history almost as completely as you or I.

XXVIII

THE ARMY MARCHED overnight, four hundred foot-soldiers, another hundred and fifty cavalry, more in wagons. Ever since Hippolyta's capture they'd been preparing for this battle, always hoping it would be proved unnecessary, hoping Hippolyta would murder her abductor and vindicate the rights of women, but licking their wounds and strengthening their numbers anyway, until the needs of honour could be deferred no longer. There was no hesitation in the way these proud women marched and rode, backs straight, shoulders high, chins and breasts pointing firmly forward. They knew surprise was a great ally when meeting a force of superior strength. Emily's infantile letters had been little help in ascertaining the precise number and disposition of the tyrant's troops, so the Amazons had set out without expecting to win a decisive victory. What they wanted was to die fighting in the lair of the oppressor, and they were truly terrifying because nothing but abject surrender could sway them in their purpose. Their diet, exercise, healthy living had all been in preparation for this conflict. Death was their goal, and they were in a state of taut, controlled ecstasy as they closed on it.

Gloria had received their advance message and she crouched at the little side gate in the dark to let Emily's rescuers in – naively, Gloria had expected a few Scythian matrons to come, find Emily, and make off into the night again, disturbing no one. When she saw what was about to happen she fled and locked her doors and

—— 199 ——

made Lysander's children hide under the bed in the sick room with her.

Her egress had been noticed by Helena, who was staying with her family at Lysander's place. Helena told Demetrius, who sighed and said he'd follow the girl at a distance. Helena was asleep by the time Gloria returned, and so didn't hear her husband tapping at the door of the sick room and telling Gloria that she was every bit as beautiful as her late mistress, Hermia, had been. Helena didn't hear him slip outside and round to the window, which he threatened to break if Gloria wouldn't admit him. Helena failed to hear Lysander's sons defending Gloria in their father's name. All Helena heard was her brave husband suddenly yelling to her hoarsely to block the doors and arm herself and hide their children. She heard his sword clashing against many swords, and the cries of the determined young women assaulting him. She got her children through to Gloria and, leaving the five boys together, these two women grabbed short swords and went out ready to fight. But the Amazons were gone, and all they could do was retrieve the heroic corpse.

'What a man!' Helena cried through her tears. 'He never let on that he loved me so much!'

'There was too much love in him,' Gloria added quietly. 'Come, we must bind him – his brains are on the carpet.'

'Yes, clean him, the children mustn't see him like this. Oh, what a man, though! Deep down the truest that ever lived – I always knew!'

A couple of guards making their unhurried rounds of the peaceful city were killed silently as the first group returned, then the main gates were opened and as light stole upon the city the invaders poured up the hill and spread through every street. At first they ignored the lesser dwellings if no one met them, most heading straight for the garrison, the remainder taking the palace, which appeared entirely unguarded.

Nick Bottom watched the opening stages of the conflict from the top room in the tower, Molly and her father behind him, and with every door locked and bolted beneath. It was remarkable how smoothly the invasion went. Nick thought it far less sickening than the sack of Thebes or the tournament; no formal speeches, no attempt to impose an ethics of justice on the inexorable flow. If this was how women went about war, he thought, they were on to something impressive. Even as he watched the last riders rounding a bend and the dim dawn streets resuming their calm, the leading fighters had commenced their bloody struggle at the garrison, and a crack team of ruthless commandos had entered the palace.

Palamon had slept badly. To begin with his mind kept filling with brilliant rejoinders and the gratifying sight of a humbled Emily begging him to be her lord; this fantasy took the edge off his appetite for authority and, calmer, he thought over the encounter from Emily's point of view. He soon saw that he'd been wrong to treat her like any other woman – that wasn't why he'd loved her. Essentially she was more like a child, frightened of the unknown. He'd woo her with sweets, tenderness and a pace so slow as to be beyond detection.

He thought he heard a noise from the bedroom, and smiled forgivingly. If she was still awake he might as well pop his head in, just to reassure her. First he washed and perfumed himself so as to look as unlike a slavering beast as possible, then he opened the door and peeped around in a friendly, boyish manner designed to win affection and remove fear.

The room was crammed with pretty-well naked women, a few with tiny skirts or loincloths, most with amulets, lucky charms and leather belts about the waist or worn across the shoulder. All were heavily armed. At a glance he saw innumerable rounded bottoms, spears, bows and swords, a few large breasts and, through that fierce fantastic forest, he saw Emily, almost as he had last seen her, standing on the huge satin bed draped from head to foot in his rich red nightshirt.

And Emily somehow saw Palamon. And pointed, just as she'd done long ago at Nick Bottom. 'There!' she cried out. 'He's the wicked man!'

As the women turned Palamon glimpsed axes too, and just

—— 201 ——

managed to swing his door shut before weapons thudded into it. Attack! He threw the lock and dragged a chest of weapons against the door. Amazon attack! He grabbed his best sword and held his ground as if nailed to it. He soon could be! What to do? Arouse the palace! Defend Theseus! *Shift!*

Palamon cautiously opened the small door into the long internal corridor, saw no one, and slipped out. He knew which room a dozen knights were sleeping in, called a warning into the dark, then hurried on. At another room he stopped. Entered swiftly. Hurried to the bed. Here was Theseus's son, Hippolytus, sleeping peacefully. Palamon gathered him up and made for the short corridor connecting that room with the great bedchamber of Theseus.

Hippolyta had snuggled up to her husband even before the women entered the main gates, for she liked to bring him lazily from sleep into lovemaking, liked that evidence of her sensual prowess, liked to feel his old sensitive parts grow hard as youth against her body, to hear him go from snoring to low groaning and, sometimes, tender words. And instead of resuming sleep they had taken a light breakfast and lain comfortably side by side, talking idly and joking pleasantly about the fine time Palamon and Emily must be having, how much fun it was to be young and so forth.

One of the guards had burst in to warn them then, and they just had time to reach for weapons before a spear emerged through the guard's belly and he dropped, a mass of bristling warriors where he had stood.

Theseus had his mighty club in his hand and the women hesitated. Several had shaved heads but he saw that they were all striking examples of womanhood, and he sighed, suddenly weary. He let his club rest on the rumpled bed and then sat heavily at the foot, laying one hand over Hippolyta's covered ankle and twisting to gaze back sadly at his wife.

'So,' he said, accepting his defeat, 'it's come this way after all! Impressive, my love, you've used your freedom to chain yourself to your past, and I am done.'

Hippolyta said nothing, did nothing, and the women edged in closer until one separated herself and took the initiative.

—— 202 ——

'Have you no stomach for this part, Theseus? When women catch you unprepared you stand no better than we did. You choose the coward's collapse, but it makes no difference. Make your peace with your gods, watery man, and we will dispatch you shortly. As for you, Hippolyta, it's as we feared: we find you a willing accomplice to this tyrant's bed. This is not your rescue, Hippolyta, so do you elect an honourable death along with your sister, or will you beg to rejoin us like the schemer you always were?'

'I am your Queen,' Hippolyta said, and then paused as if she might indeed be assessing any options for survival.

'No longer,' the new apparent leader jumped in. 'We need no queen. We are many and strong. Perhaps you may keep your miserable life if you submit to re-education, but Queen you'll never be!'

'Why did you plan this, sweet?' Theseus asked softly, not having taken in anything of what was being said. 'It was hardly necessary. Do these ladies know we've made it a capital offence for any man to assault a woman? Would they care if they knew? What are they after from us? We have no defence now against an army of women. When did you plot against me? All this while, as you won me over and reformed the laws?'

'No, Theseus,' Hippolyta declared, leaping from the bed and standing up naked beside him, urging him to stand with her. 'I didn't plan this, nor do I sanction it. These bitches are after me, too.' She faced them head on and snarled, 'You, you crawling heap of shit – dare you face me in single combat? You with the voice! Any of you? By God, you're a sorry crew! What *are* you fighting for? Emily's prissy little secret letters? To conquer your fear of men? Eh? Well, most of them are limp and vicious enough to fear, I grant you. But not this man of mine!' From the corner of her mouth she whispered, 'Arm yourself, lover,' and then she snarled again defiantly, 'I'm a married woman, by my choice – is that what you can't take, that I'll let a man be my equal? Then take this!' And suddenly she sprang down like a lioness upon her spitting enemies.

Just then the side door opened and Palamon rushed through, carrying Hippolytus. He set the lad safely aside and raced for-

—— 203 ——

ward. The swords of three women slashed at Hippolyta. Suddenly Theseus burst from his trance and in a moment was using his club generously, Palamon working away nearby. Neither man suffered a serious injury and in no time their assailants lay dead. But so did Hippolyta.

As he knelt cradling his brave wife Theseus's anguish almost exceeded the love he had had. How very like his living wife she looked, warm from their bed and with his seed within her even now, this dead warrior! Her blood clung lovingly to his arms and cheek. How could the gods permit this, when she had fought so bravely? His massive shoulders heaved and a rage for justice shook out the tired muscles and coursed through every vein as he stood and stared madly at the broken forms.

'Kill the women!' he spat venomously, and again, 'Kill the women!'

He saw his son crying near the bed and rushed over, picked the boy up and tucked him under one arm. 'Come on, Palamon, come beside me to protect my boy. I must get him away to safety.'

The fighting was already intense in the main corridor and they began beating a way through. Palamon insisted that he had to reach Emily, despite Theseus's warning that it was she who had brought down this savage retribution without cause. A number of women lay dead and bleeding around the entrance, and there were more bodies inside the door, but no more fighting. No one was in the room. Palamon looked about him anxiously, then looked again at the bed and touched Theseus's arm so that Theseus followed his gaze. On the bed was a dash of red, the nightshirt, with Emily's little feet protruding. A cry broke from Palamon's heart. 'Emily!'

And then he started, aghast, as the corpse moved, slowly sat up, and in a weightless way stood. Emily stood on the bed as she'd done before. She stretched out her arms, palms outwards, and there were arrows through her hands, and there was an arrow in her ribs, and she looked through Palamon and made a step forward on the satin sheet, and he saw no agony in her face but an expression he had seen on no face living, and no dead face come to that. Her lips parted. 'I am delivered,' she sighed.

Theseus pulled Palamon away. 'All is corruption here. We have to defend the garrison.'

By now it was nearly full day, and all over the city people were screaming and houses blazing. The Amazons were winning. Seeing this, Theseus passed his son into the care of Palamon, and gave Palamon instructions. Thus it was that Palamon arrived outside the tower. The main doors had been burnt and smashed aside and he entered cautiously and made his way over burning furniture, through other broken doors and up the stairs. As he neared the top he passed the first body. A naked woman, sprawled upside-down, her head caved in. Sheltering Hippolytus as well as he could, Palamon pressed on. Two more bodies. He reached the top and the final door, which hung ajar.

Sword ready, he called out, 'Is there a man called Nick Bottom here?'

'Here, sir,' came a frightened but unhesitating reply.

'I have orders from Theseus. Come out, man.' He only had to wait a moment. 'You've held your position, Nick. Remember me?'

'Aye, sir, you gave me the kind advice once.'

'Stop shivering, Nick, you've done a man's work here already.'

'No, sir, only necessary work. We thought ourselves safe enough till they fired the doors and used a battering ram. Even then I couldn't have defended myself, but when the first wanted to run me through Molly clanged her with the frying pan, such a whack it killed the poor girl on the instant. The next pair said they were for Molly, so I had to grab each by the neck, sir, to stop them hurting Molly. And I stopped them. It's a horrible thing we've done. They're young girls, sir, as innocent and hopeful, no doubt, as I was in my other life.'

'There's no time for this – they may be back in force any time, and I have to rejoin Theseus. If we lose the men in the garrison we've lost.'

'Stay here with us, then, or run.'

—— 205 ——

'This is the son of Theseus. Protect him at all costs. Flee the city.'

'I'm not leaving.'

'You have no choice – orders from Theseus.'

'I go nowhere without Molly – orders from myself.'

'We'll go, Nick,' Molly called to him. 'Father says there's nothing to defend, save us, and we'll do better on the open road.'

'Here, then,' Palamon said, and shoved the child forward. 'Get to a harbour. Here's coin. Bring him up as your own until he can take his rightful place. Good luck!'

'Good luck to you, sir, and to your lady wife.'

Palamon could have knocked Nick over for that, but he growled strangely instead and hurried away to add what strength he could to the dismal battle.

Nick, Hippolytus, Molly and her father managed to sneak through the side-streets and out of the city gates. Dewdrop was waiting down by the river. None of them looked back until they had passed the great empty arena, then all they saw was a black pall of smoke. The boy was exhausted, probably in shock. Nick lifted him carefully and set him on Dewdrop's back. 'If he gets too much for you I'll carry him on my shoulders,' he whispered. Dewdrop snorted, which seemed to mean he could carry such a small load well enough.

And so the slow disheartened band of refugees left Athens for the last time, with no illusions left to break, no hopes for a more settled future, no plans whatever, and nothing to say that could light a spark of cheer.

XXIX

ALL THAT DAY the battle for nothing raged. By nightfall many more had fled and found Nick Bottom's band camped in the grove near the headland. Some had food, others boxes of valuables which they clutched tightly; one man had three horses laden with tables, chairs, rugs, pots – he said he wasn't leaving the city, just waiting till he could go back. Once aired, this possibility seemed to be the hope of at least half the refugees. They didn't mind if Theseus had lost. Whoever ruled would claim to represent their best interests. *They* had no enemies. Gloria feared she might be obliged to walk the streets bare-breasted and refused to go back if that was likely to follow. Helena said it wouldn't be so dreadful and one or two men were still bold enough to voice agreement.

Peter Quince scorned talk of returning under a new régime, and he was listened to, as the most eminent man in the grove. 'I was minding my business,' he said, and his wife kept nodding agreement, 'when my door was kicked out and in comes a giant woman with an axe tall as herself. She spits on her hands and takes one swipe and lops off my head, easy as knocking an acorn off its cup. It flies away and strikes the mantelpiece. I says to her, "Mind my head, if you please," and she lets out a scream and scrams. "Come, wife," I says, "we're leaving while we still have legs beneath us." Now, if a tribe of women rule I'll not make peace. I rose to some fame under Theseus. He never

—— 207 ——

entered my home uninvited, for he respects a working man's need of privacy. What's more he never took an axe to my head. No, Athens is finished.' He stopped, then remembered he had left out the essential humorous touch. His blushing wife handed him what had been his familiar and outlandishly tall hat, and he held it up for all to see how much had been whacked away. 'We must build elsewhere, I say, and you're lucky to have me along. In short, you are more fortunate than those who stick to Athens, since I shall not be on hand to rebuild her as I rebuilt Thebes. I have my designs on the future.'

Quite a few supported Quince, but Nick Bottom kept his own counsel. He thought people should make up their own minds what to do and then do it, without being swayed by rhetoric. He didn't mind the way so many had barged into his little camp but he had no intention of following or leading anyone anywhere, except for the small band he had accepted responsibility for. A man had no real capacity, he reasoned, for caring about bigger numbers of human beings than that.

The little boy stayed close to Nick Bottom all night, and slept holding his hand, snuggling between Nick and Molly. Everyone assumed he was their son, and he was likely to stay safe as long as that assumption was made.

'Well, Nick, what's it to be?' asked Peter Quince directly at daybreak. 'Are you lingering with these backward-looking folk who'll adapt to any new indignity rather than decide anything for themselves, or will you be the free man you once were and join my people in embarking on a new life?'

'Do come with us, Nick,' Francis Flute pleaded. 'You were dead so long it's cruel to have you back and lose you right away. Come with us to the new country and make us happy again – think what times we'll have!'

'I'm sorry, Francis,' Nick said regretfully. 'Large numbers bring misfortune, and if I've learned nothing else, I've learned that I love Molly and want to miss misfortune. If we stay all together something bad will happen, because people are different and differences don't settle for long. I'm sorry, I won't risk it.'

'Which way are you heading, then? Do you know a good town somewhere? We can adapt, Nick, can't we? Let's all follow Nick – he'll know good places and think up happy schemes.'

'No, Francis, let Peter lead you. A carpenter's more valuable than a weaver at the start of a venture like this. Besides, I don't know where I'm going – just to go and be gone is the point of my movements.'

He wouldn't be dissuaded, so finally they had to wish each other well and part company, and by the time the last of Quince's followers had shuffled out of the grove Nick Bottom was leading Dewdrop after them, but at a distance and a slower pace.

'Are we going with them?' Molly's father asked, perplexed.

'No, Father, we're on the same path awhile, but our way is separate. Trust Nick.'

'I do.'

Molly held the frail old man's arm and kept back a couple of yards because she thought Nick wanted to talk to Hippolytus. Actually it was Dewdrop he confided in, but even Molly didn't know about Dewdrop. Fairies she'd seen with her own wondering eyes, but a discoursing donkey demanded another order of credulity. Nick had tried to tell her once, but she'd only laughed and kissed him for his delightful imagination.

After about an hour's trudging along the coastal track in the dust raised by Peter's party, Nick noticed a solitary figure leaning on a staff some way ahead. He was noticeable because of his size and stillness. A wanderer, but immovable as a statue, he acknowledged no one.

'Dewdrop,' Nick said softly, 'I don't know who that may be, but if he's an assassin waiting to pounce on your precious young rider, be ready to charge away the moment we draw abreast, and don't stop for me or anyone till you're sure Hippolytus is safe.' He patted Dewdrop and then stepped back to speak to Molly. 'If I'm stopped by the hooded fellow ahead, Moll, you and your father must keep walking. Never look back.'

—— 209 ——

Nervously trying for nonchalance Nick strolled on. As he got close he watched the staff and the way the two hands held it – to use it as a weapon the man's grip would have to change, but as yet no movement was discernible.

'There are many travellers on the road today,' came a voice from within the hooded cape. 'Is this usual in your country?'

Though the question made Nick jump it was reasonable, and he was unable to pass on without offering a civil reply. Uncomfortably he stopped, reaching to push Dewdrop along and ensure the others kept moving. 'No, sir, uncommon – are you a stranger? Are you for Athens?'

'Not Athens – I hear a tyrant lives there, named Theseus.'

'Well, you'd have had no cause to fear entering Athens when Theseus was there, but these travellers represent a change in fortune.'

'Stay, tell me more. I'm anxious to learn of this man and his downfall.'

'I'd rather keep up.'

'You are in a hurry?'

'Why hurry when you may be approaching danger greater than you left behind? No, I do not hurry, but I'd rather move along just the same.'

'I must insist that you wait with me.'

'I cannot, unless I know your purpose better.'

'Why are you so nervous, man? Have you a great treasure on that decrepit donkey, perhaps? Have you plundered Athens?'

'Those I will protect are with my donkey, sir, and I can't protect them unless I'm with them. My only treasure is those breathing creatures, sir, and I plan to keep them.'

'Very well.' The voice seemed to shrink back inside the hood. After a moment it came out again but sounded different. 'Nick, you are indeed a clever fool worth all my trust.' The wanderer straightened and flicked back his hood, revealing Theseus.

Nick was so taken aback he fell involuntarily to his knees.

'No, no,' Theseus protested quickly. 'Stand up, you are no worse a man than I. Stand, and call Molly back with my son.

— 210 —

There's no more to fear. We won the day, Nick. The women are dead or caged that would revolt. The battle is done. The law of Athens survives.'

The news was good yet it somehow failed to make Nick leap about; even Theseus didn't deliver it with any flourish.

'I'd like you to come with me,' Theseus continued amicably. 'I've known Molly since her father showed her to me as a baby; it was my plan that you should meet her. Her father helped me when, an unknown youth, I entered Athens as a stranger . . . but no more of that now. You, Nick, though you cannot know this, are of good stock and almost my relative. This will astonish you: your mother was Ariadne. I knew you were no traitor, but how was I to break the hold of the forest and force you to stay long enough to appreciate Molly? Do you believe me?'

'Well, you are Theseus and your powers are clearly beyond my ordinary comprehension. I think I'll believe in patches.'

'Well enough – you'll prove a good companion.'

But Nick refrained from an absolute faith in Theseus's omniscience. He didn't know he'd lain with Hippolyta; he didn't believe in Oberon and Titania. Theseus didn't understand the irreparable tragedy he had performed on the forest, either. All in all he was a man of cities.

'I hope you won't take me amiss,' Nick added, 'if we don't latch on to you, despite the indebtedness you've outlined for me. I prefer to mind my own business when I can, and I can't be transformed into a knight, sir, I am too resistant to heroic qualities. I'm dyed as I am for good or bad, and can't be made more without wreck to my fibres.'

'You think knights are bad men?'

'I think I should stay outside the law and live peaceably, the rest is not my business. I admire the work you attempt, but I think it ends in despair regardless of the good deeds woven through it. Whereas a man alone hurts no one, usually. If I can raise a few children and see them straight till they can see for themselves, I'll have done my duty so far as being civilised goes.'

'Well, that saddens me. Crete would be a happier land for

you, and I'd be happier with your company. I'm going on to Phaedra, who lacks a husband. I think my son will be loved there, and I too hope to find solace for all I've lost.'

'But you said the Amazons were subdued?'

'So they are, and my duty is done. But I count it a failure, and my people count me a failure. I won't impose myself further – perhaps if my wife had survived, but as it is let them elect new blood and discover if they can make a kinder constitution. I suspect I wasn't meant to settle any more than you. We're wanderers, you and I, and must make the best of it.'

They talked longer than Nick wanted to. It was touching that Theseus deigned to be so candid, but also embarrassing. Nick knew they could never be friends and still wondered why Theseus had singled him out. It was almost as if the great man saw something of himself in the simple weaver, or imagined a less burdensome life, maybe.

By mid-afternoon they'd reached a spot above the harbour and it was almost time to part. While Theseus conversed with the old jailor Nick walked aside and lifted the boy off the donkey so he could have a few private words with Dewdrop. But the boy didn't run over to his father and Nick faced one more surprise.

Dewdrop spoke. 'Leave the lad, Nick,' he said gruffly, wishing to sound abrupt and businesslike but failing obviously. 'You will have your wife for company from now on. I shall go with Theseus.'

'But Dewdrop, you can't!' Nick gasped, gobsmacked. 'Don't desert me, old friend!'

'It's no desertion, but this vulnerable lad Hippolytus can talk to me just as you used to, and I must travel with him.'

'Have you spoken to Hippolytus?' Nonplussed, Nick looked from Dewdrop to the boy, who smiled freshly. 'Hippolytus,' he asked in disbelief, 'does Dewdrop talk to you?'

'Of course. I love him. He's the best donkey in the world. And thank you, Mr Bottom, for all you've done.'

— 212 —

Innocence, Nick realised with awe, is not my property – just as well! And so there is hope yet.

'Very well, then,' he said, his voice like Dewdrop's thick with emotion. 'Very well.' He shook the boy's hand, and then flung his arms around Dewdrop's scraggy neck and kissed his long old nose. 'Goodbye. I'm glad for you, honestly, though my eyes sting. Good luck!'

'The best of it to you, Nick. Goodbye. Goodbye!'

And Theseus, standing tall, took Dewdrop's rein and began to walk slowly down the hill towards the glittering harbour, and only the boy looked back once to wave and blow kisses to the three silhouettes.

'We'd best be moving too,' Nick muttered eventually, sniffing.

'All will be well, Nick,' Molly said tenderly, taking his hand and recalling evenings when she'd watched him leaning on his spade and feared he would go and never return. 'Nothing is lost if memory is more fond than foul. There's a ship that waits for us as well.'

'Aye, there is, that's true. But from up here the sea looks a lonesome country.'

'No planting in it, to be sure,' the old man said shrewdly. 'But I have a sack of seed about my neck, and hope to see them in before the season's out.'

'And I have in me a somewhat similar promise,' Molly blushed shyly, 'conceived before your amnesty.'

Nick gazed gratefully into the face of the old man, then looked in astonished awakening hope into Molly's smiling face, and he felt ashamed of his own doubts. 'By gum, then,' he declared with braver resolve, 'I'd say we are a lucky crew, no matter what's gone before! Come, good Father, walk alongside us, and Molly, take hold of my arm in case you slip. Come, we'll cross that sea as if it was a springy meadow, and find a forest on the farther side, and there, far from meddling mortals make our cottage and our garden. I promise we'll not be wanderers long, for I am not like Theseus and the earth is still my friend.'

★

— 213 —

I told Oberon that that was all I had, and right away he made it obvious he was disappointed. He pressed so hard I admitted I did know a bit more, though it had nothing to do with Nick. Oberon insisted.

'Well, Theseus lived with Phaedra and Hippolytus grew up straight and strong. Then Phaedra noticed how handsome he was and fell for the boy, became obsessed, desperate. He was too innocent to know how to cope with that – I dare say he'd have talked it over with Dewdrop, if the donkey hadn't died of contented old age by then. Anyway, Hippolytus kept rejecting Phaedra and at last her lust went vicious. She ran crying to her husband and told him his son had raped her. Theseus went mad. And what he did was this: He knew Hippolytus liked racing a chariot along the coast, so he appealed to Poseidon who conjured up a huge bull from the depths. When the horses saw this terrifying thing they bolted, overturning the chariot. Hippolytus was dragged along until the life was out of him. Theseus learned the truth later, and Phaedra was so ashamed that she killed herself. Lives aren't happy.'

'It's all misery unfolding, isn't it?'

'One thing after another, Oberon – that's how you told me to tell it, though I thought it might come out jollier.'

'And you can't tell me if Nick had a happy ending?'

'It isn't in the nature of storytelling to check out such details as that – we finish at a point where you can assume the rest. But I'd say he had a good chance, being the man he was, and having Molly to look after him. But how about you? I've finished and you're still breathing normally. It looks as if your big worry was unfounded. You *do* go on from here.'

'I confess I'm mystified, Rob. Tell me, then, what happens now? Having written it out, do you burn it?'

'Don't talk so daft, mun! It's a *book*! There's no telling the sorts of people that might read it and find out you're still knocking about. I thought you'd banked on that.'

'No,' Oberon said thoughtfully, then he jumped up on to the typewriter and I had to stick out my finger smartly to stop him

— 214 —

falling into the keys, which were dangerously wet because I'd put a new ribbon in. 'But you give me an idea. Quick, explain all these buttons to me!'

'What for? They're just the symbols we make words and stuff with. These are the letters of the alphabet, the numbers are along the top row, and the rest is mainly bits of punctuation.'

'Yes, the punctuation – which is the smallest one?'

'This,' I said. 'It's called a full stop, or period.'

'How can it be both? One's an end and the other has duration. Never mind, I like ambiguity. I'm thinking of Molly's father, see.'

'You've lost me. I thought you were interested in language.'

'His sack of seeds, that's what I'm thinking. Dormant in the dark.'

'I'm sorry, Oberon, you're probably travelling somewhere else right now, because you're not making sense to me.'

'If I hide and go out in your book, maybe eventually I'll be opened by another mortal like Nick Bottom – one who believes in me. *You're* no use. It's not enough that I'm here chatting, I have to explain how and why, and where Titania's got to – I could tell you didn't believe we were in Hollywood, or that poor Puck's trapped himself on the moon.'

'You have to admit it's odd, if you're the King of the Fairies, that you bother so much with Nick Bottom, and that you don't seem able to protect yourself or your people.'

'The only powers we ever had were powers of movement. Our lives are of little consequence, but at least we know it, unlike your lot. We depend on those mortals who welcome us, so you could say we're just parasites, though in return we reduce a little of the misery of their existence. It isn't very important to you, perhaps, but that's the sum of it, and a more believing fellow would have given us a stronger part in the story. Now – watch me carefully.'

I shrugged, mildly exasperated, and watched. Oberon suddenly sprang up and stung the end of my nose. Then he leapt from it across to a blank sheet of A4, shrinking in flight, and

— 215 —

when he landed he looked for all the world like a full stop or period.

I waited, rubbing my nose (later I figured this was a sort of combined thank you and goodbye kiss, but you may think he just wanted to hurt me after such a long wait).

I waited, beginning to regret my attitude (though in fairness he was often tiresome, interrupting just when I had a good sentence going).

I waited. Nothing happened. So I went out and made a mug of coffee. While I sipped it I stared at the reduced Oberon for another five minutes or so, thinking over what he'd said about seeds and so on. Then it dawned on me what he was attempting and I laughed out loud, 'Hah!' just like that. I wish I'd asked him earlier if he was stuck to his particular form, or if he could reproduce himself throughout a print run. In any case there's no point trying to explain his whimsical turn, but I've typed my way down the blank sheet and now I'm coming right up to Oberon's hopeful hiding place . and jumping over it. I'd intended to hide it better because I know some people will just pounce on any inoffensive creature in pure malice. Sorry, Oberon!

Anyway, there he is, the living proof, if you go for living proof, of the truth of what I've written. Take a pin if you don't believe me, though if you don't believe me you wouldn't hear his cries anyway, you'd scratch him out and be on your way, happy to have destroyed another myth. I can't help that any more than Nick could.

But I don't suppose Oberon will spring out at you. I've been trying to coax him back, promising to be kinder and more imaginative, more patient, what have you, but he won't budge; so there's nothing left for me to say, except that he was here and told me most of this. And that I wish I had more faith.

A NOTE ON THE AUTHOR

Robert Watson is the author of two previous novels and a forthcoming study of film in education. He is married, has four children, and works at Bretton Hall College, where he is a senior lecturer in English and inter-arts.